Gorillaz in the Bay

DE'KARI

**Lock Down Publications and
Ca$h Presents**
Gorillaz in the Bay
A Novel by De'Kari

DE'KARI

Lock Down Publications
P.O. Box 870494
Mesquite, Tx 75187

Visit our website
www.lockdownpublications.com

Copyright 2018 by De'Kari Gorillaz in the Bay

First Edition December 2018
Printed in the United States of America

Lock Down Publications
Like our page on Facebook: Lock Down Publications @
www.facebook.com/lockdownpublications.ldp
Cover design and layout by: **Dynasty Cover Me**
Book interior design by: **Shawn Walker**
Edited by: **Lashonda Johnson**

Stay Connected with Us!

Text **LOCKDOWN** to 22828 to stay up-to-date with new releases, sneak peeks, contests and more…

DE'KARI

ACKNOWLEDGEMENTS

Okay, this is my very first book so yall know this gone be long. First and Foremost, Heavenly Father, you gave me the ability and creativeness. No matter the outcome, "I love you, Lord!"

Now, I give everything I am to my spirit, my heart, my soul, Black Pearl. For without my spirit and my soul, my heart wouldn't beat. Even in death, I will have my vibrant Black Pearl. To My Queen, I love you so much. Thank you so much for loving a fool and not giving up on a nigga when everybody told you to dip. I don't know if God will grant this miracle. Innocent niggaz get washed all day. Just know, I love you and this is for you. That's why you getting the money!

To the best things that ever happened to me, my children, I am sorry I let yall down, but I will always love you.

To CA$H, brah, good looking for the opportunity. But I'm telling you, big brah, my pen game is evolving at a rate so rapid, I'm not gonna be able to stop it. I'm on my way to your level. I'mma stop by for a second so we can holla bout where to go from there. LOL! Mad love, big brah.

To Neva Die those I can name Dok Holliday - forever big brah I luv you, Rogue, Rel Isaac, Day Day (in book you DeeDee), Lil Thomas, Lil Rel, Scooter, Mike Vegas, Pee Wee and the Dragons I can't name, I love all yall 'til the fire go out.

One Aim, One Struggle, One Goal, NEVA DIE!

My Goons & Gorillaz dragging their knuckles on the steel and concrete behind dem walls: Clarkola – my Big Brother, I love you, nigga, and look up to you. The realest nigga I eva met: my cousin G-Boi, nigga can't nobody eva copy you, I know you keeping you head up (ABCG)! Just know I always looked up to you. Ken Jr. I don't know where you at my nigga but keep you head up, cousin. Big Dame, get at me on F.B. aint from you in a minute. Lil Dame, Big Joe, Greg, Lil Ya Ya, Twan stay cased up I love you niggaz. Joe, I told you, you would be in the book. Chilly Willy, Funky Len (Menlo Nigga), Prince Mel, Paul Oliver, Low Key (what dat 415

GORILLAZ IN THE BAY

look like), M.A., Zoe and the rest of my A-Team niggaz, Free Lil Drew.

My P.A. Niggaz: Filthy, Ali Bob, Money Jaba, Lil Jabari, Shitty, Butchie, Kev, Sutton, Bear, Big Pep, Pup, Blood James, Lil Nate, Band Aide, Black Boi, Lil Vic, Jermaine, Boodladden, Boo Banger, Fresh, Pill Clinton, J-Roc, CJ, "L" (Linell) & Neal (Cornelius) niggaz I had to put you in book 1 & 2, Lil Rodney, Starrprina aka Cantelope, Lenita aka French Tip, Randell, Dusty, Lil Bit, Lil Steve, Kareem, it's too many P.A. & Menlo niggaz, Bunk what's up.

P.A. stand up, Menlo stand up!

Now the last group (last but not the least fo sho)! My best friend and role model, Levell Batman Evans, I luv you for real, blood, I respect yo Gangsta nigga, keep doing it! My mother and father, thanks for giving me life! Uncle Pete, you will always be like a father. Big Hank I need my roof fixed, LOL. Momma Nevida I really wanted to make you proud of me!

To all my ndugus ninakupenda ni upendo!

DEDICATION

I first and foremost dedicate this book and my struggle to my Angels: Mrs. Emma B. Beckum, La'Trisha Combs and Patricia Anne Beckum. Each time I lost one of you I lost a piece of me. Jamal Harris, what's up cousin!

Matasia, meeting you ndugu was the best thing that ever happened to me during my prison experience. To ALL my mwezi's all I can say is what's understood aint got to be spoken. For eva!

Big Skinny aka Kenny Hamel, I miss you cousin!

Lastly, if you eva hated on me, spoke ill of me, doubted me, tried to stop me, wanted me to fail or wished me ill, thank you! Because you created a monster. Book 2 will be ready before the end of the year and book 3 will be soon after. And I am just getting started!

DE'KARI

GORILLAZ IN THE BAY

Prolouge

Tommy could hear the loud sirens approaching in the distance, as more police cars arrived and surrounded his house. The sounds of screeching tires on top of the gravel outside punctuated the cops urgency to diffuse the situation with force. He could hear the constant pounding of footsteps as members of the Milpitas SWAT unit circled the building in preparation for a second charge at the house. He had sent them running for cover under a hail of gunfire the first time they tried to come for him, just thirty minutes ago.

"Y'all bitch muthafuckaz back? Is this really what the fuck y'all want?" He mumbled to himself as beads of sweat formed across his forehead.

The night breeze enveloped his body like a silk bathrobe due to the wind blowing through the windows that were blown out. The acrid smell of the gunpowder filled the house like the stench of burnt popcorn. His shoulder was aching and beginning to throb like hell from the 9mm bullet that penetrated him in the first hail of bullets. Yet with his pulse racing and the blood in his veins rushing through his body from his overly pumping heart, all he could think of was finding a lighter amidst the garbage on the floor. He needed to take another hit, to slow his mind down and gather his thoughts. The only way he could do so was by taking a full-pull.

The police had been in front of his house for over two hours. What started out as a simple search and arrest warrant quickly became a battle to the death. When the loud knock first came, Tommy Smith known to the hood as 'T'Rida was in the back of his five-bedroom house, buying nine more ounces of crack cocaine. He'd invited a few close friends and associates over for a little smoke-fest and get together. Upon hearing the announcement of the police at the door, everyone got nervous and acted solely on impulse. The first shot penetrated the night like a shooting star and what would follow was the biggest shootout with the police in California, since the SLA shootout, way back in 1974, when The Symbionese Liberation Army

DE'KARI

supposedly kidnapped newspaper heiress Patty Hearst. The kid-
nappers engaged almost five-hundred law officers in a standoff
that was broadcast on national TV, culminating in a shootout and
fire leaving six members of the group killed.

Tommy found a Bic lighter on the floor under what was left
of his five-thousand-dollar coffee table. Next to the lighter were
a bunch of jaw-breaker sized crack rocks that spilled in the
chaos. He picked the largest one off the floor, like a panther
snatching meat off the bone of a fresh kill. In seconds he had the
rock on his pipe and took another hit. He took a long, slow, and
deep drag. The sweet taste of the smoke filled his mouth and ca-
ressed his throat as it made its way slowly down to his lungs.

As he pulled harder and harder on the pipe, his eyes became
fixated on the melting rock as it slid its way down into his
lungs. He watched as it sizzled and melted, transforming into a
clear light-brown liquid. He twirled the glass pipe as he removed
the flame from the lighter, while still pulling on the pipe.

When his lungs would no longer allow him to pull anymore
smoke out of the pipe, he removed the pipe from his crusty burnt
lips and hungrily inhaled all the smoke into his body, like it was
a breath of fresh air. He held his breath as long as he could to
keep the potent smoke in his lungs until they ached. He sat down
on the couch, tilted his head toward the sky and exhaled the
smoke in a long stream of ecstatic bliss.

Instantly, he became light-headed. His senses were heightened, the tips of his fingers felt as if they were surging with pure
power. His entire body surged with power like he was shot up
with pure adrenaline. He was oblivious right then to all that was
going on around him. It was as if at that moment, he didn't have
a care in the world. Tommy lifted the pipe back to his lips to take
another pull Just then, the ringtone to his cell phone went
off. He ignored the phone and took another hit.

This time the hit he took was bigger than the one before. Finally, he exhaled the smoke and answered his phone. "Who
Dis?"

"T'Rida, we on the way, my nigga! Just hold the
mothafuckaz off for a few more minutes! Nigga da Mob on the
way!" Jason Voorheeze his long-time friend and brother yelled
in the phone.

GORILLAZ IN THE BAY

"V, my nigga, you gotta stick to da plan," T'Rida responded.

"Fuck dat shit! Nigga, we gon' turn dat bitch into the O.K. Corral," Voorheeze shot back.

T'Rida smiled at the metaphor Voorheeze used. His nigga was always using metaphors. T'Rida had so many emotions flowing through his body at that point that tears fell down his eyes.

"Look, V, I love you, cuzzo, and you know you, my nigga. I know it's nuthin' to a Boss. But, Blood, we knew this day was coming. I've been fucking up for too long, brah. That's why I been getting you ready to take over and run da family." As the tears flowed freely he continued.

"Nigga we built this empire on blood, sweat, and tears. My nigga, I can't sit here and just let what we've built go up in flames behind my stupidity."

T'Rida held the pipe upside down as he talked, allowing the residue to run back into the brillo as the pipe cooled down. "V, I fucked up when I started smoking this shit, it ain't shit I can do about it now but ride it out. But you my nigga, you can. Why you think I chose you instead of Gunz to take over? I know you can take dis mothafucka where I wanted to take it in the beginning. You won't be able to do shit as long as you're working wit' emotions. Remember nigga show no love, cause love will get you killed."

"This is the Milpitas Police Department! Thomas Smith, we are giving you one last chance to surrender and come out of that house with your hands up! There's no need for there to be any more bloodshed today. Come out with your hands in the air. We are only giving you five minutes. After that, we're coming in full force and bringing you out." Voorheeze could hear the voice of the police captain on the bullhorn through the cell phone.

"Rida we're getting off your exit now. My nigga, I'm almost there—"

Voorheeze was cut off by Rida before he could finish his declaration of Loyalty til' Death. "V, hold on for a minute, cuzzo," T'Rida spoke before he dropped the phone in his lap and reached into his pocket for his blue tooth.

DE'KARI

He put on the blue tooth and connected it before continuing to talk. He reached down and picked up another solid from the floor and packed his pipe with it. This time he didn't pull on the pipe slowly. Instead, he pulled hard and deep almost as if he was trying to suck the entire flame through the pipe and into his lungs. The smoke burnt his lungs, but to him, it was a good burn. His ears popped as he blew out the smoke and sweat instantly began to form on his forehead as his heart rate accelerated.

Voorheeze could hear T'Rida inhale and knew what he was doing. At the thought of his brotha being in his house with the police outside in full force, moments away from taking his life, made tears swell up in his own eyes. The emotions were too much for him to control and the tears escaped from his eyes. He made no attempt to wipe the tears away.

"Rida," Voorheeze choked into the phone.

"I'm good, V, look I ain't got much time left, so listen to me, listen good, my nigga, and let this jewel I drop on you pay." Rida put the pipe on the couch and began walking around picking up the extra clips for his Mack-90, while he barked out his final orders to Voorheeze.

Although they weren't face to face talking, Voorheeze could hear in T'Rida's voice that he was back to a clear state of mind at that moment.

"V, stop the mothafucking truck and pull over. That ain't a request, my nigga, it's an order! Pull over and get out of the truck," he told him.

Voorheeze didn't want to do it, he couldn't bring himself to do it. All he knew in his heart was that he had to get to his folks. In his mind, Voorheeze knew T'Rida didn't know what he was talking about. It wasn't him talking. It was that shit, but deep inside he knew T'Rida's orders were going to be his last. So, out of respect for his Boss and brother, he pulled the Lambo over and signaled for the vehicles following him to do the same thing. Tears ran down his face like waterfalls, he stepped out of his truck and finished listening to T'Rida with the phone on speaker. When Lenard 'Two-Gunz' Johnson saw Voorheeze pull over and step out of the Lambo, he pulled his

GORILLAZ IN THE BAY

Aston Martin over and walked over to find out what was going on.

T'Rida continued speaking, "V, by the time you make it to me dis shit gonna be over. You know I'm not gonna let these mothafucka's put me back in a fucking cage!" The venom in his voice was all too familiar to Voorheeze. It was the venom of a man who had death on his mind and blood in his eyes.

"I'ma gangsta, nigga! You hear me, nigga? Gangsta! I came in dis bitch wit' nuthin' and ready for everything. Blood we knew the consequences to dis shit, yet we accepted dem when we chose dis game. V, I've done something that most niggaz only dream about, but are either too scared to do or don't have the balls to do it. But along the way, I fucked up. Nothing you do is gonna change that—nothing! But, I'll be damned, if I'm going out like some bitch and not like the Savage I am. I'm going out the only way a gangsta should go out. Blood don't rob me of that. Don't do that to me, V."

Voorheeze closed his eyes and listened to his brotha with a heavy heart, as he poured out his soul in his last confession. "You want to help me, my nigga? Den my nigga keep it lit. Make these mothafucka's regret the day they took a real nigga. Make this family stronger than eva. I want you to build on this shit and take it to the next level. I'm talking so big that mothafuckaz will remember us forever. They will know what this *'Neva Die'* shit is all about. I luv you, my nigga, but it's ova for the kid. Tell da fam it's *Neva Die Foe Life!* I gotta end dis shit, right here and now. So, I gotta go, remember, *One Aim, One Struggle, One Goal 'NEVA DIE!'*

Instantly, after that T'Rida was off the phone. Or at least that's what he thought. He thought he had hit the end button on the phone, but in actuality, he pressed the record button instead. So, Voorheeze and the rest of the soldias with him were still listening while the phone was recording on T'Ridas end. Recording his last moments on earth. A recording that would be saved and played over and over by thousands to come.

"Okay these mothafucka's wanna take it there, then nigga let's take it there!" T'Rida could be heard mumbling to himself while he reloaded the choppa.

DE'KARI

After cocking the assault rifle, he picked up his pipe, placed another rock on it and lit it. Not worrying about the residue, he smoked five rocks back to back before the voice of the police captain came back on the bullhorn.

"This is your last chance. Come out with your hands in the air."

By now the cocaine-filled T'Ridas body and mind. God himself could not reach or reason with him if He tried. All rationale and understanding were long gone. All that remained was pure Beast.

"Mothafucka, do I look like I give a fuck about your last warning!" T'Rida yelled as he rushed to the front window with his pipe in one hand and the Mack-90 in the other.

He took one last full pull and tossed the pipe aside on the floor. He held his breath until he got light-headed, and his ears popped once again, and the sensation that he loved returned. The feeling of real uncut power. When he blew out the smoke this time you could hear him yell "Nigga it's Neva Die or nuthin'!" The next sounds that could be heard over the phone was that of the Mack-90 as T'Rida let off round after round like a hillbilly protecting his farm.

By now everyone was circled around Voorheeze listening intently as T'Rida made his final stand. The assault rifle sang a song only gangstas could understand and love. A song of power, respect, fear, and peace. Because when that song is played all of them feelings come out. T'Rida stood in the middle of the front door holding the choppa like Al Pacino did in Scarface. Glass shattered and erupted as squad car windows were blown out. The whistling sound of bullets hitting car doors sounded like a swarm of yellow jackets and blended in with the screams of the cops that were shot. The heat of the bullets that penetrated their skin was a violent contrast to the cold night air. It was just now a little past 10 p.m. and the wind coming off the Calaveras Mountains was just blowing in.

"Come on, fuck boiz!" T'Rida yelled as he continued squeezing the trigger.

The flame from the muzzle flash illuminated the night. The police were caught off guard by the quickness in which he swung the door open and began firing. The moment the door swung open bullets flew and bodies began to drop all in one motion. As a result, nine cops were caught by surprise and gunned down immediately. The other cops quickly recovered however and returned fire. T'Rida laughed at their lame attempt to kill him. He continued laughing even when two bullets tore through his body. One through his bicep and the other his upper chest smashing into his bulletproof vest.

"You, bitches' think that shit is gonna stop me?" He spat out, as he tightened his finger even more on the trigger and continued to let 7.62's fly through the air.

When the firing pin clicked on empty, he swiftly ducked back into the house, out of the doorway and switched clips. Assuming he was reloading, more cops attempted to use that moment to rush his front door. This mistake too cost them their lives. T'Rida was way quicker than they thought he would be reloading the rifle. He yanked the empty clip out and slid the full clip back into the rifle so fast that he was pivoting back into the open doorway and firing before the cops could realize their fatal mistake.

The captain didn't even have time to yell for his men to fall back and resume their position before his men were mowed down like grass in front of his eyes. The cops that held their positions couldn't return fire because their comrades had run directly into their line of fire.

"I told you mothafuckaz this is Neva Die!" T'Rida yelled out mocking and antagonizing them.

Just then, two more bullets ripped through his chest causing him to stagger backward. He coughed twice and spit out blood, but he didn't feel the pain due to the amount of crack cocaine in his body. He just laughed. Over the phone, Voorheeze and his men could hear the entire exchange of gunfire. They held mixed emotions as they listened. They cheered their Boss on as he rained down bullets of fire on the cops. Yet their hearts were still heavy as they heard T'Rida gasp every time a bullet hit his body.

Another slug hit his leg and cause him to drop to his knees. Still, he returned fire determined to leave his mark. This time when the rifle clicked empty, he ducked into the house, but instead of trying to reload he reached into his pocket and pulled out a grenade. This time no police rushed the door when he

DE'KARI

ducked back into the house. They assumed he was reloading again and wasn't going to make the same mistake their dead buddies had made. Once again none of the police was prepared for what happened next.

T'Rida stepped into the door frame and threw something as hard as he could. One of the officers screamed *"Grenade,"* and as soon as the echo landed on their ears the blast of the grenade was felt. It sent one of the squad cars three feet into the air. The moment the car landed T'Rida was in the doorway again getting ready to throw another grenade. He had no way of knowing that the captain tired of his men dying, never took cover from the blast.

Instead, he had his gun drawn and aimed at the doorway. The moment T'Rida appeared with the grenade in his hand a slug from the captain's 9mm shot through his already bleeding and bullet-riddled chest, piercing his lung. He coughed and blood ran over his lips as he reached for the rifle, but his body no longer had the strength to lift the gun, and it slipped thru his fingers clanking against the floor. He reached down for a piece of the pipe that he had tossed earlier instead. As he did so a sniper's bullet tore thru the wooden door frame and hit him in the head, knocking the blue tooth off his ear. Silence was all Voorheeze and the rest of Neva Die could hear. They were all quiet after that as a feeling of dread filled their bones and the space around them.

GORILLAZ IN THE BAY

Chapter I

Time Waits For No-One!

Some people pray for the right opportunity, some people spend years waiting for that opportunity, while some people simply make shit happen!

It was 9:45 in the morning and the air was nice, chilly and extremely calm on this October day, as Tommy 'T'Rida' Smith sat on the Greyhound bus bound for Oakland California. He was on his way home from the Duel Vocational Institution, a State Correctional Facility in Tracy, California. He was returning home after serving thirty-two months on a three-year stint for a possession for sales case.

T'Rida was a dark chocolate brotha standing 6'1. At the time he went to prison he was only one-hundred and ninety pounds. He had toned muscles and a bee-hive of waves in his hair. His skin was smooth and even-toned with no blemishes. As he sat at the Greyhound Bus Station everything about him was the same with one exception, he'd gained one-hundred pounds of muscle. He was now a hulking two-hundred and ninety pounds.

T'Rida had no clue what exactly he was going to do with his life, but he did have two-hundred dollars in gate money and one-hundred and fifty dollars, that was left on his books when he was paroled.

His baby momma Monique was waiting for him at the West Oakland Greyhound Station. So, he was using the time during the ride home to gather his thoughts and put a plan together. One thing that was certain for T'Rida, was that he would not allow himself to ever be caged up like an animal again in life. He was so deep in thought, he hadn't noticed the bus pulling off the freeway hours later, nor did he realize it was pulling into the station. He was jarred from his thoughts when the bus came to a stop inside the parking lot of the station. He gathered his small bag of letters and paperwork, he figured was too important not to take home.

He walked through the entrance, across the lobby, and out the front door, onto San Pablo Avenue. Monique was waiting for him when he exited the doors. She was standing next to a 1991 Buick LeSabre. The blue jeans she wore hugged her thick chocolate thighs extremely tight and the little white halter top was sadly losing the battle holding in her big ass titties. The minute she saw her man, she rushed into his arms and gave him one hell of a hug and kiss. That was when the reality of being a free man finally hit him and sunk into his head.

"Damn, Moe, you look sexy than a mothafucka!" He said grabbing his hard dick.

"What? No, I was rushing, I had so much to do." She turned toward him for a minute. "But, you, oh my God you got a girl scared with all them muscles you done put on." She left out how wet he had her pussy.

"You know I gotta be able to throw you around and remind you who's King," he joked making all types of gestures.

"You ain't gotta remind me, Daddy, cause I neva forget." Her rapid beating heart was proof of her honesty.

He'd been gone so long she feared him sexually. But wasn't gone long enough for her to forget, she was his.

"Why?" This was their ritual.

"Because I'm your, Kipaka," she giggled.

"You damn, right!"

They rode back to her three-bedroom apartment in Fremont engrossed in conversation and excitement. When they finally pulled into the apartment there was no large waiting party of family and friends. There was no huge reception and no miraculous feelings. Just a sense of despair and embarrassment at the sight of the rundown, cheap apartment complex on Sundale Avenue. She had moved into the apartment two years earlier after giving birth to T'Rida's son Titus. Their daughter Na'Shay was just a year old. That feeling didn't improve or disappear once they entered the apartment unit. The front room was small. When he walked into the front door he was standing in the dining room looking directly at the living room in one direction and the kitchen in the other. The carpet looked as if it hadn't been shampooed in over five years. It was a dark brown color turned black from all the dirt built up. Here and there were even darker spots on the carpet where someone spilled something but was too lazy to properly clean up. The walls were a dull ass beige, off-white eggshell color.

The walls were in desperate need of cleaning. The smell that engulfed and molested his nose was that of a rundown gambling shack. It smelled of old burnt food and grease long embedded into the walls with the stale scent of weed, cigarette smoke and God only knew what else.

He followed Monique down the hall to the bedroom in the back wondering where his kids were.

"Where the kids at?" He wanted to see his babies.

"That's what took me so long. I had to get them dressed and ready. Then I took them to Mama's," She replied setting her keys down.

"Oh, so, you knew you was getting some dick? he teased, she didn't need to respond.

He placed his bag of letters on the floor next to the closet and looked at the room. There was no improvement in its condition from that of the front of the house. The walls were just as filthy, and the carpet had even more stains in it than the carpet in the living room. Monique flew into her man's arms again, hungrily attacking his lips and body. He wasted no time as an erection rose in his pants. She could see the flame of lust burning bright in his eyes. Years of pent up testosterone possessed his body and he ripped her clothes off like they were made of tissue. She gasped as his actions threw gasoline on the fire burning inside of her. She welcomed the passion. They collapsed onto the bed in a heap of hot passion and desire.

The lust in her eyes, as he looked into them, was intoxicating. As she rubbed her hands all over his back and bit him on his shoulder, three years of pent-up sexual tension was released. T'Rida lifted himself up from Monique's luscious naked body and violently snatched his clothes completely off.

He gazed back down at the mother of his kids and his eyes took in a body that was succulent in every aspect of the word. Her 38-DD breasts laid perfectly against her body with her hardened nipples sticking out, begging to be sucked and bitten like gumdrops. Her flat stomach was nice and firm, with just a hint of baby hair that was shaved in a thin straight line, that spread out into a triangle leading to her hot, awaiting pussy. Her thighs were a deep dark chocolate like the rest of her body only it glistened with a firmness that made any man want to get his head trapped between them.

The sight of her body commanded attention and T'Rida had to discipline himself enough to appreciate every curve. He bent his head down and took one of her nipples into his mouth. The warmth of his watering mouth caused Monique to moan and arch her back slightly off the bed. She closed her eyes, tilted her head back, and worked her hands up and down his muscular back and shoulders. He worked both of her breasts, sucking each of her nipples, then kissed his way down to her stomach, on down to the hot warmth of her pussy. He stopped to inhale her sweet, musky scent, his chest swelled with the breath he took, and when he covered her pussy lips with his mouth. He let the hot air of his breath rush into it.

His hot breath felt like steam coming out of the furnace of hell. Yet, it was so delicious to her. She moaned loudly from the sensations his hot and experienced mouth awakened in her pussy.

"Sssss—ooh, baby. Yeah, Daddy, lick that kitty." She threw her head back and closed her eyes, in the throes of passion. She grabbed the back of his head needing him to give his best.

"Make me cum, Daddy. Yes, please make me cum."

Tommy had the best head she'd ever had in her life. They had been together since junior high school in Fremont. At the age of eleven, they each surrendered their virginity to one another and Monique was the first woman he had ever given oral sex. Over the years he grew to enjoy eating pussy, just as much as he enjoyed fucking and it showed. T'Rida took his time around the pussy. He was like an artist sculpting a painting when he was performing oral sex.

Though over the years they would break up and makeup just to break up again, they were always drawn back to one another. Expertly, his tongue circled her clitoris, then slid in and out of her wet tight hole, while his lips massaged her pussy lips. He began fucking her pussy with his tongue, sending jolts of electricity through her body. Monique started rocking her hips back and forth, shoving her pussy deeper and deeper into his mouth. But, when T'Rida enclosed her clitoris between his lips and began sucking on it like a cough drop she really went berserk.

She howled out in pure ecstasy and grabbed the back of his head, forcing it against her pelvic bone. T'Rida never let go of her clit. Instead, he sucked even harder on it while he slowly slid one of his fingers inside of her. Once his finger was coated nicely with her juices, he commenced to fingering her pussy, while sucking on her clit and massaging her lips. His dick was throbbing so hard against the bed, it hurt. He kept control of himself and held back.

After Monique's first orgasm ripped thru her body, she bucked her hips even harder against his mouth. Now she was fully in sync with the motion of his tongue and the rhythm of his finger. She fucked his face while his finger and tongue fucked her. One finger became two fingers and the pleasure multiplied and grew beyond her belief. Another orgasm shot through her body, this time she screamed out his name so loud her ears popped.

"Oh, Daddy," she moaned over and over again. "Oooooh, yes, yes! Eat it, Daddy, eat this pussy!"

He looked up at her. "That's right fuck my face, Momma. Give me that pussy," He mumbled while sliding his tongue in and out of her as fast and far as it would go.

Unable to continue taking the sweet abuse Monique cried out. "Now Daddy! I need you inside of me now."

The smile that came across his face was hidden due to her pussy smashing up into his face. Shortly after, when she felt his strong arms wrap around her thighs, Monique knew her ecstasy was just beginning. As he held her thighs in a vice-like grip, T'Rida continued to eat her pussy, for fifteen more mind-blowing minutes. Once he was no longer able to hold back his own hunger and lust, he rammed into her soaking wet pussy in one long stroke. Monique screamed out from the pain of receiving all nine and a half inches into her so abruptly, but, soon the pain subsided.

Once it passed, all she felt was pure pleasure. T'Rida fucked her hard, fast, and strong. Giving her three more orgasms as he did so. He turned her over onto her knees and his dick jumped at

DE'KARI

the sight of her big, dark, round, tight ass. This time as he slid into her hungry walls from behind, he slow stroked her, which really drove her crazy. He was hypnotized at the sight of her juices flowing over and coating his dick. All the excitement began to take its toll on him and as his balls slammed against her clit, he could feel his own nut building.

He grabbed both of her ass cheeks tightly and fucked her with all his might. As he stroked Monique it manipulated her inner walls so that they contracted against his shaft and soon Rida erupted. His climax was so powerful, that an electrical current shot through his own body. After they were drained and satisfied, they collapsed on the bed, exhausted.

"Uggh, God damn, Moe." He could barely breathe.

Minutes later after regaining some of his strength, T'Rida rolled over and reached into his pants for his cigarettes and lighter he bought from a stand at the Greyhound station.

"Sshhh, don't talk." Right now, everything was perfect and Monique didn't want to mess that up.

He lit one of the Newport 100s and took a long drag before laying back down on his back and blowing out the minty smoke. As he thought, *"Yeah, a nigga finally home!"*

"Monnie, damn baby, I missed you. It's good to finally be home. But, you can't understand the feelings inside of me, right now," he sincerely told her.

"I know baby, I'm just glad, you're finally here with me," she replied, as she rolled onto her side, so she was looking directly into his face.

As he stared up at the ceiling, he continued. "Baby, I'm proud of you for getting up out your mom's house and shit and doing yo' own thang. But, Daddy home, now. Baby this ain't it for us. It ain't good enough for you or my kids. Now that I am home we gonna get out this shit hole and jump into something phat."

His words stung Monique's heart. She knew that the apartment needed some work. Hell, she wasn't stupid, but she had gotten this place all by herself and was proud she was on her own, at the age of twenty-one, and not on section eight like everybody else. But, she knew what kind of nigga T'Rida was. So, she knew deep down he wasn't going to be happy in the tiny rundown apartment.

"Daddy, I don't want you to get into any trouble or have to do anything illegal. The kids need their father and I need you here with me. I know this isn't the best, but as long as you are here with me it's good enough for me and the kids."

"Look, I'm not going to get into any trouble or leave y 'all again. Believe that, but you know I gotta do me. You already know what type of nigga I am. So, I'ma need you to ride wit' me and play yo' position like you do." For the first time, he looked at her, took a long drag of his cigarette, then asked her in a serious voice. "Can you do that?"

Monique looked at her first love with all sincerity in her heart. "Daddy, whatever it takes, wherever it goes I'ma always be right here with you and for you."

T'Rida put his cigarette out in the ashtray and held her tightly in his arms and they fell asleep. T'Rida was thankful to God, he'd made it home. Monique was even happier, but she was wondering if he was home for good.

DE'KARI

Chapter II

Later that evening, T'Rida awoke to the smell of fried pork chops, collard greens, cornbread, and macaroni and cheese. The aroma of the home-cooked food made his stomach growl, he was glad his baby had gotten up and cooked for him, instead of getting fast food. As he entered the kitchen his stomach growled again. This time it was so loud, she heard it and smiled.

"Walking up in here sounding like a Bear straight out of hibernation, guess all that exercise took away your little energy?" she teased.

He wrapped his arms around her and kissed her on the neck, smiling. Instantly, his dick became rigid again. He looked over his shoulder at the counter to see if anything was on it. T'Rida softly bit her on the shoulder and bent her over the sink where she was standing, instead of moving her over to the counter. Monique was already wet with anticipation, so he slid his shaft into her with relevant ease. She moaned out loud as he slid inside of her. He reached around grabbing both of her large breasts into his hands and gently nibbled on her earlobe, as he pumped into her.

"Not all my energy," he whispered in her ear.

"Daddy, damn I've missed this dick," she cried.

"Not nearly as much as I've missed you."

He let go of her breast which dropped into the salad bowl she was holding. The coolness and wetness of the chopped tomatoes felt wonderful against her taut nipples, she closed her eyes enjoying the pleasure she was receiving. T'Rida then grabbed her large hips and controlled her ass. Making it rotate in a circular motion, which caused his shaft to reach and touch every inch of her pussy.

"Oooh, fuck, I'm cumming already! I'm cumming, Daddy!" She shouted as a strong orgasm shot through her body covering his dick with her love.

T'Rida picked up his pace and began pounding into her harder and harder until they both erupted. Once she gained some composure, she went to the bathroom to quickly wash up before heading back to the kitchen, to finish preparing dinner. Butt naked and starving, they ate their dinner while listening to *Jill Scott's 'Who is Jill Scott?'* Afterward, they showered together and went to bed where they made love one last time before falling asleep for the night.

Monique's peaceful sleep was invaded with nightmares. Visions of the future, visions filled with violence and pain, such unlike anything she'd ever known. Yet, she would not remember these dreams in the morning when she awakened. They would not be recalled by her for another four years. Not until it was already too late to do anything about it. T'Rida, on the other hand, slept peacefully and dream free for the entire night. When he woke up in the morning an idea would come to him, that would forever change their lives.

It was the sound of the telephone that woke T'Rida. He wasn't going to leave the warmth of the bed and answer the phone, getting all cold and shit. Hell, it's November, shit it's cold in November.

"Moe, go get the phone, babe" When she didn't move he smacked her firmly on the ass, "Get the phone!"

Besides he didn't know why the phone was way the hell in the front room and not on the nightstand. She was mad, he'd woken her out of her sleep instead of getting the phone himself. But, she knew how much he hated the early morning chill, so she got out of the bed and answered the phone. The sight of her round ass jiggling firmly back and forth, with every step gave T'Rida an instant hard-on. She walked back into the room moments later, with the cordless phone and handed it to him.

"It's Jason, baby," she told him as she climbed back into the bed.

"V, what's hood wit' it, cuzzo?" T'Rida said into the phone.

"T-Mothafucking Rida! Welcome home, my nigga. I thought niggaz woke up early on the yard mothafucka?" Voorheeze joked.

"This ain't da pen cousin. And how you get dis number anyway, nigga?"

Monique and T'Rida exchanged puzzling looks. Hell, T'Rida's own mother didn't know his house numbers. That's just how he got down. Ever since he was a teenager, he never gave out his home number, back then it was only his pager and as an adult, all he ever gave out was his cell number.

"Come on Rogue, you know, how I fucks wit' it. So, why you gon' ask me some dumb ass shit like that?" Voorheeze laughed into the phone. "I got a couple of connections down at the phone company." By connections, he meant a chocolate honey he was laying pipe to.

"Yeah, I heard that nigga the president ain't supposed to have this number. Anyway, what's hood wit' it, though?" T'Rida responded.

He and Voorheeze had known each other since they were kids. They were more like brothers then homeboys.

"Rogue, I got some shit to take care of out yo' way, when a nigga done I'ma swing by yo' spot. I should be sliding through in like three hours." Voorheeze had always been a morning nigga.

As far back as Rida could remember, he was always the first to wake up and always the first to make some shit happen. Most importantly, Voorheeze was always the first to show up when needed. T'Rida couldn't understand how the nigga always wakes up so early, but V was a good nigga and he loved him like they were blood brothers. So, he really wasn't surprised, that Voorheeze was the first person to get in touch with him. Knowing Voorheeze that nigga had probably already been up for a few hours bussing moves.

As far as T'Rida went, shit he needed his sleep. After they hung up, T'Rida rolled over and climbed on top of Monique. Shit, he wasn't going to let the image of her walking across the room slip from his mind. After their lovemaking, he asked her if she had any weed. She took out an eighth from the nightstand and handed it to him. When T'Rida went to prison niggaz were smoking Dro in backwoods and grape swishers. Now they had something out called blunt wraps and she handed him one of these too. He rolled his blunt and smoked, while Monique went back to sleep.

The grape flavor of the wrap made the Grand Daddy Purple taste that much better. As he smoked he noticed, the weed burnt hella quick. After his conversation with Voorheeze, he couldn't go back to sleep so T'Rida got up and went to take a shit. After he finished and cleaned up he grabbed his smokes and went into the living room. T'Rida sat in the living room watching the news, thinking of a plan, while sipping on some Patron Silver. This was his favorite drink. While most niggaz be on that Remy and Hennessy hype, T'Rida had been fucking with Tequila ever since junior high school.

When the knock came at the door he was halfway to the door already. In prison, he had become accustomed to hearing footsteps approaching, even while he was doing something. His subconscious was trained to listen in. One thing prison had given him was an acute sense of awareness which sharpened his senses. When he looked through the peephole, he mentally kicked himself in the ass for slipping. One thing he stopped doing years ago was looking through peepholes. That was an easy way for a nigga to get his shit knocked off. When he saw Voorheeze he swung the door open, with a big smile on his face. The two embraced like T'Rida had just come home from a ten-year prison term instead of three.

"Brah, you want a drink?" T'Rida asked him.

"Nigga, do a bear shit in the woods and wipe his ass with a rabbit?" Voorheeze responded.

"There you go with all dem riddles and shit," T'Rida responded with a smirk.

"Yeah, I want something to sip on nigga," Voorheeze shot back.

Voorheeze himself had just come home three months ago. He was paroled from Pelican Bay Maximum prison. Voorheeze was a good nigga, with real authority issues that kept him getting into shit, inside and outside.

"On some real shit, V, nigga we gotta eat my nigga. I can't do this small shit no more, brah." T'Rida told him as he handed him his drink.

"Rogue, you ain't saying nuttin' the kid ain't been thinking myself. A nigga so hungry, I'll eat a bowl of soup wit' a fork around dis bitch," Voorheeze responded using a line from Turf Talk.

"My nigga I've been thinking about shit and dis here ain't da business," T'Rida told him.

GORILLAZ IN THE BAY

Just then Monique walked into the living room wearing some sweats and a long t-shirt. Even as she was walking into the room T'Rida told his folks about a plan he'd been thinking of all morning. Monique made breakfast, while the two of them talked about what T'Rida had been thinking that morning. Monique listened to every word as she cooked.

T'Rida was from the shady 80's in East Oakland. All while he was serving his bid, he stayed watching the news. He stayed up on all the current events in the hood and around the world. He remembered not too long ago an armored truck was driving through West Oakland and dropped four bags of money out of the back. The bread was never recovered and word on the streets was niggaz in the West was eating. A week after that a couple of young niggaz robbed another armored truck off San Pablo. Them niggaz weren't just eating they were eating phat, right about now.

To T'Rida them little niggaz would be their means out of poverty. Not that he was a hater or nothing. He just figured if they had it and wanted it, they needed to be able to keep it. If he was able to take it, they didn't deserve to keep it. Monique didn't like the idea, because it was well-known that West Oakland niggaz were grimy as fuck and really with the bullshit. She'd already committed herself to ride until the wheels fell off, and right now them bitches were just getting put on. So, the way she saw it, she just had to bite her tongue and play her position.

Voorheeze had come up on a few pistols and one Calico in the time he had been home, but for the shit, T'Rida was talking about they were going to need at least another person and a couple more choppas. Shit bangas wasn't going to be good enough for what they were talking. V told Rida they should bring in Gunz.

Lenard 'Tommy Gunz' Walker was a cat they went to school with. He never was close to the two of them, but they all fucked around from time to time, and he was one solid mothafucka. He favored the 44-long nose whereas Voorheeze favored the 45 Dragoon Colts. Lenard was from Berkeley but had moved to the 69 Village in East Oakland years ago. He was a hungry lil' nigga and loved getting down and putting in work.

DE'KARI

T'Rida and Voorheeze knew that if they wanted Gunz he would be found right there in the Vill, rain, sleet, or snow. So, they ate breakfast and headed to Oakland to find Gunz. Voorheeze didn't have a car. In fact, he had caught the Bart to T'Ridas spot that morning after bussing a couple of moves. So, they drove Monique's car.

When they got off the 880 freeway, they exited on the Coliseum exit. T'Rida was loving the feeling of really being back in the hood. Messy Marv's Turf Politics was playing on the cheap system, the sun was shining bright as fuck, niggaz were out in full force, and the hoes were thicker than all outdoors. They drove through the village looking for Gunz. While they drove T'Rida couldn't believe the dramatic changes that had taken place.

The village, although he could tell there were still some niggaz making money, it had fallen far. He thought back to the days when machines were running in the Vill. Days when that mothafucka had money flowing through it like water. Sometimes you may have up to eighty mothafuckaz hustling and moving. Everybody had their own job or function, and they did just that. From lookouts to runners, to drop boys and so on. Everyone did their share and as a collective, things worked like a well-oiled machine. It takes many individual pieces to make a machine work.

He remembered when he was a youngsta, you had real goons like Siege and Wu. Mothafuckaz that really lived the game and set an example for cats to follow with this Mob Shit. T'Rida was just a youngsta back then, he listened to Siege's music like it was the Bible and watched how them older cats held it down. He knew he would one day grow up to be a block cat and just waited for the day, he would get to the level they were on. Soldias died in the game by the dozens, real mothafuckaz sacrificed their lives making a way for the young niggaz to really get it. But these niggaz he was seeing now weren't following the blueprints laid out for them.

They had forgotten what it meant to be Gangsta. Just getting money, wasn't it. You had to live and die by a certain code. Any lil' nigga could sell dope, but you had to be a different breed of nigga to be a Gangsta. These niggaz he was seeing wasn't that breed. But he would remind them, he would show them, and everybody else for that matter what the business really was.

Like flies on shit, Gunz was posted on his spot doing his thang. When he saw Voorheeze and T'Rida pulling the Buick to a stop he smiled his signature smile. The one he was so famous for.

"These two niggaz always bring life to the party," T'Rida thought.

These were two niggaz who would always talk about one day doing it big, really doing da fool. Although they did their thang, Gunz had never heard of them doing anything on a serious level. Silently he always knew that with T'Rida's ambitions and Voorheeze' s analytical mind, that one big day they always talked about was just around the corner. Maybe today was that day. Why else would these niggaz be coming through the Village?

"Well if it ain't Jason mothafucking James and T'Rida the kid," Gunz joked as the two got out of the car.

"What's good wit' it, family?" Voorheeze asked as he embraced the one person he felt was more dangerous than he was.

"T Gunz what it do, cuzzo?" T'Rida called out as he too embraced the young gunslinger.

"You know me, brah, posted like a thumbtack making dis dough."

"Well, nigga we need to get at you on some serious shit," Voorheeze told him.

Gunz looked at him with the look of a man silently respecting an adversary or a chess opponent, as Voorheeze made that comment. One of the traits Gunz admired about Voorheeze was that he always got to the point. Never was Voorheeze the type of nigga that would beat around the bush.

Gunz shot back, "Shit I was just thinking that now would be a good time to grab something to eat." Gunz knew these two niggaz wouldn't have come all the way over here to see him unless it had something to do with money.

Gunz never hesitated or overlooked an opportunity to make some money. He grabbed his bundle he had stashed and the three of them walked upstairs to Gunz 's apartment where Gunz fired up a blunt. They had a couple of drinks with the weed and Rida told Gunz about the plan, he and Voorheeze had in mind. Not knowing what Gunz response would be, he was careful not to get into too many details.

"Fuck! You niggaz really wanna do the fool, huh?" Gunz said as he took a swig of his Remy Martin.

He looked from T'Rida to Voorheeze and back to Rida seriously. The look turned into a smile, then a grin. "Yeah nigga, I'm wit' whatever! Keeping it one hundred, I don't know why I didn't think of that shit," he told them.

Reading the young killa's eyes and seeing what he was looking for, Voorheeze passed the blunt to T'Rida, took a swig of his Don Julio, which they picked up on their way. Then he sat straight in his chair, looked straight into Gunz's eyes, and laid out the full official plans they had constructed. Regardless of how he felt, Gunz would handle himself like a pro and this Voorheeze knew.

They went over the plan a few more times making sure everything was on point. Gunz had a few ideas that sounded good to Voorheeze and T'Rida, so they adjusted them into their plans. They would use multiple getaway cars stashed in different locations in case things didn't go as planned and using heavy artillery instead of little shit cause the niggaz in the West was holding big shit. He also told them he would supply the guns they were going to need to pull the job off. The three agreed to meet over at T'Ridas spot the following night to go over shit one more time. Gunz would bring the choppas to the apartment with him.

T'Rida dropped Voorheeze off at his spot and instead of heading back to his apartment he decided to hit the gas station and drive out to the west to do a little homework. He came up San Pablo, cruised down Adeline driving slow enough to look at shit, but not too slow to draw any attention to himself.

First, he went through Acorn Projects, then he hit the Lower Bottoms, Ghost Town, and even Dog Town. After he was satisfied with everything and how it all looked in his mind, he headed back down the freeway. Again, instead, of going home he went to Fremont where he had this female named Tanya who lived on Pennsylvania Ave. He parked the car in the back of the apartments on the opposite side of the complex, then made his way to her door. He hadn't called her due to losing her number a few months back.

This bitch was a stay at home type of broad, so he didn't worry too much about her not being there. As he climbed his way up her stairs, he made sure to take in everything around the building for security reasons and store everything in his memory.

When she opened the door, she was wearing sweatpants and a t-shirt with no bra under it. Her little titties sat up straight and perky under the cotton shirt, with her nipples poking through. When she looked at her best-kept secret, Tanya's pussy immediately came to life and moistened at the sight of him. She knew her young stud was a hood cat, but around her he was so sweet and gentle. She couldn't find it possible to believe he did the things she heard he did in the streets. The way he made her feel when they made love, she could care less about what she'd heard about him.

She could overlook anything he did because she could see the potential in him, that he didn't see and plus the dick was that good. That is why she never said anything to him about Monique or the other females she'd found out about over the years. Besides she was forty-six years old and had lived her life already, so she knew what it was like to be young.

She let him in and as soon as he locked the door behind them, she attacked him like a lioness attacking her king. She'd only had sex three times while he was incarcerated. Not out of loyalty to him, but out of respect for herself. To her the person you had sex with was everything. Her body desperately needed the loving that only T'Rida could give, and give it to her he did. Altogether, he fucked her three times that night.

They fucked up against the refrigerator, on the dining room table, the floor and finished with him bending her over the couch in the living room. The entire time neither of them said one word to the other, except for the vulgar expressions and remarks of pleasure. After they finished Tanya got up and made T'Rida a drink. As she walked away, he couldn't take his eyes off her five-foot-eight frame. She only weighed one-hundred and twenty pounds and each little pound was spread out very well. So, watching her walk away from him was an added delight.

Her ass wasn't big like he was used to, but it was smooth and succulent. She was the total opposite of Monique. Tanya was small and petite, but every curve of her body had its own unique signature.

He lit a Newport and smoked while he sipped on the drink she handed to him. While on the floor, he allowed his mind to drift to the plan for tomorrow. They were going to hit three different spots all in one night. niggaz they knew were eating and making a name for themselves. Catching all those niggaz off guard in the process would have a very nice effect. At the same time, if they didn't do the shit just right, shit could go bad for them real quick. He allowed his mind to clear itself as Tanya brought the food into the living room. Seeing the tacos she'd made, caused T'Rida to start laughing. While in prison he had seen the movie Baby Boy with Tyrese in it and his mind flashed back to the scene where Tyrese told his baby momma to make him some tacos after they had sex.

"What's so funny?" Tanya asked as she sat on the couch and watched him eat.

"Baby Boy," was all he said.

It took her a minute before she caught on to what he was talking about. Once she did she playfully hit him with a couch cushion and laughed herself.

"Are you staying the night?" She asked him already knowing the answer. He neva stayed the night. He was always too busy chasing his street dreams in the fast life. When he didn't answer, she'd received the answer she knew she'd get. A tear rolled down her eye, but she quickly wiped it away.

After he finished the tacos and they talked for a little while, T'Rida took a shower with just hot water and headed back to his place with Monique. When he walked through the door she didn't ask him anything about where he had been or was up to. Instead, she asked if everything was okay. He reassured her that everything was okay and informed her about the meet tomorrow. They went to bed early because in the morning Rida was going to show her the routes he mapped out mentally for them to take.

34

GORILLAZ IN THE BAY

He had already made up his mind, he would use her as their driver he just hadn't told the fellas. He knew Voorheeze wouldn't question his judgment. Gunz, on the other hand, was a different story, but he would deal with that tomorrow if the situation needed to be dealt with. One thing he wouldn't do was second guess himself.

Over the years as they were growing up, Monique had aided T'Rida numerous times when he was putting in work. She'd done everything from driving the getaway car to tucking the burner. He knew Monique was a Ride or Die bitch. Never bringing himself to sleep with two different women in one day, T'Rida just held Monique as they went to sleep that night.

The next morning, after eating breakfast, they drove through West Oakland, he showed her the routes they would be taking. After he was satisfied that she was comfortable and would be cool and relaxed later, they drove to Milpitas where he stole a black 1992 Cadillac Seville. They drove back to her complex and he parked the stolen car a block down the street in another complex. He made sure that he parked it in a visitor's space, so the car wouldn't draw attention from any of the neighbors.

It was a little after 6:30 that night when Voorheeze knocked on the door. He told T'Rida he had stolen a Chrysler New Yorker and parked it a down the street. An hour later, Voorheeze's cell phone rang. It was Gunz telling him to come downstairs and help him with the duffle bag. T'Rida was sipping on a glass of Patron when they came back in. Monique made the other two niggaz drinks and gave them to them when they came in. When he told them his plans to have Monique drive no one said a word against it.

"As long as having them two kids ain't mess up yo' barz." Voorheeze joked.

Monique was always T'Rida's getaway driver. It's been that way since they were kids. Gunz didn't give a fuck. If shit got real his choppa was his getaway driver.

"It's yo' call Blood."

As they went over the plans one more time, Voorheeze inspected all the metal Gunz had brought. The first was a pistol grip pump shotgun which held twelve rounds, there were two AK47's with extended clips, and two brand spanking new

Dragoon Colt 45's. Along with the guns, there were a double shoulder rig and three bulletproof vests. Of course, there was extra clips and ammunition for everything. One of the AK's was old, but still in good condition. Everything else looked fresh out of the box and knowing Gunz they probably were. When he was done going over all the guns, Voorheeze instructed everybody to put on a pair of non-powder latex gloves and clean a gun. New or not Voorheeze wasn't taking any chances.

Thirty minutes past 10:00 p.m. All four of them headed out. T'Rida was driving with Monique in the Cadillac, Voorheeze followed them in the New Yorker and Gunz was behind them in his 2000 Chevy Impala SS. They all drove back-to-back so no-one could drive between any of the cars. The Impala they parked next to the Coliseum in the East. They parked the New Yorker on the corner of Chestnut behind the California Hotel. All the guns were placed in the Cadillac with Monique and T'Rida before they left.

The plan was simple yet complex. First, they would drive down 34th Street, until they hit Campbell, then turn right and drive until they hit the Lower Bottoms. T'Rida figured they would lay down this nigga who was doing his thang in Campbell Village. After leaving the village they would drive over to Acorn and hit their next target. Then they would lay down all the niggaz on 34th and Adeline. Afterward, they would dump the Cadillac on Chestnut and take the New Yorker back over to the east and hop in the Impala and keep it moving.

Not too difficult of a plan on the surface but considering that all the areas were located just blocks from one another and somewhere even hooked up with the others. It was going to be a hell-of-a-job to pull off. They were now all piled into the Cadillac and headed off for the village.

Chapter III

Meanwhile, Bamma had just sold these little niggaz four birds last week. So, he wasn't tripping when Money called and told him, he wanted to cop six more. Bamma who was a little greedy mothafucka, never thought twice about them coping six birds so soon after the first four. Although niggaz were getting jacked left and right, he was Bamma! Who would fuck with him—*no-one*! The little niggaz weren't smart enough to pull a jack move on him. So, the greed of the money he was making off them clouded his decision-making.

He even told Money if he'd get eight instead of six, he would drop him two more. Money agreed and told him he'd hit him in an hour. After he made this drop he was coming back to the spot, to drop off the bread, then he was heading over to Tommy T's to kick it for the night. Even though he didn't think anything would go wrong he still packed an all-black 9mm Glock. Once everything was in order, he headed out the door with the small duffle bag carrying the ten kilos of cocaine in his hand.

He had stumbled across some money roughly nine months ago when he was driving back from one of his bitches' house in North Oakland. As he was driving down the street he noticed an armored car driving toward him. Not thinking anything of it, he was surprised when the truck hit a large pothole and the back door of the vehicle flew open and dropped two money bags out of it. His first thought was that it could be some type of set up, but when the truck continued down the street and turned the corner Bamma slowed the bucket and jumped out.

Cautiously scanning the area, he snatched the bags up and got out of dodge. When he got to his apartment he counted the money unable to believe his luck. On the floor of his dirty ass apartment, laid out in stacks of twenty thousand, was almost a million dollars. He was so fucking happy, he almost pissed his pants. He didn't know what the hell to do. For the next two weeks what happened was all over the news. They claimed the truck lost over two million dollars, but Bamma knew that was some bullshit.

The police and the Feds were all over this shit. But, Bamma was smart enough to play it cool, and stashed the money on the floor of his closet, under some dirty clothes instead of running out and spending it. A dummy would have done that and drew all kinds of attention toward themselves.

Wisely, he took a rack here and a rack there and went out of town, to buy some much-needed clothes. He went all the way to Seaside to get the clothes. They had a little spot out in San Diego he liked as well, called Gioni's that had some cool shit, too. He knew it was too soon to rock like that. A week after he found the money bags, some little niggaz robbed a Brinks armored car out in North Oakland. This only made shit that much crazier in Oakland for a while.

After the robbery police started harassing all the street hustlers. Anyone who looked like they were getting money or in the streets, the police were all over them like flies on shit. Bamma stayed grimy and maintain his normal lifestyle. About four months after the harassment by the police settled, things began to quiet down.

By then most of the niggaz that were really trying to eat and do their thang got cracked and were locked up fighting cases, shit was crazy. Nine months later, Bamma took forty-thousand-dollars and got a deal on three birds, which he broke down to ounces, half, quarters, and even solids. It took him over eight hours to cook, cut-up and weigh all the dope by himself. But, as soon as the third brick was done he was out the door, and on the block serving stone for stone, while giving niggaz double ups on the sly.

A little while later, he began selling half ounces and whole thangs. Although he kept the price for a half the same as everyone else, he let the whole thangs go for four hundred a piece. His name slowly began ringing in the streets, but not enough to draw too much attention. Just enough for niggaz to begin noticing him. However, Bamma did get the attention of Young Money, a little up and coming jacka that hadn't yet made a name for himself.

As he made his way through West Oakland, these memories replayed in his mind for so long he waited for his turn. Often asking God when he would get a chance for an opportunity, he didn't think would ever come.

The first reason Money hadn't made a name, was that he hadn't knocked off anything or anyone on a major level, yet. The second and most important reason, he hadn't made a name, was because every nigga he robbed, he killed. Dead men tell no tales. For the next six months, Bamma went from moving zips to pushing quarter birds up to whole thangs. What he didn't know at the time, was that there was talk on the block about him moving up the ladder and food chain so rapidly.

Two months earlier, Money began plotting on Bamma. If this nigga had it the way Money figured he had it, this would be the move that gave him the name he wanted, and it would also give him the money to take over shit the way he'd always wanted to. He knew he had to play his cards right, so the shit could slice like butter when he pulled the move. Bamma was always slipping, which made plotting on him way too easy.

In fact, Money had caught him slipping so hard on two separate occasions, he wanted to make it happen right then instead of waiting for the time he'd planned. But, he held himself in check and stuck with his plans. Bamma walked down the stairs of his apartment complex, just after eleven-thirty with his two-hundred-dollar Roc-A-Wear sunglasses on. He used his electric car opener to unlock the 2001 Lexus GS44.-When he got into the car, he sat under the parking stall, rolled a blunt, and smoked half of it, before pulling off.

Bumping the *Luniz 'Oakland Raider'*, Bamma cruised down the streets of Oakland feeling invincible. The Lexus was midnight black like his outfit with twenty-two-inch rims. The windows had a slight smoke on them. Just dark enough for someone to see a silhouette behind the tints, but not be able to make out the driver. As the music knocked on full blast and the weed aroma floated in the air, he was feeling like the million-dollar man, Ted DiBiase. He rolled down 34th without a care in the world.

***

Just as they were driving down 34th getting ready to stop on the corner of Adeline and turn, Guns couldn't believe his eyes. Young Bamma had just turned the corner on Adeline, right in front of them. He knew that car because he'd come across it and its driver a few times at different events. He wondered what he'd done so good that the game was sending him such a good blessing at a time like this. Especially, on a night when they were out on a terror.

"Cuzzo, slow up a bit," he spoke softly

"What's hood, my nigga?" T'Rida responded as he looked at the car in front of them.

"Man, we gotta be some lucky mothafuckaz or something. I'm telling ya," He spoke with a shit eating grin on his face. "That car right there, my nigga, that's that nigga *Bamma*, in dat bitch," He said with emphasis on the name as if they all should've known who he was talking about. When no-one reacted to the name, he continued. "That nigga, right there is the mothafucka that got those bags dem armored truck niggaz dropped a while back." He waited for their reactions, this did get their attention. "I'm telling you if this nigga is out it's either to go clubbing or make a drop. Those are the only times this nigga comes out at night. And the way that nigga is heading he ain't going to no freeway."

Voorheeze realized what Gunz was getting at and instructed Monique to follow the Lexus at a safe distance. Either way shit went down, Voorheeze had already made his mind up to get the mothafucka. Just as he was giving Monique the instructions, the Lexus pulled into an apartment complex in front of them. Following the instructions that were given to her, she waited a few seconds before pulling into the driveway behind the Lexus.

They watched as the car parked at the end of the driveway and saw a little nigga get out of the car, just as another cat emerged from the shadows and walked up to the car. Bamma exited the Lexus carrying a small duffle bag and the two walked off.

Relying solely on instincts, T'Rida opened his door. "Wait in the car for a second. I'll be right back." Was all he said as he reached into his pocket for a cigarette and stepped out of the car, making sure to close the door softly behind him, so it wouldn't make a sound.

As the little nigga and Bamma walked, he followed them from a distance of twenty feet or so. When he saw what apartment, they'd entered he continued to walk aimlessly by as if he was just strolling and enjoying an evening smoke. Just in case someone was on the lookout, that he couldn't see, he didn't turn immediately around. Instead, he followed the path all the way around back to the car. When he got back into the car, he gave Voorheeze and Gunz a report on what he saw. Immediately, all three of them grabbed their respective weapons and were out of the car walking casually to the apartment Rida saw Money and Bamma enter.

Before leaving, however, Rida told Monique to turn the lights off and leave the car in park, but to keep it running. He also told her to honk the horn twice if she saw anything that looked out of place. If nothing out of the ordinary took place she was to wait for them to come back around the corner and the moment she saw them put the car in drive.

As Bamma pulled his car into one of the parking stalls, Money was already calculating how he and his goons were going to split this fool's wig and get paid. The two cats were waiting inside the apartment waiting to play their positions. The plan was simple, Nate was waiting in one of the back rooms for Money to come and grab the digital scale. Which would be his clue that the shit was about to go down. Smalls was sitting on the living room couch playing Madden "02" with a .45 automatic behind him.

Bamma got out of the car as Money was approaching. "What's good, cousin? Let's make this shit happen," Money said as they embraced.

"Real spit. When we get up in yo' spot, my nigga, ya boi gonna need a drink," Bamma told him.

Still oblivious to what was about to take place, Bamma walked with his mind on the night he was about to have. When they walked into the apartment Bamma was shocked at how filthy these lil' niggaz were living. Although he struggled most of his life, he always made sure he lived in a clean spot. Just cause a nigga was broke, didn't mean a nigga had to be dirty.

41

"Smalls, fix the big homie a drink, while we get shit sorted out." Money gave the order so naturally, Bamma respected the lil' niggaz leadership qualities.

Qualities he himself did not possess, but he didn't notice the smirk on his face. On the floor next to what was supposed to pass as a coffee table was a black duffle bag similar to his. Too distracted with his greed as he looked at the bag, he never saw Smalls pick up the cannon that was laying behind him as he went into the kitchen. Inside the duffle bag on the floor was one-hundred and fifty thousand dollars.

He asked Money, "That the dough?"

"Yeah, big homie. niggaz been out here twenty-four seven getting it."

"Alright, bet, check dis shit out," Bamma told him as he opened his bag and grabbed one of the kilos.

Smalls handed him his drink, a glass of Remy XO. As adrenaline pumped through his body, Money grew excited. When things were going the way he'd planned, he always got a little excited. Money stood up to go and retrieve his scale from the back room, calling out over his shoulder to Bamma, asking him if he wanted to smoke a blunt. When he opened the door, he looked at Nate and smiled. Then he walked back to the living room. Instead of a scale in his hand, there was a .50 Caliber Desert Eagle, which he had pointed directly at, Bamma.

"Nigga, you, done lost yo' fucking mind? Don't play wit' me, wit' no fucking pistol!" The venom Bamma spat out with the words were deadly and cold. Although he seemed outraged and pissed, the stench of fear seeped through his pores like steam.

"Ain't no game, Fuck Boi! niggaz is hungry in dis bitch and you da meal!" Money shot back.

To let Bamma know that shit wasn't a game and for his disrespect, Money shot the nigga in his leg. The pain that shot through Bamma's leg sent fire throughout his body.

"Fuck you thought, pussy? niggaz was just gonna sit back and watch you eat while we starved? You charging a nigga twenty-five when a mothafucka coping eight of them joints off you!" Money yelled at the nigga crying and bleeding on his floor. "Now, I'ma only ask you this shit one-time, nigga. Where the rest of the bread at? Nigga dis ain't no Hollywood movie and it damn sho' ain't no game. So, where it at?"

Being too cocky, like most young wolves were, Money wasn't really paying attention to Bamma. He was too busy making the nigga look like shit. So, he didn't notice the nigga grabbing his gun from under him as he laid bleeding on the rug. Nate came running from the back room after hearing the gunshot. His running drew Money and Smalls attention, a rookie mistake. That brief distraction allotted Bamma the split second he needed. He whipped his pistol around, as quick as he could and with a body filled with anger and adrenaline raging through his veins, he aimed the banga at Smalls' head and fired.

The force of the slug smacking into his head was so powerful, it broke Smalls' neck and jerked his head back real quick. As Money turned his attention back to Bamma, he heard the shot in his head before his mind could register what his eyes were seeing. He lifted his arm out of pure reflex and instincts and fired two shots. At the same moment, he fired, Bamma fired at him. However, Bamma's shot was just a little quicker and the results were life-altering.

His shots landed, sending the big mouth mothafucka staggering backward. Thinking quickly, Nate jumped over the couch landing hard on the floor, when Bamma's first shots rang out. The sight caused the seventeen-year-old wannabe gangsta to go into shock. He never saw the slug that smacked into his skull like a train hitting a car crossing the tracks.

***

Just as they were getting ready to kick the door in, T'Rida and the rest of his squad heard the shooting in the apartment and cries of agony coming thru the door. Hearing the gunshots that followed, they first thought someone had spotted them and got the drop on them. Then they quickly realized the shots and the screams inside the house were connected. Voorheeze figured someone was trying to beat them to the punch. He looked at T'Rida with a puzzled look on his face. T'Rida returned Voorheeze' s puzzled look, with one of his own, but shrugged his shoulders like *fuck it*.

Gunz looked at the two of them and did the same thing, only there wasn't a puzzled look on his face. Instead, there was a sinister smile.

"Let whoever is up in that bitch do all the dirty work, when the shit quiets down den we just clean up," Gunz told them. They waited crouched outside the door listening to the battle. When they didn't hear any more shooting, Voorheeze called out, "Game time niggaz!" Just like that, the size fifteen Timberland boots he was wearing sent the door crashing open with one mighty kick.

***

"Stupid ass mothafuckaz thought it was going to be easy to jack the kid? Thought you'd get young Bamma, like that! I'm Bamma, Bitch! I knock niggaz down! I don't get knocked down!" Bamma was staring at all three bodies on the floor as he yelled. In his outrage, he didn't give a fuck that he was yelling at dead bodies. His long dreadlocks hung like a lion's mane, while spit foamed out the sides of his mouth. The pain from the gunshot didn't even register in his mind.

"You, dumb ass, niggaz!" He spat out again continuing his tirade. As the last words left his lips, the front door came bursting in and he could only think, *'Now what?'*

"Alright! Alright, more of you motha—" He began as he turned around lifting his pistol.

The sentence was never completed. Instead, he screamed out in agony as a slug from the AK47 tore through his shoulder, shattering the shoulder blade and spinning him back around. A second slug ripped through his back and exited out his chest. Bamma stumbled forward, but his body only allowed him to stagger forward twice, as all the life escaped his legs causing him to fall flat on his face. All the bullets that hit him came from Gunz. Holding the shotgun in his hands, Voorheeze briskly stepped past Gunz and the bodies and moved toward the hallway making sure no-one was still alive hiding in the back, waiting to jump out on them like Jack in the Box.

He found the room empty and called out to the front room, "We good back here."

A few seconds later, he was heading back into the living room with five Kilos of cocaine and what looked to him to be about fifty-thousand in cash, which he found in a shoebox in the closet and a bunch of jewelry. By the time he came in, Gunz and T'Rida was ready to leave themselves. T'Rida had a duffle bag on his shoulder that he'd picked up off the floor in the living room and Gunz had the bag with the Kilos in it, that Bamma was just dropping off. Each of them carried a duffle bag on their shoulders and guns in their hands, as they left the murder scene and walked calmly toward the car.

DE'KARI

Chapter IV

Monique sat in the car with the engine idling and her hands nervously drumming against the steering wheel. Her heart was speeding in her chest and her breathing was past rapid as she waited. When they were younger, T'Rida had done plenty of things and she was always the get-a-way driver when he needed her. But, that was so many years ago. Back then they were kids and fear was something they never acknowledged. They were the Bay Area's real Bonnie and Clyde. But now, sitting in that Cadillac, all she could think of was that she wasn't a child any longer.

She was a mother, thoughts of her two children flew into her mind, as she heard the first shots ring out. She was scared for her man, but she had faith in him and his gangsta. T'Rida was good at what he did. Even still, twice she reached for one of the extra guns and wanted to race to her man's side in case he needed her. But, she knew her man and she knew how he'd feel about her not following his instructions.

What if things went wrong inside there and they came speeding out needing to leave in a hurry and instead of finding a waiting getaway car, they found a disobedient Monique out of the car and that would cost them? It was this logic and the faith she had in T'Rida, that kept her in the car, frantically scanning the complex for anyone who may have heard the gunfire and wanted to come play hero. As shot after shot erupted the silence, the night sounded like a war movie was being filmed outside. She couldn't believe her eyes in her paranoid state when she first saw them. The niggaz were just walking casually like they were leaving out of the house going to the corner store.

Voorheeze was out front with the shotgun in his hands and the other two were directly behind him, one walking on either side of him. But, she had to admit that walking instead of running was always best. Running would only draw attention to them, plus the way they were walking, they were covering each other from every angle. Nevertheless, the sight fucked her up. The shit looked like a scene right out of a Hollywood

Gangsta movie. She was very close to pissing her panties and here these mothafuckaz were just walking like they were in the Military patrolling the barracks or something.

She threw the caddie in drive and turned the lights on as the three of them got into the car. T'Rida was the only one to speak and his only words were, "Drive normal Mo. Don't draw any attention to us by speeding."

Again, going against her feelings of wanting to get the fuck outta dodge, she listened to her man's instructions. She wondered if the niggaz knew how all that gunfire sounded outside. If they did she thought, they would want her to do it moving. She drove out of the complex, just as she would if she didn't have a car full of niggaz who'd just robbed and possibly killed a bunch of niggaz. As she was approaching the entrance to the complex, a Navigator pulled in blocking their way. Politely she gestured toward the other vehicle, requesting that the driver allow her to leave.

Instead, the tinted windows rolled down and some nigga stuck his dreadlocks out of the window. Since the windows in the Cadillac were tinted as well, the nigga in the Navigator couldn't see the killers inside of it. All he saw was the woman sticking her head out asking him to move. So, being the bitch nigga that he was, he called out. "Bitch, back yo' stanking ass up and let me through."

T'Rida never could figure out why niggaz were so stupid and did so much dumb shit. Give a bitch boi a little money and they thought they were John fucking Gotti or something. Right now, he didn't have time to play games with this faggot nor could he waste the time to teach the dumb mothafucka a lesson. Which he wanted to do so bad. Instead, he opened his door and stood up with the AK in his hand. Gunz and Voorheeze both did the same thing. It was as if the three of them were thinking in unison or something.

"Bitch, put that thang in reverse and get yo' punk ass out the way!" He told the fuck boi.

The nigga was so scared he threw the truck in park instead of reverse, he was shaking so hard. Seeing all the bitch come out of him, Monique made a nigga please smirk and started to drive off.

GORILLAZ IN THE BAY

"Stop the car," T'Rida quietly told Monique.

She already knew what was coming, but she still stopped the Caddie. T'Rida climbed back out of the car and sprayed the Navigator. He couldn't just drive off, even though, he wanted to. Nobody disrespected his queen like that. He climbed back into the vehicle silently as if nothing happened. The night's activities happened so fast and so unexpected, they decided they didn't need to change into the other cars. Instead, they jumped straight onto the freeway and headed to the East. After switching cars, they hit the freeway again and mobbed to Hayward. All four were engulfed in their own thoughts as they drove. It wasn't until they were passing the A Street exit, that the silence was interrupted by Voorheeze after seeing Gunz pull a bottle of Remy out of his jacket.

"I don't even wanna ask yo' ass where in the fuck you got that bottle from," Voorheeze said smiling.

Gunz smirked at Voorheeze' s remark, took a long drink and replied, "Dem niggaz can't drink dis shit no mo', what I'm supposed to do? Let a perfectly good bottle go to waste?" They all laughed and took turns passing the bottle back and forth.

All except Monique, she was focusing on getting their asses to the house and nothing else. Once they got there, *'Fuck Yeah!'* She needed a strong drink, maybe even two! When they arrived at the apartments, Monique parked in the back of the building, so they could put the guns in the trunk without anyone seeing them. The men had their hand-guns still tucked in their waistbands and with the duffle bags on their shoulders, they climbed the stairs. It wasn't until, they were inside of her place and she had herself a drink, that Monique was finally able to relax.

All four of them had their own drank and blunt in their hands as they relaxed. She wanted to play the radio on low just to have some noise in the apartment to calm things down, even further. But, Voorheeze insisted they left the radio off, so he could hear and pay attention to the surroundings outside, as they counted all the shit they had. Although to them it seemed like it took longer than it actually did, four and a half hours later, they successfully counted all the money three times.

DE'KARI

The extra counting was to make sure they had an accurate count. On a fluke, they ended up coming away with two-hundred and fifty thousand dollars, and fifteen kilos of raw cocaine.

As she got up to pour another drink, Monique said to no-one in particular. "Now that's what a bitch call being in the right place at the right time."

If they split everything equally, the four of them would get a little over sixty-two-thousand apiece, with three and a half kilos to go with it. Instead of splitting the shit equally among them, T'Rida had a different idea. One that would change the game as they all knew it. He got up himself to fix another drink, then planned on sharing his idea with all of them.

When he came back into the living room and sat down he began. "A'ight, look, smell ya boi on this." He took a drink from his glass before continuing.

He mapped out his mental thoughts verbally to them and painted a fucking beautiful picture of a plan to bring dreams to reality. It didn't take long for everyone to get on his level and start thinking how he was thinking. If they all kept the money together along with the fifteen bricks, they had enough shit to start their own machine. For quite some time, there hadn't been any major machines in the Bay. Niggaz was too busy on their own hype.

Years ago, T'Rida, Voorheeze and Dok Holiday had envisioned a plan. They dreamed of building an organization that was true and could stand the test of time. This could be a jumpstart to that. They sat up drinking, smoking and discussing the possibilities over and over, playing out scenario after scenario for another four and a half hours.

Before anyone had realized, it was seven o'clock in the morning and the news was coming on. Shit, T'Rida couldn't even recall who turned the television on in the first place. Voorheeze knew because it was him. He'd turned it on thirty minutes ago. He always paid attention to the details, he knew the shit from last night would make the morning news. So, he wanted to see what theory the cops had come up with.

There was nothing on the six o'clock news about the shit or at least if it was he'd missed it because he hadn't turned the tube on until a little after six thirty. Then just like he figured, the

GORILLAZ IN THE BAY

Channel 2 Morning News was covering it. The reporter stated that the police suspected the murders were somehow gang-related, due to the severity of which the murders occurred. There was no mention of a possible robbery. To them, one gang got the upper hand on another gang in some type of turf war. Turf wars weren't uncommon in Oakland, they usually were over territory for drug sales.

The police did say however, they suspected that there was another party who'd gotten away even though, they didn't elaborate on why. The niggaz inside Monique's apartment knew why. Both the bullets from Bamma's body were from an AK47 which was not at the crime scene. It didn't matter because in a few hours all the choppas would be at the bottom of Niles Canyon.

After the broadcast, they picked right back up on the conversation the four of them were having. They discussed shit for another couple of hours. Monique got blankets out of the closet for Voorheeze and Gunz. She knew that with all the drinking and smoking they'd done, it wouldn't have been smart to drive, especially this time of the morning. They all eventually fell asleep sometime around ten or so. When they awoke, it would feel as if they'd somehow awaken in a different time zone. Shit was about to get thick! *Real fucking thick—real soon!*

DE'KARI

Chapter V

SHIT OR GET OFF DA POT

Gunz checked his watch to see what time it was. Afterward, he stood to stretch his tired limbs that threatened to fall asleep from resting so long. Time seemed to crawl along at the slowest pace imaginable. The trap house had been moving non-stop since six o'clock that morning, now at five in the evening, Gunz was silently hoping this shit would hurry the fuck up. The two bitches he was watching, worked silently and methodically. They each sat on the couch in their bras and parties with gloves and masks on, while they worked.

Tamika was the dark skinned one with an ass like you wouldn't believe. She was born and raised in the Village. In her twenty-two years she'd seen a lot, been through even more, and always kept it moving. She knew how to keep her ears open and mouth closed. So, it was natural, without thinking that Gunz called her and told her, he had something for her to do if she was trying to make a little bread. Being the hustla she was, she didn't waste any time when he told her to grab one of her homegirls who could keep her mouth closed as well and meet him at the apartment.

When she showed up that morning with Stephanie, she was told he wanted them to sit in the living room all day weighing and bagging dope with no clothes on. Stephanie had a problem with the no clothes part. But when Gunz told them they'd get two racks apiece, she came out of her shit faster than Tamika. Gunz watched as Tamika worked the triple beam weighing the work. Then she would dump the dope onto a tray and hand it to Stephanie, to bag and tie it up though they'd started off weighing up and bagging ounces. Tamika had lost count after the first hour of weighing the dope. Before she had lost count she was at two hundred and sixty ounces.

Then T'Rida had come in with five extra-large Round Table Pizzas and a bag of drinks in his hands. During that first break, he told Tamika he wanted her to start weighing up half ounces for the next few hours.

***

Jason Voorheeze sat at a big wooden dining room table underneath a mountain of cocaine. Next to the cocaine were two smaller mountains one containing B-12 and the other baby lax. The cocaine ended up being so raw, he could step on it twice and still have some good shit. But, who wanted *'that shit?'* Keeping that in mind he only hit it with one and a half. It was magic, Voorheeze would take three kilos of work or one-hundred and eight ounces of raw cocaine and throw it in the mixes with eighty ounces of baby laxative and eighty ounces of B-12.

After letting all two-hundred and sixty-eight ounces mix for ten minutes, he sifted all of it, turned three kilos into six and a half. Turning the fifteen kilos to thirty-five was the easy part. Although, it too was time-consuming because Voorheeze had to make sure it was done right. The laborious part came when it was time for him to weigh up and package ounces, half ounces, quarters and grams.

T'Rida stood in the kitchen with an actual apron on. It was one of them aprons that read kiss the chef on the front of it. His pistol was tucked in his lower back like in them old gangsta movies, you couldn't tell him shit! T'Rida had visions, he didn't know if Voorheeze or Gunz could fathom what he saw in his mind, but he really didn't give a fuck. If they didn't see it yet, they would. T'Rida got the game from his uncle and just like his uncle, he didn't fuck with them new digital scales.

One slip of the finger or mistake could cost a nigga a lot of money. So, just like everybody else in the apartment, T'Rida rocked wit' a triple beam. Putting forth, the skills of Betty Crocker, he turned every thirty-six to forty-eight ounces of that real cake! As T'Rida put a fresh forty-eight in the freezer to cool and harden even more, he looked over at Voorheeze lost in his own world. Voorheeze never saw T'Rida shake his head and smile at the sight of him working with one of his dragons on the table for any and all to see and the second hidden under the table sitting nicely on his lap.

GORILLAZ IN THE BAY

Voorheeze always stayed on his shit. T'Rida knew a mothafucka could say what they wanted about Voorheeze, but everyone had to agree on one thing, that nigga stayed on point when it came to safety and security. So, when Gunz told them that his lil' cousin A.J. would be posted at the front door with a choppa making sure they wouldn't have no problems. Voorheeze still had his lil' cousin across the street from the apartment ready to go apeshit! T'Rida turned his attention back to the next kilo waiting to be rocked up.

By the time, all the work had been fluffed, weighed, cooked and sacked up, all six inside of the apartment were tired as fuck. There were only two kilos of crack left inside the apartment with them. T'Rida hit lil' Cantelope on the hip three times throughout the day so that she and her she-wolves could transport the shit to a safe house. As they now sat in the living room unwinding and massaging the cramps out of various muscles they passed around four blunts at once and sipped on a little drank. Seeing how beat the two bitches looked and knowing he himself was tired, T'Rida hit them off with an extra rack. After all, good workers were hard to come by.

Shortly after they began to unwind, Voorheeze noticed that the sun was going down. He wished he could go home and climb in bed. But, time waited for no-one and neither did money. Tired or not they had work to do. As he stood to take a piss, he downed the glass of Patron Silver. He told everybody to put their blunts out and get ready. Voorheeze didn't give a fuck about the women. They could get as high as they wanted to, but the niggaz had work to do. They needed to be on point. When he came back from the bathroom, he noticed that Tamika and Stephanie were already gone. He chirped Tut on the two-way, letting him know they were coming out.

Cantalope's timing was always impeccable, and with that signature precision she was pulling up in her hot pink Camaro just as the three of them hit the sidewalk. She popped the trunk of the Camaro once she came to a stop. T'Rida opened the trunk and tossed in a Gucci bag with the two kilos inside of it. As the trunk closed and he walked up to the driver's window she rolled it down.

"What's up, big brah, this it?''

"Yea, but, don't take it to the spot." Handing her a set of keys, T'Rida gave her new instructions. "I need you to take this to the spot, on Sundale and toss it in my trunk, then take the keys to Moe. She already knows you're coming."

"Alright, big brah, you need anything else?" she asked.

"Naw, it's good, I'll hit you tomorrow, sis."

Cantalope was Voorheeze's first cousin, but she and T'Rida hit it off the first time they met, and he saw her as a little sister. At first, everyone thought it was more to it, but the bond the two of them shared was that true gangsta shit not to be tainted by any bullshit. As she pulled off, T'Rida made his way over to Gunz's all black Buick LeSabre. Voorheeze was already inside the black on black Jeep Cherokee with Tut Tut. Once T'Rida was in the car, the four killas pulled off.

The dark blue and grey three-bedroom house sat just little ways down from the 69 village. The house was bought in the early sixties by a young black man who worked at the rail yard in Richmond. The young man was barely in his twenties. Both he and his twenty-year-old wife were God-fearing people, with their fourth child on the way. He was proud as ever at the greatest of all his material and worldly achievements. A home for his wife and children, whom he was raising to be God-fearing like himself.

That young man's name was Earnest Berthard Williams. Earnest and his wife had long since been dead. Three of their four kids were still alive; however, the house was passed down to Earnest's youngest child, his daughter Jeanine. Although Jeanine was a devout Christian growing up she had gotten swept up into the crack epidemic that plagued most in the black community in the eighties.

The memory of God-fearing, Bible-toting and hardworking Old Man Williams had long been forgotten. Nowadays when anyone in the community of East Oakland drove by the old worn-down house or even spoke of it, only one name came to mind, Earnest Lamont Williams known to everyone in Oakland as Big Roc. He was a bi-product of Jeanine turning a trick one night for a hit. Big Roc was the meanest and most feared man in all of Oakland. No one ever knew if it was having a crack head for a mother, never knowing his father, or hearing the silent whispers and rumors that he was conceived by the filthy life crushing desire of a crack Jones that made Big Roc so vicious.

No matter the reason, the outcome was the same. He had a vendetta against life and he took it out on almost any and everyone he came across. Big Roc was a highly unstable and evil son of a bitch. None of the normal shit that made most hood niggaz tick mattered to Big Roc. Not money, not fame, not even bitches. The only thing that excited him was destruction. The infliction of pain, he bestowed on so many people is what drove Big Roc. Because of this, he did whatever he felt like doing to whomever he happened to feel like doing it too. Murder, robbery, and extortion was his game and he played it wickedly. Because of that, the four young killas sat in their parked cars a couple houses down getting ready to unite Big Roc with his grandfather Big Earnest.

Growing up, Gunz heard about all the terror Big Roc reined in East and West Oakland. Rumor had it that both the Firm and the Moe Moe's had tried to stop Big Roc and had paid dearly for their mistakes. Gunz didn't even care if the rumors were true, he knew the only truth he needed to know and that was that Big Roc was a predator! You didn't play with a predator. You didn't try to reason with a predator or wait for it. You simply hunted a predator! As Gunz was getting money in the village he knew he was going to have to get at Big Roc before the Beast came looking for him. Their recent luck and new plans sped up that timeline.

Gunz chirped once on his Nextel, signaling to the others that it was time. He tossed the mobile phone in the glove box, and then he pulled the ski mask down over his face, cocked the shotgun and climbed out of the car. The other three poured out just as silently and walked with stealth and precision toward the house. As they approached T'Rida made a silent clicking sound with his tongue calling Samson. The massive one-hundred and ninety-five-pound Rottweiler, Big Roc let loose in his front yard. Before he could hear the thump of the heavy paws T'Rida tossed two very big and very bloody potter house steaks over the gate. Both of which Samson devoured in a heartbeat.

DE'KARI

As they reached the front of the gate T'Rida tossed over the remaining four steaks and slowly lifted the latch on the gate. Samson paid them no attention as they crept past him. Big Roc hadn't fed Samson in four days, the delicious meat was all that was on his mind. Maybe if the animal wasn't so hungry the weird smell would have given it pause, but as it was Samson woofed down the meat. He hungrily licked his massive chops as he stared at the four intruders wondering if they would give more.

Even if T'Rida did have more of the fat steaks, it wouldn't matter. For two whole days, they'd marinated in a Bar-B-Q sauce that had so much cyanide and sleeping pills in it, the dogs breathing was already becoming laborious. Voorheeze looked at T'Rida as they walked past him and Gunz. Voorheeze nodded his head in understanding as T'Rida made two zero signs with his fingers and proceeded to the back of the house. In twenty seconds T'Rida was coming thru the front door no matter what!

The nightlife of East Oakland was always buzzing with activity, so all noise was masked. Even still the duo stepped with caution as they made their way to the back door. Voorheeze climbed the two steps of the porch and got ready to kick the door in. Tut placed a hand on his shoulder stopping him. Most dangerous niggaz were cocky and cocky niggaz didn't lock doors. Just as he figured, when he tried the doorknob it turned silently with ease. He glanced over his shoulder at Voorheeze and smiled'll. While holding his Desert Eagle in his right hand, Tut quietly opened the door and stepped inside with Voorheeze right behind him, with his .45 pointed toward the sky.

Just as Voorheeze closed the back door and turned back around to face the kitchen, a big, fat, black-ass nigga rounded the corner with a plate of food in one hand and an empty glass in the other. His laughter was cut off by the sound of the loud Desert barking in Tut-Tut's hand. The two bullets hit the fat mothafucka directly in his chest causing him to stumble backward and drop the dishes he was holding. When they stepped out of the kitchen they were in a narrow hallway. To the left and around the corner was the dining and living room, to the right were four doors which no doubt led to the bedrooms. They headed that way.

GORILLAZ IN THE BAY

The thunderous sound of the Desert Eagle snapped Big Roc into action like a horse out of the gates of the Kentucky Derby. Without thought or hesitation, he threw the bitch that was grinding on his lap onto the floor. The commotion caught Rhino who was sitting in the recliner eating a plate of food off guard. Before he had time to respond, the front door came crashing in.

Boc! Boc!

The dark night erupted in flashes as two bullets flew from the Glock .40 in T'Ridas hand. The first bullet punched through the flesh of Big Roc, while the second tore through his shoulder knocking him back into the wall as his body fell over the couch where he was standing. Finally, snapping out of his momentary paralysis, Rhino reached with one of his big meaty paws trying to grab the 9mm he had tucked in his waistline. As his fat fingers gripped the handle of the banger, he knew in his heart that he was too late. Confirmation came in the form of a *Boom*! As the blast from Tommy Gunz's shotgun sent him flying backward over the recliner. Pellets from the shotgun burrowed deep into his upper chest, neck, and face. He was dead before his body completed the flip.

Leading the way down the hallway, Tut-Tut had the Desert Eagle aimed and was on high alert. He kicked the first door open and stepped in swinging the cannon across the room ready to let it buck. Directly, behind him, Voorheeze was doing the same thing to the second door. Seeing that the room was empty, Tut, moved on to the third door, which no doubt had to be the third room. Kicking that door open, he quickly noticed that room was empty. As he turned around Voorheeze was quietly approaching the last door, which sat directly at the end of the hallway.

As he got ready to lift his size fifteen boot to kick the door in, the floorboards squeaked.

Kaboom!

Voorheeze was sent flying backward and knocked off his feet. Before his body hit the ground, Tut had already dropped to one knee and started firing.

Bocca! Bocca! Bocca!

DE'KARI

He sent three of the .50 Caliber Missiles soaring through the door. He stood up and continued firing as he kept walking toward the door.

Bocca! Bocca! Bocca! Bocca!

He kicked the door in with the large cannon pointed ready for whatever. Some high-yellow nigga in a wife-beater and sweats was slumped on the toilet with a sawed-off Mouse Berg pump sliding out of his hands. Although he was already approaching death, Tut, decided to help him reach his destination a little quicker.

Bocca! Bocca!

He shot him twice in the head at point blank range.

He turned around and took a deep breath! Not his big cousin, fuck! As Tut stepped over to where Voorheeze was laid out on the floor, he was praying his big cousin wasn't dead. Voorheeze coughed and groaned, as Tut kneeled down. His chest felt like he was hit by a cannonball. As he winced from the pain of just breathing, he thanked God that he had his bulletproof vest on under his hoodie. Voorheeze knew now was not the time for reflecting, so he fought the God-awful pain and climbed to his feet. His chest felt like a plow mule kicked him square in it.

Tut handed him his dragon that flew out of his hands when he got shot, and the two headed to the front of the house. Even though, he had complete faith in T'Rida's and Gunz's capability in handling their shit. Safety and security were always of the utmost importance, so Voorheeze was still on point, as he and Tut entered the living room.

T'Rida stepped into the middle of the living room. Not even the sound of the shotgun going off in Gunz's hands made him break his stride. Though he did a quick scan of the living room, his focus was on the midnight black nigga standing with a big ass gun in his hand. T'Rida had to hit him two times when he walked through the door. The bitch on the ground stared up at the masked gunman and opened her mouth to scream.

"If you open yo' mouth, I'ma blow yo' fucking head off!" T'Rida sounded like the Grim Reaper himself, as the words spewed out of his mouth.

Mocha wasn't stupid, so she swallowed the scream back down her throat. Although, her heart was racing like Jackie

Joyner from fear. She kept control, praying to King Jesus, she'd make it out of this alive. She knew all them years breaking her mother's heart ripping and running the streets would one day catch up to her. But, *'Lord'*, she thought, *'If you protect me and get me out of this. I will be in the front pew of Mount Zion Baptist Church Sunday when daddy takes the pulpit.'*

"What the fuck? Blood, why you niggaz in my shit?" Big Roc spat. The heat from his stomach making him grimace.

It was the second nigga that addressed him. The one with the pump in his hands. "I'ma keep it all the way one-thousand with you, big homie. You're too dangerous blood!" Gunz didn't see any reason to beat around the bush or bullshit the nigga. Those niggaz name alone made niggaz in Oakland glance around out of fear. "I'm about to take over this City. And we both know once I do you gonna try to come and take what ain't yours."

As Roc started to speak the sound of a shotgun went off in the back of the house, followed by what could've only been Tut's Desert Eagle responding. No other gun in the world made the sound a Desert Eagle made. Although T'Rida wanted to check on his brother, he had to hold his position, but he prayed Voorheeze was alright.

"Instead of waiting on that day to come, I figured fuck it! I might as well make sure it neva does!" Gunz told him as he pumped the shotgun.

Mocha couldn't believe her ears, *'There is a God! And he is good!'* She didn't need to look under the mask. The voice was unmistakable. She knew that God heard her cry and she would live. There was no way her little cousin would kill her or allow his people to kill her.

"Gunz, I'ma shoot it straight young hitta. I knew it was something special about you years ago!" Seeing the masked gunman lower the shotgun a little, showed Big Roc that he had his attention, so he continued. "I neva took from you or knocked you down because I wanted to see what that would be. Now, I ain't neva gone go out like no bitch. So, I ain't begging foe my life! But, I'll tell you this, if you let me breathe, I'll ride by yo' side! You will neva have to worry about my loyalty. You will know, you spared my life, so I'll always owe you a life!"

That shit caught Gunz completely off guard. He'd always heard that the man's word was his bond. Time seemed to stop and stand still as three sets of eyes stared at him to see what his response would be. The suspense and tension in the room was equally thick. Just as Gunz started to speak, Tut came rounding the corner with a stumbling Voorheeze, who was holding his chest tenderly.

"If you know me, Big Roc, you know not to make me regret this shit!" Gunz vowed. He turned to Mocha, "Get up and take yo' ass home!" She had neva heard the authority, she'd heard in his voice before.

Gunz looked at Tut-Tut and Voorheeze, "Let's go! We done here!"

The two of them didn't know what the fuck was going on. But they didn't hear any protest from T'Rida, so whatever it was, fuck it! They wouldn't question the call. Instead, all of them walked out the front door.

Chapter VI

Voorheeze pulled into the parking lot of Three Brothers Tacos on University Avenue. It had been a productive day so far and as *'Hood Reality'* bumped from his speakers, Voorheeze was feeling like new money. Fuck a machine! That was too much work. It may work for the niggaz across the Bay in Oakland, but for Voorheeze it was all about networking. So far, just running through Menlo alone, he'd dropped off five kilos. As he thought about the mechanics of how he was gonna formulate his team. He smiled at how easy the shit was going to be.

He would drop his price a hundred dollars for every ounce. Two-hundred if you bought four or more. His nine packs would be a rack lower than anybody else's shit. Two racks for a half of bird and a full four racks for the whole thang. Sure, profits would be marginally smaller in the beginning, but as the clientele grew, so would the paper. Give him three months and the city would be his, *both Menlo and P.A.*

Once he entered Three Brothers Tacos, Voorheeze saw that his older brother was already inside at one of the booths on the far side of the restaurant. His stomach growled as he placed his order. He couldn't tell if it was from his hunger or the smell of the delicious food. He and his brother acknowledged each other with a head nod, then Voorheeze turned back around and waited on his order. Once the plate of super nachos arrived, Voorheeze walked over to the booth where Clarkola was seated and sat down.

He put the Gucci backpack he was holding under the table between their legs before he blessed his food and started eating. Neither of the two spoke until Voorheeze had woofed down half the plate of nachos. It was he who broke the silence. "What's' up, Rogue?"

"Shit, nigga, you knocking down those nachos like you fresh out!" Clark told him as he looked at his baby brother in astonishment.

"Shit, you, know me and food, Rogue," He responded just before tossing a couple chips with a mountain of toppings in his mouth. After chewing, Voorheeze took a swig from his Corona and continued. "Check me out, Rogue, it's four birds in dat thang. You owe me for two of 'em. The others are a gift to you, cause you my big brother." He paused to allow it to sink in. "Clark, you a grown ass nigga, blood. So, you gon' do you. But, Rogue, I gotta plan and if you, wit' it, I want you to fuck wit' me. But, seriously blood if you gonna fuck wit' me, Fuck wit' me!" Voorheeze stopped eating and stared directly into his brother's eyes.

Clark sat listening to his little brother talk. Oblivious to everything and everybody else in the small restaurant. Even while he listened, his mind was racing a million miles a minute. Voorheeze didn't sell dope he played with pistols, so, where was all this coming from? This was his little brother, yet, he sat talking as if he was a made nigga or something. Not to mention, hearing that the bag contained four kilos of coke. Where in the fuck did the little mothafucka get that kind of work?

The craziest part of all was hearing his brother tell him that two of them were free. That did two things. First, it told him that Voorheeze had to really be holding, to just give away two kilos. Second, it played on Clark's conscious a little making him feel guilty because over the years his little brother had always looked up to him and went out of his way to be there for him and look out for him. Clark, however, had always looked out for self. Never doing shit for his little brother.

"One way or another I'ma 'bout to take the City! I need to know if you, wit' me or what?" Voorheeze told him bringing Clark out of his thoughts and back to the present.

"Rogue, I'm listening to what you talking?" Four birds under the table and the prospect of more had Clarkola all ears! "Look, I don' already hit Roc and P. Clinton and dem niggaz off in da Low today wit' some small packages, so they can see what it do. Trust me though, it's gonna do da fool! And when it do niggaz gon' be at chu. But we gotta have an understanding on three things."

"What's that?"

"First, the prices I set, you keep unless you holla at me! Second, no matter what, neva step on the work! I don't care if God himself tells you it's good. And third, nigga we ain't taking no losses—none! For any sign of disrespect, we getting it like Dracula—" He paused to let his words sink in. After taking another swig from the Corona he finished. "Nigga, I can guarantee you two things: the City will be ours and it won't stop until we want it to! Get yo' niggaz together and do what you do! Blood, the play is yours. You need to know and make sure they know that at the end of the day, my word is *'Law'*! If I make a call, the shit ain't negotiable!"

Voorheeze spoke with no wavering in his voice whatsoever. Wasn't no room for mistakes and there wasn't gon' be no chances! Clark felt a tinge of heat from the way his brother addressed him. Yet, he also felt admiration toward the little nigga. Shit, he wasn't a little nigga no more. But, could he actually take orders from his little brother? The last time they had a chance to fuck with each other they were kids. Voorheeze had been locked up since he was twelve. He'd come home once for two months then went to prison.

Now, he sat before Clarkola a grown man with gangsta ambitions. How would he look to his niggaz taking orders from his little brother? Just then his foot nudged against the Gucci pack. Shit, fuck what niggaz would think! Clark was about his chips.

So, his only response was, "Let's eat!"

***

T'Rida and Johnny Spitz sat low in the seats of the stolen car, in all black with their bangers cocked and laying on their laps. As they passed the blunt back and forth, the two of them sat in silence listening to *DMX* declare his loyalty to his niggaz on *'My Dogs'*. A nigga named High-Top had the park over on Berry Ave in Hayward on lock. He also had A-Street, too. Initially, T'Rida wasn't going to move on High-Top. Top was a real poodle, his older brother was an active Dove for Kumi, so High-Top used that to buffalo niggaz.

Now, T'Rida didn't give a fuck one way or the other. Since T'Rida was Black Guerilla Family, he figured he would extend an envelope of diplomacy. The three Birds that Cantelope had placed in his trunk, he gave to Johnny. Johnny was supposed to give them to High-Top as a way of showing respect before they opened up shop and did their thang. If he had just refused the package, it would've been one thing, but he disrespected T'Rida. Because of his disrespect, he would be an example to niggaz.

Hayward Lanes was popping that Friday night. Niggaz was out stuntin' and showcasing their whips, while bitches were out showcasing their bodies tryna catch a trick. Even the gold diggers were out tryna find a sponsor, each one telling herself, she had what it took to be wifey to a Boss. T'Rida could see the bitch in High-Top from across the parking lot, as he and Johnny watched him and his weak ass crew, as the nigga acted like he was the king of the Bay.

The longer T'Rida stared at the pussy, the angrier he got. He hated cowards that paraded around like they were Gods. He also knew that killing High-Top would present a problem with his brother. But fuck it, an example had to be made so lessons would be learned.

T'Rida put the blunt out and got out the car. Johnny Spitz was right behind him as they both reached the front of the car and made their way across the crowded parking lot. No one paid attention to the two killas. Johnny carried a baby AR under his black leather jacket, while T'Rida walked tall with a .45 magnum in his hand down by his leg.

High-Top was tipsy. He had the two baddest bitches all over him. He was surrounded by eight niggaz from his team as they relaxed and chilled in front of their whips. He was sitting on the hood of his Black on Black Drop Corvette, with one bitch in his lap and the other kissing on his neck. Shit, a mothafucka couldn't tell him shit! Just as Sonya stuck her tongue in his ear, High-Top spotted T'Rida and Johnny Spitz walking up to him.

Tasha felt his body tense up and turned her head to see what he was looking at. High-Top's heart immediately began racing, but he knew he was surrounded by his team, so his false bravado outweighed his common sense. His mind was screaming danger, but the liquor and courage from having his team with him silenced his common sense.

"Well, well, well, if it ain't Mr. Major League himself!" Even as he said the snide comment, High-Top's fear screamed volumes to the trained ear.

GORILLAZ IN THE BAY

"I was shocked, you wouldn't accept my gift and simple gesture." T'Rida feigned hurt as he spoke. "Man, I don't need that chump change nigga." A little more courage seeped into High-Top's voice.

Some of the niggaz who were with High-Top noticed the banger in T'Ridas hand, began getting nervous and whispering to one another. Still, High-Top was oblivious to what was taking place. He didn't even notice Johnny Spitz move his hands from under his jacket in response to the niggaz around him getting nervous. Immediately, they got the message, shut the fuck up and stopped moving. The move was not lost on Tasha who began easing her body from between High-Top's legs and out of the line of fire.

"But on the real though, I wanted to hear what you told my little mans to tell me from your own lips." T'Rida now spoke with the deadly venom of a hissing Black Mamba.

Again, danger alarms were sounding off all through High-Top's mind. But shit, he had eight niggaz with him. What the fuck was this lil' nigga gon' do?

"Nigga, I told dat lil' bitch to tell ya pussy ass to take that shit and shove it up yo' candy ass! And go fuck yourself, nigga!" High-Top spat out as all his courage fully returned.

"I knew yo' punk ass was too stupid to see the real. Yo' bitch ass so caught up on your own hype, you couldn't see I was trying to save your brother's life!"

The puzzled expression on High-Top's face proved he didn't have a fucking clue. T'Rida didn't give a fuck. He slowly lifted the big gun.

Boom! Boom!

Two shots point blank in the face followed by three in the chest sent High-Top spread eagle on his windshield clueless and soulless.

"Not to worry though, when he comes to avenge you, I will make sure he follows you," T'Rida told the corpse that continued to bleed.

Pandemonium broke out in the parking lot, as people screamed and yelled, bumping into one another frantically trying to evacuate the scene after hearing the gunshots. All except the twelve that surrounded the dead body. No one moved! They all stood frozen waiting to see what the next play was.

It was T'Rida who made it. "I don't hold any of you niggaz responsible for the idiotic shit, your Boss did. So, ain't none of us got a problem. But, if any of you feel the need to represent a dead dumb nigga and come for me, you will follow him—" He paused to look each man in the eyes to make sure they understood. Then he looked at both women who stood as still as a deer in headlights. "You two look, too smart to have seen what happened here, right?" he asked.

Immediately their heads nodded vigorously! Accepting what he'd done, T'Rida turned around and calmly strolled back across the parking lot with Johnny. They got back into the stolen car and drove off like they were leaving the bowling alley after a friendly night of bowling.

***

"Alright, look family, I know you about yo' shit big homie, so wondering if you gon' get down ain't even a question for me. I need to know that you, 'bout to stick to da plan." DeeDee looked over at Big Roc starring the killa directly in his eyes.

It was as if he was staring into a deep abyss of dark black nothingness. The soulless orbs of Big Roc would terrify most just gazing upon them, but not DeeDee. To him starring into Roc's eyes was just like staring into the mirror at his own soulless eyes.

"I need you to understand that my lead is to be followed no questions asked and no improvising.

Big Roc's response reflected the Old Killas feelings to the whole situation. "It's yo' play lil' Homie." Roc had no feelings.

DeeDee slowed the all black Camaro down and came to a stop in the middle of the street a block away from their location. Roc climbed out of the Camaro. He pulled his jacket closed against the winter chill, to actually conceal the chrome pistol in his waist. As instructed he walked up 82nd headed toward E-14th. DeeDee drove to the corner of E-14th directly in front of the liquor store. Instead of turning the car off, he checked his rearview mirror. Right on cue, he spotted D.J. reaching the corner of 82nd.

DeeDee climbed out of the Camaro with a P-90 in his hands and rounded the corner. Though he was on the opposite side of the street, D.J. was a few steps ahead of DeeDee with an FN in each hand. The group of hustlas standing on the back side of the store was unaware of the dangerous net that was closing in around them. Just as D.J. came parallel to the group, a 4-door Ford Bronco skidded loudly to a complete stop directly in front of the group of hustlas.

The sound of the tires screeching violently against the asphalt got everyone's attention. While everyone's attention was on the truck with the tinted windows Big Roc did his thang!

Booca! Bocca! Bocca! Bocca!

The first two niggaz dropped right where they stood, because of the bullets Roc put in their heads. As soon as the gunshots rang out, the Ford Bronco pulled off. Everybody standing in the group turned their attention to Big Roc who was beginning to side step toward the middle of the street. No one saw D.J. once the truck was out of the way *Faaaaaaaa! Faaaaaaaaa!* The F Ns began to sing. The moment DeeDee was sure, Big Roc was out of the way, his P-90 added to the violent chorus the guns were singing.

Taat! Taat! Taat! Taat!

The Bronco stopped just before rounding the corner of East 14th Street and Gunz climbed out wit' his .40 Caliber Glocks.

Boom! Boom! Boom! Boom!

The killas knocked down any and everything that moved with speed and precision. This being a BGF dope corner they were hitting, Gunz didn't want to take no chances. The organization birthed women too, so there was no telling who was affiliated and who wasn't. Which is why Gunz wanted everybody laid the fuck down! It was complete chaos for the hustlas. Bullets were flying from every angle. They didn't know which way to run. A couple of the hustlas returned fire, but it was useless. As they shot in one direction they were gunned down from another.

Big Roc saw a skinny dark nigga duck down low, running behind the chain link fence, that led to the parking lot behind the store.

"Oh, where you going, bitch?" Big Roc yelled as he sent missiles at the nigga, hitting him in the back of his head and back.

In a matter of seconds, an entire Cadre of the Black Guerilla Families *NuMan* – *NuWoman* were annihilated. Bodies were laid everywhere. DeeDee and Big Roc jogged around the corner and jumped into the Bronco.

Later, when the crime scene was secured, the death count totaled twenty-four and Gunz was just getting started!

Chapter VII

Voorheeze was just getting off the phone with his play sister Margo when his phone rang.

"Hello?" Voorheeze answered it right away.

"Habari Gani ndugu?" *How are you doing brother?* The greeting threw Voorheeze off. Although he and his folks in prison spoke Swahili, no one really used it in the streets.

"Habari Gani wewe aku?" *I'm fine, how are you?* Voorheeze responded back in Swahili as a courtesy, but he wouldn't hold a full conversation in Swahili unless he was talking to one of his comrades.

Pulling out into traffic, he continued, "Who dis, though?"

"Brah, it's me. We need to talk," the caller said.

"Who da fuck is me?"

"Nigga, dis Dame." It had been a while since Voorheeze heard from his crazy ass comrade.

"Yeah, nigga it's me," Dame yelled into the phone sounding juiced as always.

"I ain't even about to ask yo' crazy ass how you got dis number! Mwezi, *Comrade.* What's up wit' it?" He said as he navigated through traffic.

Voorheeze knew, whatever it was, it was a problem. That's usually the only time niggaz reach out to you, out of the blue.

"You know how shit is, V. When niggaz make moves, the streets talk. When it's power moves the streets be yelling. Like dat move yo' lil' niggaz been making." The laughter and excitement was gone. Dame's tone was very serious and political.

"Mwezi, we need to have a little baraza, *meeting,*" Dame told him.

"It's cool, lil' brah. We talking family shit or some otha shit." Voorheeze tried to decipher the magnitude of a meeting he was talking 'bout.

"The Family, good, Big Brah. I'm on some Case shit."

"Say no more, brah, I'm on my way." Voorheeze hung up.

Dame was Jamaa, just like Voorheeze and T'Rida. All three stood firm on their oaths and guidelines, and all three wore two

DE'KARI

hats that were very rare. Two hats mean being committed and loyal to two separate factions at the same time. Along with being Jamaa, he was also Nutt Case. Them niggaz were young and wild and extremely dangerous. Voorheeze had extreme love for them niggaz. He'd been knowing the Founders for years. He was closest to Dame and Big Joe, but cool with all of them.

If Dame wanted a meeting it could only be about the moves, Gunz and them had been putting down. Hell, the entire Bay Area knew that them niggaz weren't playing fair. Since they came on the scene, they came smashing shit. Hence the name Nutt, the average person would probably take some back up with them, but not Voorheeze. These were his niggaz, he didn't have shit to be worried about.

He got off the freeway at 98th. He went down until he hit E-14th and made a right. He made another right pulling into Church's Chicken. He parked at the back of the parking lot, popped the trunk and grabbed his double shoulder rig. Before the phone call from Dame, he had just come from visiting his Auntie Pat. He loved and respected her too much to have his guns on him in her house. So, he put them in the trunk.

Putting his Dragons on, he jumped back in the car and headed to his destination. He arrived at the house ten minutes later. The first thing that caught his attention was the number of niggaz, who were in the front. That wasn't normal, just for a brief moment he got nervous. After all these niggaz were the most feared niggaz in Oakland. But, that moment was brief. He got out and made his way to the front door. Every set of eyes mugged him. Voorheeze knew better than to poke a bear. So, he didn't mug back, but he didn't bitch up either. When he made it to the front porch the door swung open.

"Crazy ass Jason mothafuckin', Voorheeze!" Dame greeted him the way he always did.

"What's up, Mwezi?" Voorheeze greeted as they embraced.

"Nigga, look like Case getting ready to go to war," He said gesturing to the niggaz who'd just walked through.

"Nah, ain't no war. We just about to go make our presence felt, though." Dame opened the door wider and stepped out the way. "But fuck all that, come in nigga."

GORILLAZ IN THE BAY

The room was so hazy from the weed smoke Voorheeze could barely see. A house full of Jamaicans couldn't of had the room cloudier. niggaz was chilling, playing video games and smoking. When Big Joe saw Voorheeze he paused the game, stood up and embraced him.

"Long time no see, brah."

"What's up with my big brah, tho?" Voorheeze responded.

"Shit, you know just casing it." It sounded so normal.

They made their way to the back so they could talk. Dame was smiling. People always mistook and underestimated him because of that smile. He looked harmless and his good-hearted nature didn't help. However, in a room full of killaz he held his own.

As they sat at the table, Greg came and joined them. "V, you smokin'?" He asked as he sat down.

"Nah, brah, but I'm drinking," Voorheeze replied pointing at the big bottle of Remy on the table.

"Shit do you," Greg told him.

There wasn't no cups at the table. When it's real luv amongst niggaz they just pass the bottle around. Voorheeze cracked the bottle and took two swigs. Greg lit the blunt. Dame produced his own blunt and lit that. Joe was always quiet and thinking, he may have been Kumi, but he was all Guerilla.

"Brah, nigga, reached out to you because you, my loved one. Why should I reach out to Gunz when you're my folks—" He paused to let that hit home.

"Niggaz see what y'all on and we respect it. Spot smashing and running over shit. That's the Case way, but mothafuckaz tryna see how far y'all tryna go wit' this shit. Cause that last play by the store was a little too close for comfort. V, you my brotha and I love you. I hope I'll neva have to go to war with you, but I'm Nutt Case all the way and we confronting that, that gets in the way of Case!" Joe didn't say any of this in a threatening manner. He didn't have to. Real niggaz knew it wasn't how you say something but what's being said.

First of all, you right, we family. All of us—" He paused and looked at each man. "Now, what we on? We getting money, brah that's it. Period, point blank!"

"Ya mean that shit by the store wasn't on no smash shit."

"Really, ain't none of it been no smash shit. We got a plan that's all. And everybody we felt would get in the way of that plan or have a problem with it got removed—"

Voorheeze paused and took another swig of the Remy enjoying the burn as it slid down his throat. He turned his head toward Dame.

"Brah, you already know, I'm an old guard. I ain't got no time to be getting into it with mothafuckaz over policies. So, that's what that was."

"V, I know you ain't gon' lie to us, but from over here it look like y'all tryna take over the Town. Now me personally, I don't give a fuck about nothing, but Case shit! Y'all can have whatever else y'all want. But, don't fuck wit' nuttin' dats Case!" Dame spoke for the first time.

"Dame, on the spirit of Lil' Dude we ain't taking the Town. What needed to be done is already done. Now it's get money time." The Remy had him feeling good.

Greg and Joe exchanged a look. Nothing was spoken but a whole lot was understood. Brothas or not, Voorheeze knew that if they weren't feeling what he had to tell them he wasn't eva going to leave that house.

"Well since it's get money time. What you talking?" Greg was about the money first and foremost.

"That's easy. We'll beat whatever price you're at. But before we go any further, we got to have an understanding."

"What's that?"

"As long as our product is A1, you buy solely from us."

"As long as the shit is A1, we good."

"A'aight, so, tell me where y'all at on the package and how many you can handle."

"Right now, we at twenty-four doing about ten a week." Greg figured telling him two grand less than he was getting would get them a better price overall. He didn't know Voorheeze already knew what he intended to do.

"Well, we at nineteen." He knew that would get their attention.

"Shit, lil', brah at nineteen we'll take five now." Big Joe couldn't help himself, he had to speak up. All he saw was money.

GORILLAZ IN THE BAY

"Look I'ma hit my folks and let 'em know what's good. The package will be dropped off tomorrow. Don't worry about the dough, he gon' drop off twelve, pay for ten of them next week when you ready to re-up. Two of 'em just cause we brotha's. And because I'm walking out of here." All four of them started laughing. Voorheeze was far from a dummy.

Back in the car, he picked up the phone to let Gunz know what was what. He figured he would fill T'Rida in when he saw him. Having Nutt Case on board was a good thang. Of course, it would bring more money to the table but more muscle as well. He smiled at first, then began laughing. They neva knew, he had seen lil' Boonie standing behind him with a chopper through the reflection of the window.

When you want it all, you gotta go Hard as a Motha-fucka!

'I can feel it coming in the air tonight/hold on/I've been waiting for this moment for all my life/hold on/ hold on.'

As the words to *DMX's 'I Can Feel It'* blasted out of the speakers, Voorheeze cruised down highway 101 on his way to the East side of San Jose. He was on his way to hook up with his folks, Johnny Blaze over in the King Ocala neighborhood. On that first night so long ago, the three had developed a strategy and plan that would reshape the face of the game. Johnny 'Johnny Blaze' Ramirez was in Pelican Bay State Prison a few years ago and had gotten into some shit. Voorheeze had been dealing with Johnny for a minute, on some getting money shit with them cell phones while on the yard. Blaze is a Norteno and six Sureno's got the drop on him inside the infirmary.

When the shit kicked off Voorheeze happened to be there. Shit wasn't looking good for Johnny and since he was fucking with him, Voorheeze decided to even things out. From that moment on their relationship wasn't just business, they became patnas. They stayed in contact since they'd been out. Johnny told Voorheeeze that he was holdin', and if he ever needed him Johnny would be there for him. Of course,

Voorheeze never called him on that because he didn't feel the time was right.

Instead of going straight to him when he first got out, like most niggaz would've, he figured he'd wait. Knowing that if he went looking for a handout, Johnny would've put him on. But if he waited until he put something together, Johnny would not only put him on, but would also see that a nigga came correct and respect him even more. Naturally, making whatever blessing he received that much better.

So, the night that Rida and them decided to put their plans in action, Voorheeze turned to Johnny. A lot of things had gone down in West Oakland. As Voorheeze cruised down the freeway in his limited-Edition Chevrolet Suburban, he reflected on the moves they had put down and the efficiency in which they built their organization.

The three of them agreed, they'd come together and do the damn thang for real. They played their positions, combined their resources and began a complete *take-over*. Their plan was first the Bay, then California. Sure, you had a couple of major playas moving weight in a few cities. You had niggaz networking for real in the bay area. But, one thing has never happened in the Bay Area, and that is one machine and one family controlling it all. These three had visionary hearts, discipline, and knew it could be done.

It would be a simple plan given the fact that Voorheeze had roots and family ties in East Palo Alto and Menlo Park, Gunz had them Village niggaz ready to get gutta, and T'Rida had niggaz who had Hayward on lock and had pulled in the shady Eighties. No one ever expected the amount of gunplay that followed, would occur. They were like a boxer rolling with the punches thrown at him. They met every situation head-on and made their presence felt. The bloodbath was vicious and lasted about eight months and claimed the lives of over one-hundred and fifty young street soldias.

The residents of the Bay Area would remember and talk about that summer for years to come. Gunz and Rida first united the Village with the Shady Eighties, then took over East Oakland altogether. Once they were in position to take over the West as well they did, it wasn't difficult at all. Rida would give niggaz an option, they could either fuck with them or get lifted. On some real life *'Paid in Full'* shit. Most niggaz and crews fucked with them, but a few chose to try and do it on their own. Those were the ones who paid with their lives.

Rida and them were niggaz on a mission. It was *'Ride or Die*, straight the fuck up. Bodies fell in the streets like leaves falling off a tree in the fall. Gunz, on the other hand, operated in a way that would make Rida seem like a saint. He gave no one options. He picked out the niggaz he thought would pose a problem and eliminated all of them, no questions asked, no chances. The message was quickly understood by those that were spared. *"God Forgives, but Gunz don't!"*

Now Voorheeze was a completely different story. There weren't many machines operating in East Palo Alto like they did in Oakland. You just had blocks where niggaz did their thang. Instead of muscle, he utilized his mind and simply gave niggaz a new and better plug to fuck with, and a chance to fuck wit' some real niggaz. P.A. niggaz being about their money, before anything else, made things real easy. Aside from the name he'd made for himself, his family was one of the families that controlled shit in the city.

Even still, there were a couple of small situations, but they were quickly taken care of. Within those eight months of violence, hard work, and strategic planning a team was being built and a family was being formed. The *'Neva Die Mobb Family,* was born, bred, nurtured and operating strong.

Voorheeze exited on Story Road and drove down King Road while wondering how Johnny still lived at home with his parents. All the money he was making, he could have gotten a nice large spot up in the San Jose hills or something. That wasn't Johnny, he had to be with the Homies, he had to remain in the neighborhood. The clientele they provided Johnny was so lucrative, constant, and problem-free, that they soon began getting kilos for fifteen thousand a piece, while everyone else was still paying twenty-five.

They were moving product faster than McDonald's moved ninety-nine cent double cheeseburgers. Johnny and Voorheeze had worked out an arrangement that suited both of their schedules. Voorheeze would send someone to meet one of Johnny's boys and bring him two-hundred thousand and the following day, he'd personally pick up the work from Johnny. This was a weekly arrangement and it was cool in the beginning, but with the family growing so fast, Voorheeze's time was needed doing other things. On top of that, he would never personally pick up work from anyone else. For Johnny, however, it was a different story.

Johnny was extremely paranoid and wouldn't deal with anyone, but Voorheeze under no circumstances. Regardless, today Voorheeze was going to let Johnny know, they needed to work out another arrangement. As he always had done, when Voorheeze reached the corner of Ocala, he picked up his phone to let Johnny know, he was rounding the block. Voorheeze pulled in front of the house and jumped out with his bottle of Brisk Iced Tea in his hand and made his way to the garage.

The door was already open and he could see Johnny playing Madden on the Xbox 360. Like most cats in the hood, Johnny had turned his garage into a small den sort of like a man cave. He had it loaded with everything from an entertainment system, pool table, mini bar, and a few other things.

"What's good, homie? Grab a controller, I'll restart the game, so I can get in yo' ass." Johnny always talked shit but couldn't win to save his life.

Voorheeze was the only cat in the game that Johnny trusted enough to invite to his house. No one else had that privilege, not even his own homeboys. They say when you build a bond with someone during drastic times such as war, that bond will be stronger than any other and would last longer than any other. Shit, Voorheeze had saved Johnny's life. Shit couldn't get anymore drastic than that.

When he got into it with the South Siders, they had actually hit Johnny four times. If it wasn't for Voorheeze being there to stick three of them and back the mothafuckaz off him, it would have been a completely different story. So, not only was this bond established in testing times, it was dire times.

After beating Johnny thirty-five to fourteen, Voorheeze told him, they needed to discuss a new arrangement. Although Johnny didn't like changes, he knew 'Neva Die' had gotten huge and Voorheeze was essential to their expansion and operations. Voorheeze assured him, he'd personally pick some-one to make the pick-ups. All things considered, the family was spending well over eight-hundred thousand a month with Johnny and was working on making that over one-point-six-million, which was in a month from now. This was more than double the amount they were pushing.

The two decided on a system where Johnny wouldn't have to meet anyone personally. So, all was good for them. After fin-ishing things with Johnny, Voorheeze decided to head over to Kim's Nails and Boutique in Sunnyvale off Lawrence Express-way. Once all the violence had slowed down and everyone was able to start relaxing, Voorheeze began taking the time out to treat himself to a manicure and pedicure once a week. His mother used to always tell him when he was growing up to treat himself not cheat himself.

Later that night, he was supposed to meet up with Gunz and Rida over at Tommy T's, a comedy club in Dublin. When Gunz came back from Philly, he'd told them some of the shit he was seeing out that way. He informed them that if they implemented it into their shit, it would only better their business. Gunz had proven to be more important to the squad than Voorheeze or Rida could have ever imagined.

While sitting in the chair with Cheryl working on his hands and some little Asian thang at his feet. He decided, he'd follow up this treatment with a full body massage. They had come a long way in just a short period of time and had been putting in major work. Now that they had arrived, life was looking good.

DE'KARI

Chapter VIII

Fresh out of the shower, T'Rida was feeling like a million dollars while listening to *Messy Marv's 'Turf Politics'*. Money was good, and life itself was good, right now. He'd bought a house for Monique and the kids two months ago in Tracy. It was a five-bedroom joint complete with twelve-foot ceilings, plush carpeting, a big ass backyard and one of the best state-of-the-art video surveillance systems. He also had a second house in Milpitas. It was just a spot to lay his head when he was in the Bay taking care of business.

He also bought a beach house in Aptos. The house in Aptos was to be used as a safe house if shit was ever to hit the fan. From the beginning, it was clear, that even though, the three of them had started this shit together, it was actually T'Rida who ran the family. This wasn't verbally nor officially stated amongst the three of them, it was just how things gradually became. Neither Voorheeze nor Gunz tripped off this because they all played a certain part and each one of them played their position to the fullest. This is why they'd gotten to the level they were at now.

T'Rida's intentions were to drive out to Tracy to surprise Monique and the kids for a few hours since he didn't have anything planned for the day, until the meeting with Gunz and Voorheeze later that night. However, he wouldn't be able to carry out those plans. As he was deciding on which outfit to wear his cell phone started ringing. One of his lieutenants, C-Murda was on the line sounding very hysterical. Somebody had just robbed him and J. Styles while they were leaving one of the safe houses. Styles had gotten shot four times in the chest and was currently in the emergency room at Washington Hospital in Fremont.

"I'm on my way! I'll be at you in about twenty minutes." Was all he said on the phone, as a volcanic fire began building inside of him.

This was twice this month that someone in the organization had been robbed. T'Rida knew the game and knew that you always had to consider taking some loses. You always had to stay prepared for some type of inconvenience or misfortune in this life. He didn't think someone would be stupid enough to kick some shit off so soon after all the bloodshed they'd rained down on the Bay Area had just ended. He also knew that this wasn't a fluke. One robbery could be considered a fluke, but two robberies popping off in the same month, had to mean somebody was plotting on the team.

Fuck it, tonight would just have to be the night that he made an example out of mothafuckaz. T'Rida thought he'd already made his position known in the Bay, but he guessed he was wrong. After this though, niggaz would know that Neva Die meant just that! *'Neva Fucking Die!*

After the call from Murda, T'Rida placed two calls before leaving the house. Then he jumped quickly into his Navigator and raced to the hospital, with death on his mind and murder in his heart. Marlon, the first person T'Rida called before leaving the house, was already in the parking lot of the hospital with two trucks full of Hyena's waiting for T'Rida.

T'Rida had known Marlon since back in the day when they were in Fremont for a minute. Marlon had always been a solid cat and an effective soldier. So, T'Rida put him in charge of his *Hit Squad*. A squad that was hand-picked and chosen by Marlon himself. A squad tried and tested, loyal to Marlon alone.

"Wait here, I'll be back in a few," T'Rida told the killa as he marched into the emergency room to find Murda.

Marlon hadn't been told anything over the phone, so he didn't know why they were there. All T'Rida told him was to meet him at the Hospital with a squad. Marlon could see from the expression on his Boss's face, they were indeed about to set shit off.

T'Rida found Murda at the back of the E.R. They walked down to the cafeteria where they could be alone so Murda could fill him in on what happened. After hearing from Murda how everything went down, T'Rida instructed him to go home and lay low until things cooled off. There was no reason for him to stay around the hospital. He couldn't do anything for Styles except pray that the young goon would make it. That he could do from home. Knowing that the hospital would indeed notify the police about receiving a gunshot victim, T'Rida made his way out of the hospital as well, making sure he left in an opposite direction than-Murda.

He figured, if the hospital hadn't called the police already, they were going to at any moment, and he wasn't going to be anywhere near there when they did. T'Rida and Marlon drove over to McDonald's on Fremont Boulevard, across from the Fremont Hub while the goons followed close behind in the other vehicles. They needed a spot where they could park and discuss what T'Rida had found out from Murda. He also wanted to give Marlon instructions on what he intended for the Hit Squad to do.

They weren't in the parking lot long enough for one of the young goons to walk in and place an order, T'Rida was gone before the goon ever came back. Before the night was over T'Rida wanted to know who was responsible for the robbery.

At first, he thought of calling Voorheeze and putting him up on what popped off, but he figured why bother him? T'Rida could fill him in later tonight when they met up. So, instead of calling Voorheeze, T'Rida picked up the phone intending to send a message to Monique to let her know, he wouldn't be coming home tonight. Just as he picked up his phone it rang. He looked at the caller I.D. recognizing Big Booty Jenn's number immediately.

Jennifer was one badass red bone, in her early forties, but she was built like she was still in her twenties. She had the type of body a nigga just wanted to play with all night.

Jennifer had been a small playa in E.P.A. when she was in her twenties and thirties, but when she turned forty, she got out of the game entirely. It was the same year her brother was gunned down in the streets. His death was what made her decide to take a step back and analyze her life. Even though she wasn't in the game any longer directly, she kept her hand in something at a distance. A lot of the O.G.'s in P.A. over the years tried to fuck with Jenn after her surgery, but she wasn't fucking with them. She would never forget, they were the same niggaz who talked shit about her and her weight back in the day. She would never in a million years entertain the idea of them seeing how gorgeous her body was underneath her clothes now.

From the start, Jenn liked T'Rida. From what she saw, the youngster had a swag about him like no one else, yet he was far from cocky like most youngstas. He did his thang and carried himself like a well-seasoned vet in the game. To her, he truly was far beyond his years in maturity. He was a young man with an old soul.

"What's hood wit' it, lil dollar?" T'Rida knew she hated when he talked ghetto, but she loved it when he made up some new little nickname to call her.

"You. If you're ready, or should I say if you think you're ready?" she replied, giggling while her mind pictured his hard tongue playing hide and seek with her pearl. Thinking about how skilled he was with his tongue caused her panties to moisten as she became super wet. Forcing herself to concentrate back on her reason for calling, she continued. "I need you to stop by my place. I just heard about something I need to run by you."

"What's good, wit' it?" he asked her.

"I'm at my daughter's house in the 'G', come over I'm in the garage—"

He cut her off before she could finish her statement. "Jenn, you, know that on any given Sunday I would be all over that invitation, but right now ma, I got a situation that needs dealing with."

"Baby, you know the streets talk and my ears are always tuned in. Tonight, they picked up on something that just happened to you. So, you need to come over here and see me." She didn't have to say anything else.

Even before he responded, T'Rida was turning on the ignition of the truck. After giving Marlon brief instructions, T'Rida was pulling out of the McDonald's parking lot and heading toward the Dumbarton bridge.

"I'll be there in ten minutes," He replied to Jennifer before hanging up.

From what he'd heard, Jennifer had bought a phat-ass house out in Stockton. When she bought that house, she had given the house in the Gardens to her daughter Dominique. She'd turned the garage into a bedroom for herself for the nights that she stayed in East Palo Alto. As T'Rida opened the door, he took in the aroma of Shea Butter. He was always taken aback when he looked at her room in the garage. The shit was nice as hell, all exotic and shit. To Rida, the most impressive thing in her room was her bed.

She had it custom built, twice as big as any California King bed and actually took up over half of the garage. As he walked in, she was laying seductively on it, wearing a mint green silk negligee and smoking a blunt. For a quick second after seeing her, T'Rida had briefly forgotten his purpose for coming over.

"You heard something about what happened to a couple of my boyz today?" He finally asked, snapping back to reality.

"Straight to business like always," she mumbled, feeling slightly mad that he didn't at least acknowledge the new nightie she'd put on for him.

Handing him the blunt, she got up to pour them a drink. Once she was back sitting on the bed, she told him everything she'd heard. It turned out that Jenn has a cousin who fucks with one of the cats who pulled off the robbery. She'd overheard him on his cell phone bragging to one of his boi's about the shit, right after it happened. At first, she felt good that the mothafucka had finally gotten some money, so she could get some from his scandalous ass and go shopping.

At least that's what she was thinking until she heard the mothafucka say it was one of Jason Voorheeze's drop boys they'd robbed. Hearing this, she didn't want any parts of the money or the dumb ass mothafucka, she called her boyfriend, who took the money. In fact, she was so scared thinking about what Voorheeze would do to the mothafuckaz who'd robbed him along with anyone who was with him when he found them. She walked outside and called her cousin from her cell phone. Knowing how cool her cousin and Voorheeze were, she told her at least five times to make sure she let Voorheeze know, she didn't have shit to do with the robbery.

Everyone in East Palo Alto knew how Voorheeze got down and she didn't want anything to do with him. When her cousin first told her the business, Jenn thought about calling Voorheeze, but that nigga was too hot-headed and short tempered. No matter how cool they were, she wasn't going to be the one to bare him any bad news. Jason Voorheeze was by far the most intellectual dude she'd ever met, but sometimes his temper would override his intellect and he acted an all-out donkey. Besides, Voorheeze

DE'KARI

didn't have a head game like T'Rida did. She was also horny as hell, so she figured she might as well get a little something-something for herself for looking out for the team.

For T'Rida, hearing this news was like busting a nut on a cold rainy day. Not only did he learn who was responsible for robbing him, but Jenn's cousin told her where the little Gilligan lived and was at that very moment. It was just a few minutes after five when T'Rida picked up the phone and called Marlon. When Marlon answered, T'Rida told him to forget anything he was doing, right now about that situation. Marlon was confused, but he knew better to question his Boss's orders.

Besides, T'Rida's next comment explained everything he needed to know. *"Dress the kids for church and take them to choir practice."* This was a code they'd been using for a while. A code that meant it was time to suit up and go to war.

T'Rida told Marlon he'd meet him over by Price's Barber Shop on Clark Street, at six thirty. Voorheeze had an uncle that worked at the shop who was real cool peoples. He never allowed any bullshit to go down at the shop, but the crew did kick it there on occasion.

He got off the phone and spent the next forty minutes or so fucking the breath out of Jennifer. Blood she had some good ass pussy. To him, her fuck game was so good, that eating Jenn's pussy was his way of thanking her for what was to come after the head. At times T'Rida found himself thinking that if it wasn't for Monique, Jenn would definitely be wifey material. She was bad, loyal, and her sex game was out of this world. Plus, she knew the game inside out and respected the rules to the utmost.

T'Rida pulled into the parking lot of the barbershop at a quarter after. Big Pete had someone in his chair when T'Rida entered the shop.

"What's up, nephew?" Pete greeted him.

Back in the day, Pete was a major playa. That beast people could hear beneath his calm demeanor was in full effect back then, when he made one helluva name for himself. Yet, for those who'd only heard the stories, the respect was out of admiration for a goon who became a boss and left the game by choice, not by force.

86

"Unc, what's hood wit' da Goon?" T'Rida embraced the man he came to love and respect as if he was his very own uncle.

"Shit, Rogue, you know me just getting this money. I'm finishing up my last head, gimme a sec and we'll take a walk." After the guy in the chair paid and tipped Pete, he and T'Rida went outside and Pete lit a Black and Mild. "So, what've you been up to, Rogue?" Pete asked while lighting the cigar.

"You know, just tryna get my paper game right, while making sure I stay true along the way."

Blowing his smoke out, Pete responded. "Shit, from where I'm standing y'all look like, y'all are doing shit right to me. Just make sure y'all keep things the way you got em and y'all will be alright." He took a drag on his cigar and continued. "Niggaz fuck up when they switch up their style and go against their own norms."

T'Rida looked at his watch thinking to himself that Marlon should be pulling up any moment. He explained to Pete that he was meeting one of the fellas there in a few minutes cause they had some business to take care of.

"You straight, you need me or anything?" Pete asked. He himself had grown fond of the little nigga over the years.

"Naw, we straight, Unc. That's a good look, but yo' boi got it."

"Just make sure y'all stay safe and keep yo' eyes and ears open, nephew."

Just as Pete finished his statement, T'Rida saw Marlon turning the corner onto C Street. He signaled for him to pull next door. Out of respect for Pete and old man Price, he didn't want Marlon to pull into the barbershop knowing the truck was loaded with an arsenal. He left Pete with a warm departure and jumped into his Navigator.

Marlon backed out of the store at the same time and followed him. They turned right onto Bay Road and made another right on Pulgas. When they came to Runnymede, they made a left and drove to the end of the street and parked in front of Runnymede Charter School. Marlon let T'Rida know that the rest of the team was waiting for them in the McDonald's parking lot on University.

DE'KARI

T'Rida filled Marlon in on everything he'd found out from Jenn, and they devised a plan of retaliation. "We're not going to need everyone you brought for this. All we gon' take is two niggaz wit' us and have four more follow us in another whip. The rest of them niggaz you can tell to stay on standby," T'Rida told him.

"What about Gunz and V, are we gonna fill 'em in?" Marlon asked his boss as he picked up his phone to give the orders to his men.

"We good. Gunz ain't gonna be back for another hour or so and ain't no need bothering V with this shit. He got some other business he's taking care of today," T'Rida said as he pulled away driving Marlon's black expedition. "Tell dem niggaz to move out and meet us at the post office."

It turned out that the nigga they were on their way to see was related to this nigga named Wendell. Neither one of the niggaz were important though, but the knowledge was important. T'Rida remembered Voorheeze had gotten into it with the nigga Wendell about a year back. The nigga had this fine ass mocha chocolate, thick country sista who was sweet on Voorheeze. Anyway, due to him fucking with some cats that fucked wit' his family on some big money shit, Voorheeze had given the nigga a pass, instead of waking his game up.

In fact, he was one of only a few cats Voorheeze had ever given a pass to, either on his own free will or at the request of one of his uncles. All the while, the coward was still envious and jealous of Voorheeze, who'd eventually taken the sista away from the nigga. The envy brewed and festered, smoldering like a campfire left unattained. It was because of this that Wendell gave his cousin the information on the safe house and had him jack Murda and Styles.

Chapter IX

Wendell's cousin Melvin lived in the Midtown Court apartments in south Palo Alto by the Safeway on Middle Field Road. Although, Voorheeze had long ago warned– T'Rida that E.P.A niggaz didn't go to Palo Alto because of the police. T'Rida didn't give a fuck about any of that or the Palo Alto Police Department. T'Rida was from the Town and this was Town Business. Nothing and no one got in the way of Town Business. They pulled into the back of the complex out of sight from the streets.

Marlon and T'Rida headed for the apartment Jenn had given him, with T'Rida leading the way. One of the goons with them stayed at the front entranceway smoking a cigarette, and the second waited at the bottom of the staircase. T'Rida went up the stairs with Marlon directly behind him, alert and ready. The two lookouts had Desert Eagles with silencers on them under their jackets. That was Marlon's thang, his entire squad used Desert Eagles and nothing else. T'Rida reached the top of the stairs, with his .45 automatic drawn, and nestled gently in his right hand. He was about to kick the door open, but at the last minute, he decided to check the door handle. Believe it or not, most people usually left their front doors unlocked.

To his amusement, the doorknob turned in his hand. He looked back at Marlon, making sure he was ready and walked into the apartment like it was his. Some fat mothafucka was sitting on the couch, he looked up as the door whined quietly when T'Rida pushed it open. He tried to reach for a 9mm resting on the coffee table, but his attempts were futile. The big .45 coughed and knocked the back of his face off. Without so much as breaking stride or slowing down their pace, the gunmen entered the living room as T'Rida let his .45 spit another slug into the chest of the fat man who was slumped over like he was drunk.

They crossed the small living room together, stride for stride like cadets at a military academy. Marlon headed toward the kitchen, while T'Rida went down the hallway toward the backroom. Inside the kitchen, Marlon came face to face with nice, firm, round ass cheeks, as a chocolate sista stood with her back toward him making sandwiches in nothing but a black thong. She didn't hear the gunshots, which were barely whispers due to the silencer.

Marlon walked slowly up to her. After all her back was pointed at him, so he couldn't tell if she had something in her hands or not. She could be playing the role for all he knew, waiting for him to walk up to her and try to stab him or something. So, he cautiously and silently made his way toward her.

When he got close enough to her, he put the tip of the silencer on the back of her head and whispered. "If you so much as gasp, I'ma butter yo' bread."

T'Rida walked down the hallway toward the bedroom as quietly as a cougar stalking his prey. He kicked the door open only to find an empty room. After glancing over it quickly, he made his way back to the front. Coming out of the room, T'Rida saw Marlon standing next to the dead fat fuck with his gun pointed at one of the most chocolate sistas he'd ever seen.

"I'm not going to threaten you or yell at you," Rida addressed the half-naked woman, cowering in front of him. "I'm only going to ask you one question, one time—" He paused to allow her shocked mind to register what she was just told. "Where the fuck is Melvin?" He asked her with a *'don't fuck with me'* look on his face.

"He just walked across the street to the store a few minutes ago," She whispered barely audible, as she couldn't bring herself to take her eyes off the enormous dead body next to her feet.

T'Rida looked at Marlon, but Marlon was already thinking what T'Rida was thinking. If Melvin were to walk back and see the two goons out front he'd run. So, Marlon made his way swiftly to the door and told the one at the bottom of the stairs to wait for them in the truck. The chocolate bitch in front of him told T'Rida her name was Anne, she was Jenn's cousin. T'Rida couldn't help but think that a phat ass was genetically plentiful in their family. Anne continued trying to plead with T'Rida not to kill her.

If he had the time, he would've told her she didn't have anything to worry about. But, he had to hurry up and move the dead fat fuck before Melvin came back. Always one to take the initiative instead of being asked or told what to do, Marlon cleaned up what he could of the blood as fast as he could. When he had a moment, T'Rida told the little dime piece to stop tripping. He knew who she was and didn't plan on doing anything to her, as long as she didn't do anything stupid.

Motioning her back into the kitchen, he asked her. "How much of my shit is in here?"

"I don't know, there are two bags, one filled with money and another filled with dope. They're in the room. He gave two other bags to someone else." She managed to say as she shook like someone on the verge of hypothermia.

Marlon cleaned up as much brain matter as he could, ~~and~~ then he hid in the closet at the front end of the living room just beyond the door. What was left of the blood on the floor looked like someone spilled Kool-Aide or juice.

T'Rida was getting ready to ask Anne a question when he heard the door open. He placed his index finger over his lips, nonverbally telling her not to make a sound.

"Anne, why in the fuck is there Kool-Aide on my floor and yo' ass ain't in dis bitch cleaning dis shit up?" Melvin was furious. "Jack, nigga you spilt dis shit, you, fat fuck?" Melvin yelled as he slammed the apartment door behind him.

"Jack, went to go get his phone charger out of the car. And I just spilled the juice. I'm getting a towel right now to clean it up." amble mmm Anne turned on the faucet to make her lie more believable.

The stupid Gilligan just kept walking, revealing how close he was to the kitchen as he yelled. "I swear to Go—" Was all that left Melvin's lips as T'Rida came stepping from around the corner, out of the kitchen with his pistol in his hand.

The sight of T'Rida not only cut the fuck boi off mid-sentence, it also stopped him dead in his tracks. At that moment, Marlon came out of the closet behind him. The bitch ass nigga was so scared, he dropped the bag of shit he went to the store for. As his mouth opened to say something, T'Rida stopped him.

"You open yo' bitch ass mouth ~~to~~ utter one word, fuck boi, I swear to God I'ma knock yo' shit back, right where you stand." T'Rida pointed at the blood stain on the floor with his pistol. "That ain't Kool-Aide, you stupid son of a bitch. Sit yo' bitch ass down and listen good." The pussy ass nigga did exactly as he was told. 'Rida looked at Marlon. "Run down there and tell da boiz to wait where they are for five minutes and see if anyone comes up after this fuck nigga. If they don't see anybody in five minutes, tell 'em to head out and break wide." He looked over at Marlon. "Say, pussy, my name's T'Rida. That shit you fuck niggaz stole was mine. Do you know who I am?" Before Melvin could speak, T'Rida continued. "Now, I don't take too kindly to—"

Melvin interrupted, "Say, brah, man I didn't know—" The sound that followed was a painfully shrieking scream from Melvin as T'Rida put a bullet into his kneecap.

"Shut yo' bitch ass up, nigga," T'Rida spit out. "Didn't I tell yo' faggot ass not to say shit? Nigga, you think I'm talking for my fucking health?"

Melvin was petrified. He didn't know whether he should answer or not. He wasn't trying to get shot again, because that shit hurt like a m othafucka. He chose not to answer the question and sat there with a stupid, puzzled look on his face, silently praying he was doing the correct thing. He was so terrified, he lost control of his bladder on the couch in front of everyone.

"Now, you, learning mothafucka." Rida chuckled.

Anne looked like she had seen a ghost from the moment T'Rida began talking. It wasn't the gunshot or the blood, not even the dead body that she knew was in the closet that caused this look. It was the mention of the name of the nigga standing in front of her with the gun in his hand. She'd heard of Tommy 'T'Rida' Smith but had never actually seen or met him. If she thought she was scared of Jason Voorheeze, the stories she'd heard about the nigga standing in front of her, outright petrified her. Most females' pussies would soak, knowing, they were in the presence of a nigga like T'Rida, but not Anne. She'd always prayed she would never come face to face with the smooth killa after hearing so many stories about him.

T'Rida looked at her just then and told her to get the two bags she'd told him about earlier. When Anne came back into the front room, she was struggling to carry the two big duffle bags. T'Rida took the two bags from her with the ease of a man grabbing grocery bags, then he dumped them both out onto the floor. Marlon took up a post next to the front window after he came back from telling the two goons outside what T'Rida instructed. He remained there the entire time as lookout.

Not once did his eyes leave the window, but he was still very much aware of everything going on inside the house. Looking down at the contents of the two bags dumped onto the floor, T'Rida noticed there were only five kilos of coke and what he'd guess was only about four or five hundred thousand dollars or so. Since he distributed the same amount of dope and picked up the same amount of money from each house every two days, he knew staring at him in his face was only half of his shit.

"Alright, nigga, dis only half of my shit. Where in da fuck is the other half? Now, you got just one mothafucking chance to tell me, right da fuck now, where my shit at. Before you speak, remember this, I found yo' faggot ass this quick. So, with or without you, I'ma find out and get my shit. You might as well make it light on yourself. If not, we're in for a long and fucked up night."

Melvin could see from the look in T'Rida's eyes, everything the young killer told him was true. Before he even opened his mouth, Anne knew by the pathetic look plastered on his face that this mark ass nigga was about to snitch fast. True, she'd snitched on him when she found out, but this bitch ass nigga ran around acting all gangsta and thugged the fuck out all the time. But the moment the nigga felt some heat on his ass, he started singing like Rick fucking James.

'The nigga T'Rida was right, this nigga was a little faggot!' she thought.

She was scared to death herself, but even still, she would've had to role play things in her mind if she was Melvin. She figured nine times out of ten the nigga

T'Rida was going to kill him anyway, whether he told him what he wanted to hear or not. So, why would you give up whoever you split the shit with? If nothing else, not telling him could be your last effort at going out like a soldier. Not this sucka! She could see it in his eyes, right then, Anne asked herself why she'd ever started fucking with this sucka to begin with.

"JJJJaaac—Jack's brother Lynch. Man, he got the rest of it. I gave it to him. It was all his idea to rob you niggaz to begin wit'. You gotta believe me, man, I didn't know," Melvin cried helplessly.

"You, know this nigga he's talking 'bout?" Rida asked Anne.

When she responded with a yes, he asked if she knew where this other pussy ass nigga lived or how to get ahold of him. "Yes," she replied to both questions.

"How many niggaz were wit' you earlier?" T'Rida wanted to just erase Melvin's faggot ass, right then, but he knew that while he had the nigga singing, he should see just how many songs the mothafucka was willing to belt out.

The nigga told T'Rida it was only three of them that pulled it off. Then he just started volunteering information. He started telling T'Rida how other niggaz operations were run, who killed this nigga or that nigga, who was responsible for this robbery or that one. All the shit that T'Rida shouldn't nor wanted to know. He couldn't stand to hear the niggaz voice any longer. Right then, while Melvin was uttering on, T'Rida squeezed off five rounds from the big .45 into the mothafucka's chest.

After he shot Melvin, he turned to Anne and asked her if she lived at the apartment or somewhere else. She didn't know why he was asking her this or why he even cared for that matter, but she told him anyway. She lived in Oakland. She didn't know why she told him the truth. Together the three of them spent the next half hour wiping and re-wiping every inch of the living room and kitchen. They wiped the places they knew, they'd touched three times and everywhere else twice.

You could never be too careful. Thirty plus minutes later, they were headed back to East Palo Alto, with Anne giving Marlon the directions to Lynch's house and telling them everything she knew about him.

***

The eight-o'clock Express flight from Philadelphia to San Jose International Airport was thirty minutes ahead of time, which was quite alright with Gunz. Mentally, he was preparing for how he'd pitch his idea to T'Rida and Voorheeze. The trip he was returning from had just opened his eyes to a new avenue, on a whole different level then they were on now. What he had in mind would be sweet for the whole family, no question about it. Even still, he always made it a point to present things in the best way when he brought something to the roundtable.

He wasn't ignorant, he knew most people looked at him as just a goon. Everyone except T'Rida and V. He still sought to impress them and gain their respect for his business savvy. To further strengthen and expand the empire, he went above and beyond in all his business ventures and obligations to the family.

He headed to a bar inside the airport. After the long flight, a drink or two was exactly what he needed to relax and get back on point. So, he continued to his destination and got his drink. As Gunz drank his Tokyo Tea, he sat with a smile on his face reflecting on the turns his life had taken. Gunz was finally a Boss. Not the Boss he knew he'd one day become, but there was still time for that. Nevertheless, he was a Boss.

Done with his first Tokyo and nursing his second one, he continued reflecting and grew even more satisfied. Just when he thought things couldn't get any better, a fine ass Mulatto thang came strolling so elegantly through the front entrance, looking jazzy and sophisticated as shit.

Gunz may have been a hood nigga, but he had a deep thirst for knowledge and sophistication, and this thirst for self-improvement made him seek out other knowledgeable people. People who just like him searched for knowledge and carried themselves in the sophisticated manner of a person seeking to do just that. Never would you catch Gunz with a hood rat. He only sought out strong-willed, educated black women with elegance and class. Which is why Miss Mulatto captured his attention.

Gunz waited for the woman to order her drink and find her seat before he picked up his drink and strolled confidently over to where she sat. "Excuse me miss, would you mind if I attempted to keep you company for a while?" Gunz smoothly asked.

The smile she gave Gunz as she glanced up at him was all the answer he needed. Just as he was taking his seat, his cell phone rang. "Talk about bad timing," he joked as he reached into his pocket for the phone.

Seeing the number on the screen, he knew he had to take the call, so he excused himself. All the while she gestured for him to still have a seat while she kept a *'come fuck me'* look on her face. As he answered the call, Gunz thought Voorheeze always had the best intentions, but the worst timing.

"If this is the Angel of death, brah, you have to wait and call me back. Right now, I am staring face to face with my future at this very moment," Gunz said into the phone half-jokingly, half serious. This got a warm sensual giggle out of the woman.

"We got a problem, Rogue." It wasn't the words but the tone in which Voorheeze spoke that instantly wiped the smile off Gunz's face. Just then a cold chill swept through his body.

"Big brah, speak to me. What's wrong?" Gunz asked hoping V would speak words that told him the feeling overcoming him wasn't warranted.

Voorheeze was a nigga that would never discuss business over the phone, so if he gave Gunz some type of answer, no matter what the answer was, it would mean things weren't as serious as Gunz was feeling they were. Unfortunately, if he didn't answer, Gunz already had his conclusion.

"Can't say lil' brah, not like this. I didn't think your plane landed yet, so I was actually expecting to leave you a message that we need to meet up—" Voorheeze paused for a second then continued. "Since I got you, meet me at Mucho's after you get your bags and shit. I'm around the corner from there already. So, I'll be waiting on you."

"I'll be there in ten minutes," said Gunz, wondering what could possibly be wrong?

He already knew deep down that it was something serious. He could feel it in his bones, and the tone in Voorheeze's voice solidified his feelings. Whatever it was, it was about to alter their lives. He stood up to leave.

"I hope whatever it is, it isn't so serious, that I'm not going to be given the opportunity of finding out your name." The mulatto spoke with an actual look of disappointment on her face.

Gunz was so lost in thought, he'd actually forgotten about her. He had come to love these two dudes like they were his blood brothers. He could feel that something was up with

T'Rida. Although he tried to shake the feeling off, it just wasn't going anywhere.

He picked up his drink and finished it in one gulp. "I'm so sorry, beautiful. I wish we had the time to get to know one another. I honestly think it would've been a treat for both of us. But, I have a family emergency," He apologetically told her. "Luv my name is Leonard Johnson."

"It's very nice to meet you, Leonard. I understand emergencies. *Lord knows I do.* It's okay." She dug into her small Prada handbag and retrieved her business card, which had her work and home numbers on it.

The name on the card read: *Nastasia Stevens*. Gunz thought the name had an elegance of its own and suited her perfectly. It was such a beautiful, exotic name for such a graceful creature.

After saying good-bye as quickly as he could without being rude, he sped out the door and made his way to the front of the airport. He only had some clothes and miscellaneous items inside of his suitcase, all of which he could buy again. So, he said fuck it, and chose to leave the bag at baggage claim, heading directly for the nearest exit. He made his way as quickly as he could to his truck, which he had dropped off for him earlier that day. He found his black on black Escalade, and drove through the parking lot in less than three minutes.

As he made his way down Second Street, he rolled the windows down and lit a blunt, trying to calm his nerves. After the phone call, the slight buzz he received from the two Tokyo Tea's was long gone. Unbeknownst to him, he'd soon learn what he was about to hear would take more than weed and alcohol to calm his raging nerves.

DE'KARI

Chapter X

As they turned onto Pulgas, T'Rida told Marlon to stop at Garden Supermarket. He had to grab some cigarettes and wanted to get something to drink to wash away the taste that vengeance cause to fill his mouth. Coming out of the store, with two tall cans of 211 Steele Reserve and a pack of peach Optimum's in a bag, T'Rida was already opening his pack of Newport 100s and grabbing one out of the pack by the time he reached for the handle on the passenger door.

"What's up, Big Lynch?" Anne called out of the back window.

Hearing the name caused T'Rida to look up. He looked at Anne first to see what direction she was looking in. Then he turned in the same direction, and what he saw completely fucked him up. The nigga she was looking at was a full-blown *'look at me'* faggot! A big, buff ass faggot in drag.

"Say, Miss Anne girl, oooooh, tell me what you're doing and who you're doing it with, bitch." The mothafucka had the nerve to lick his lips looking at T'Rida when he said it.

"Girl, these are a couple of Mels friends. We were just about to go and try to find some bomb to smoke."

Lynch was now fully ignoring Anne. He stepped up real close to T'Rida, *too fucking close* and said, "If you're looking for some bomb handsome, my shit is all you're gonna need," He whispered into T'Rida's ear.

His blood instantly began boiling, but T'Rida kept his composure. "And what kind of shit is that, ma?"

T'Rida hated homosexuals with a passion, to call him homophobic would not do his feelings for them any justice at all. Marlon knew this very well, so for T'Rida to keep his composure only convinced Marlon even more just how dangerous he was.

"Follow me over here to my car and let me show you something." Lynch turned away from T'Rida, while brushing his hand across T'Rida's dick at the same time and then walked over to his car.

DE'KARI

No one saw Lynch's hand brush against the front of T'Rida's pants, but T'Rida knew what had happened and it made him sick to his stomach. It literally took all his willpower not to knock the buff ass sissy out, right there on the spot and shoot the mothafucka–in front of the store for any and everybody to see. Yet, he tossed his bag into the truck and grabbed his forty-five out of the glove box at the same time. Seeing this, Marlon made eye contact with his Boss and nodded, letting him know, he was on the same page.

One of the youngstas that was grinding in front of the store peeped him grab the cannon and said something to his patna, and the two of them walked away from the store with a purpose. When T'Rida rounded the corner of the store, he saw the punk sitting inside of a Candy Grape Lexus with the driver's door wide open. This allowed T'Rida to see the interior of the car, which was a bright hot pink. The Lexus was actually clean as fuck. It was sitting on twenty-four-inch spinners, had chrome everywhere it would fit, and had a light smoke tint on the windows. The pink interior just fucked it all up unless it was a bitch car.

Lynch lifted a Ziploc bag with a pound of White Widow from the back seat and handed it to T'Rida. "Smell that and let me know what you think, chocolate." Lynch batted his eyes and licked his lips.

Instantly he felt a searing hot pain in his chest before his eyes even registered the smoke rising from the barrel of the big canon in T'Rida's hand pointed directly at him. The force of the slug slamming into him at point blank range knocked his big body backwards into the passenger seat. The first shot was instantly followed by three more, that were determined to meet inside Lynch's body. All four of the slugs were sent into his chest, which accounted for his body being propelled backward. As he was thrown into the passenger seat the last bullet raced from the barrel of the gun not wanting to be late to the party and slammed into his shoulder.

T'Rida blacked out for a fraction of a second. The rage he was holding all the time Lynch was sex playing him erupted like volcanic lava. He felt violated and just continued firing shot after shot, sending bullet after bullet into the unnaturally large

100

body. Unaware of this or the time being wasted, T'Rida just continued to stand over Lynch's body squeezing the trigger, until the chamber clicked on empty four times.

Then, snapping out of the trance, T'Rida pivoted on his feet and walked calmly back toward the truck. He walked just as calm as if he was walking out of Sunday morning service. Lynch didn't understand why he wasn't dead yet from so many bullets, but he knew undoubtedly that his life was slowly leaving his body. However, he wasn't going to die without some type of get back. This was the only thought on his mind, as he mustered all the strength he could, and fumbled for his cell phone. He pressed one on his speed dial and prayed Dollar would answer his fucking phone.

"What's up, Baby?" Twin Dollar answered on the first ring.

"Baby listen to me, there's a black Expedition leaving out of G Market, right now."

Looking out of his front window, Dollar saw the truck Lynch was talking about pulling up to the stop sign at Pulgas and Camellia. "Yeah, I see it Boo, what about it?" Dollar didn't like the sound of his lover's voice and knew something was wrong.

"Them mothafuckaz just robbed me, Daddy."

"What!" Dollar yelled hysterically into the phone.

"Baby, I'm good, calm down." Lynch lied.

As he coughed, blood oozed out of his mouth. After the coughing subsided he continued. "Just get them mothafuckaz for me, Daddy. The mothafuckaz shot me. I'm okay, but you need to get at them mothafuckaz." After the last word left his lips, the cell phone dropped from Lynch's hands.

Dollar stared at the silent phone for a second in disbelief. Then he quickly jumped into action. He raced out of the front door and through his gate with his keys already in his hand. He jumped into the Malibu and started the ignition just as his brother jumped into the passenger seat, and they sped off.

Dollar had been sitting in his living room watching T.V. when the shots rang out. Since his house was so close to the store he'd heard them crystal clear, but this being E.P.A he didn't think twice about it. Guns went off all day, every day.

His heart wanted Dollar to make a left at the corner and check on his lover, but his mind and demon called for revenge and made him turn right in order to catch up to the truck he saw drive by his street. Meanwhile, Jeff didn't know what was going on, but he knew something was up when his big brother bolted out of the house. So, he went with him without any hesitation.

"What's up, brah?" Jeff asked his brother as they sped down Pulgas.

"Them mothafuckaz in that Expo just jacked Lynch at G Market. She called me right after it happened and told me as I saw the niggaz driving by," Dolla yelled. "They shot, my bitch, blood!" He screamed as tears began to fall down his face.

Reacting to the news, Jeff yelled. "What! Nigga speed dis bitch up!"

As he pushed his foot down on the gas pedal as hard as he could, Dollar swore he'd get the mothafuckaz in the truck. Jeff pulled out his 9mm from his waistband and checked the clip. Then he reached over into the back seat of the Malibu and snatched the AK47 off the floor. He checked the clip on the assault rifle and cocked it back before sitting up impatiently eager to make the choppa ring out.

***

As they crossed Beach Street, Marlon checked the rearview mirror and saw a Candy Red Malibu speeding down the street behind them. He didn't pay too much attention to it at first, because niggaz in the hood smashed up and down the streets all day. He still kept an eye out for the muscle car, and as he pulled to the end of Runnymede where T'Rida's truck was parked, he glanced back into the rearview and noticed the red Malibu turning the corner, heading toward them. Just as he noticed the car Anne and T'Rida were already climbing out of the truck.

"Rida I ain't feeling that Mali coming down the block, we got company, my nigga," He called out, but his words fell on deaf ears because the doors were already closing.

However, Anne noticed the car as she turned her head to check security before climbing into T'Rida's Navigator.

Her words caught Rida's attention. "That's Lynch's nigga Dollar driving up!" She knew the vehicle.

GORILLAZ IN THE BAY

T'Rida instinctively reached for his .45 as he was turning, but as he was pulling the gun out, shots begin to ring out from the approaching vehicle. The shots were coming from the passenger side window. Two of the bullets caught T'Rida in his left arm, causing him to drop the .45 he was starting to lift. The Malibu came to a thunderously loud, screeching halt, the driver jumped out with a choppa in his hand and started shooting the mothafucka like he was in Afghanistan.

Marlon jumped over the seats the moment he heard the shots, trying to get to the AK47 he had in the back of his truck. Then he kicked the back door of the Expedition open and jumped out of it. The driver of the Malibu was too focused on T'Rida and Anne. He never noticed Marlon moving inside of the Expedition, nor did he see him come out of the back of it. Marlon squeezed the trigger of the AK aiming for the driver. However, he was in such a hurry that his aim was slightly off. Instead of hitting Dollar, he ended up shooting out the back window of the muscle car.

Jeff reacted to the sound of the second AK and turned around. Spotting Marlon pointing the assault rifle at his brother, he sent two shots into his chest. After the shots hit his arm, T'Rida immediately jumped behind the big Navigator. He was trying to pick his gun up with his left arm, but the attempts were futile. Accepting that he was not going to be able to grab the gun with his left arm, he picked it up with his right arm and began firing. His aim with his right arm was useless. When she heard the shots, Anne dove behind the Navigator as well.

"Is there something in your truck, I could use, or am I supposed to just rely on you two nonshootin' mothafuckaz?" She yelled to Rida.

She wasn't just going to lay there like some dumb helpless bitch, and get her head knocked off. If she was going to die she was going to die trying to live.

"Look in the back on the floor under the passenger seat!" T'Rida yelled back at her, hoping the bitch would at least be a distraction for the niggaz and give him some extra time to catch the mothafuckaz off balance.

Somehow, Marlon found the strength to get back on his feet with the choppa in his hand. He struggled to stand and gather his balance. Blood spilled from the side of his mouth as he coughed and gagged, gasping for a breath. The mothafucka who'd just shot him was busy reloading his pistol. Once he had it reloaded he lifted his arm, this time he was aiming at the window of the Navigator, lining his sights on a shadow he saw moving in the truck.

The silhouette, he was aiming at was Anne reaching for the pistol T'Rida told her was under the passenger seat. Jeff didn't have any idea who the person was, nor did he know what they were reaching for. All he knew was, whoever it was, wasn't going to get what they were reaching for. He took aim at the silhouette and started squeezing the trigger just as a searing hot pain tore through his arm. A Pain like he'd never known before ran up and down his entire arm.

It felt like a swarm of bees were stinging his arm all at once. While that thought filled his mind, that same feeling surged throughout his chest, then his neck, shoulder, and stomach. Before he understood, it was the AK in Marlon's hand spitting at him, the entire white fire spread all through him until all feeling left his entire body completely.

Marlon watched through blood-filled eyes as the nigga who was pointing his gun at the Navigator's window danced like a ballerina, as his body was torn to shreds from the bullets of the choppa in his hands. The AK sang a song in Marlon's hands that only a choppa could produce. It was music to his soul. But, the joy he was feeling would only last a few seconds.

As Dollar heard the AK, he spun around and saw Marlon shooting his brother. Dollar aimed his AK at Marlon and filled his body with the same bullets Marlon was shooting his brother with.

When T'Rida saw Dollar turn to Marlon and shoot him, he knew his opportunity would be now or never. He stood up completely and walked out from around the front of the Navigator, so he could get close enough to shoot the nigga with his gun in his right hand. He told himself, he wouldn't allow two shots in his arm, to be the reason he checked out of this bitch. He raised his arm shakily and took aim as best he could. He took extra time aiming and let the .45 sing its own song.

GORILLAZ IN THE BAY

This time he hit Dollar, but the bullet didn't catch him in a good spot and the nigga spun around and caught T'Rida again. This time the bullet crashed into his chest and lifted him off his feet. Anne saw Marlon shoot the nigga just as she was rising up from grabbing the gun. Thankful that Marlon shot the mothafucka before he had the opportunity to shoot her. She was rounding the back of the Navigator just as Dollar opened fire on T'Rida. She couldn't do nothing but watch in horror as T'Rida was knocked off his feet.

He flew backward about two feet and hit the ground so hard she knew he had to be dead. She'd found a sawed-off Mossberg Shotgun on the floor of the Navigator. It was T'Rida's shotgun, she now had leveled at Dollar who was standing just a couple feet away from her, still staring at T'Rida. When Dollar looked up and saw her, his eyes were as big as golf balls. It didn't matter though, because, at that exact moment, she pulled the trigger of the shotgun. At such a close range the results blew Dollar's head completely off his shoulders.

His head exploded like a piñata bursting at a kid's birthday party. After Dollar's body slumped to the pavement, she ran over to T'Rida and dropped to her knees by his side. To her astonishment, he was still alive. How? She didn't have a clue, but he was indeed alive.

"Can you get up?" She asked him as the sounds of police sirens could be heard in the distance.

Anne knew if she didn't get T'Rida and herself out of the area as soon as possible, they'd no doubt be spending the remainder of their lives locked behind bars. She called out to T'Rida again. "Rida, can you get up?"

He stared up at her in a daze. He could hear the words coming out of her mouth, but he wasn't able to comprehend anything. Anne grabbed the shotgun and the .45 that was in T'Rida's hand and tossed them both into the truck. Next, she ran back toward T'Rida and used all her strength to lift him up. Although he didn't realize he was doing so, T'Rida helped her get him to his feet, while blood ran from his body like a river rushing out of a mountain.

Finally, managing to get him inside the truck. She was out of breath and sweating like crazy. Her adrenaline still pumping through her veins, she ran to the driver's side of the Navigator, jumped inside and got the fuck out of dodge.

"Hello?" Jenn said into the receiver as she answered her phone.

"Cousin it's me!" Anne frantically yelled into the phone.

"Bitch what's wrong? Why in the fuck are you screaming?" Jenn asked alarmed.

"Shit just popped something fierce and shit went bad!" Through the hysteria, Jenn could barely make out what her cousin was saying, but she listened to her. "That nigga, you sent to the house got hit a few times and bitch it's bad. Call Doc, I'm on my way to your house, right now. I'll tell you what happened when I get there, but for now bitch, you need to call Doc." Anne dropped the cell phone on her lap not waiting for a response and continued to fly back down Pulgas as fast as she could.

Jennifer immediately called Doc after getting off the phone with Anne. She didn't know the extent of T'Rida's injuries. All she could tell Doc was she knew he'd been shot a few times and it was very serious. She hoped the wounds weren't as bad as Anne made them sound. She really like T'Rida and didn't want anything to happen to him. Not to mention, since Anne didn't tell her any details she was scared for her cousin. Jenn thought something went wrong when T'Rida went over to Melvin's and she knew the onslaught of what was to come from Voorheeze wouldn't be good.

She didn't even want to imagine the bloodshed that was about to come. Doc was around the corner from her house at the gambling shack when she called him. He told Jenn since it was her, he'd drop everything and be right over. He dropped the dice he had in his hand and walked out telling the youngsta who had him faded on the dice that he won. Doc wasn't worried about his point. He had work to do.

Jennifer was standing in the open doorway of the garage when Anne pulled up to her house in the Navigator. Jenn rushed to the truck to help her cousin and both women struggled to carry T'Rida as carefully and quickly as they could into the garage, hoping no one saw them. But, you couldn't come speeding down any street in East Palo Alto like Anne just did and not expect to draw some attention. T'Rida was losing a lot of blood. By the time the girls got him into the garage, there was blood all over their clothes and in the driveway. Anne was just standing there staring at T'Rida's body with the shotgun and .45 in her hands. It was like both her and Jenn were in some type of trance, just gazing at T'Rida.

When Doc's tires stopped behind the Navigator, Anne spun toward the open garage door with the shotgun leveled in the direction of the car, ready to pop off on whoever was climbing out of the vehicle. When she noticed Doc, she lowered the shotgun, picked up the .45 she'd just dropped and smiled. It was a sad smile that said, *'I'm glad to see you. Please help us.'*

"I'm glad you took the time to look at who you were pointing that thang at instead of just shooting me," Doc told her as he climbed out of his vehicle looking forward to the money he would make.

"We put him in the garage here," She told him as she followed him in. Not particularly in a talking mood at the moment.

Jenn went inside the house to get a new bottle of Remy Martin, she desperately needed a drink. Doc was already at work on T'Rida. Doc was a celebrity in the hood. He'd been an actual doctor with a degree from Pepperdine University in Malibu. He used to work at Stanford Hospital, but he was fired after knocking the Chief Resident Doctor out one night, after a botched surgery that ended a little girl's life. Although the surgery was a success, the Chief resident didn't pay close attention to the patient's file and had ordered an anesthesia to be administered that the little girl was allergic to. She never woke up.

The mistake cost the little angel her life and it crushed Doc to the core. Instead, of taking ownership for his mistake, the arrogant Doctor placed the blame on everyone else and wrote it off like nothing happened. Doc couldn't take that and confronted the cocky prick in the employee's cafeteria where things got heated. By the time the confrontation was over, the Doctor was busted up and unconscious. Doc was out of a job, facing criminal assault charges.

After pleading guilty to a deal that kept him out of prison but cost him his practicing license. Doc did his thing in the hood like so many others who'd made it but had got sucked right back in. If you needed some type of medical help without attracting the wrong kind of attention, everyone knew to call Doc.

The two women left the garage and stood outside drinking the alcohol. Anne left the shotgun in the garage next to the door, but she had the .45 in the waistband of her pants like all the niggaz carried theirs. She drank the rest of her drink down in one big swallow and told her cousin she needed another one. When Jenn came back with it, she handed it to Anne. Anne told her everything that had happened from the time T'Rida entered her apartment. It was like a giant weight was lifted off her shoulders.

"Wow, we're going to have some major problems jumping off once that nigga Voorheeze finds out about this shit," Jenn told her little cousin after hearing the entire story.

They smoked a blunt while she thought about what she was going to tell Voorheeze, or better yet how she was going to tell him. While Jenn was thinking, Anne remembered the two bags that were in the back of the Navigator. Just before she called out and the shooting began earlier, T'Rida had tossed both bags into the back of the truck. She told Jenn about the bags and told her that she needed to take them into the house. Once both bags were placed safely in the back room, Jenn picked up her cell phone and placed a call that she wished to God she didn't have to make.

Chapter XI

H. A. M. Hard as a Mothafucka

Voorheeze was relaxing on the massage table being treated like a king. He was enjoying his Swedish massage when his business phone started ringing. The massage was feeling so good, and he was so relaxed, he wanted to ignore his phone. But Voorheeze never neglected shit, especially when it came to his business phone. What if he ignored a particular call and it was an emergency. Little did he know, the call would end up being the biggest emergency he had thus far. So, he asked the honey-brown sista who was giving him his massage to excuse him for a brief second.

As she walked over to retrieve the phone off the table for him, he enjoyed every second as he watched her ass cheeks jiggle and hungrily swallow the G-string she was wearing. When she handed him the phone, he answered it laying on his back. He noticed Jenn's number on the caller I.D.

"It's ya Boi, tell me what's hood wit' it beautiful," He spoke into the cell phone with a Chester Cheese smile on his face revealing the good mood he was in. A good mood she knew was about to be ruined.

"V, honey, I'm sorry to be the one to bring you this, but we got a problem." Now that caused him to sit straight up. His voice became ice cold and very business-like.

She began telling him what was going on, trying her hardest not to say too much. The growl she heard escape his throat after hearing his best friend was fighting for his life, sounded like a grizzly bear getting ready to attack. It sent a chill through her body, that made Jenn feel as though she was frozen in the arctic circle.

The sista giving him his massage felt the same cold, shattering chill. Letting her know, the massage was now over. She lived in the hood far too long not to notice and be able to read the expression on Voorheeze's face and his tense body language. So, as Voorheeze was sitting on the table continuing his conversation, Nikki silently gathered her equipment and left the room to give him the privacy she knew he needed.

"Look, stop talking." He cut her off. "Don't call anyone else, Ma. In fact, sit tight and don't do shit else, I'm on my way, right now." Before he hung up he added. "Jenn thanks for everything." He hung up and retrieved his things.

He made it to East Palo Alto from San Jose in less than fifteen minutes. He couldn't stop his mind from racing. Over and over he tried to imagine a scenario that would lead up to T'Rida getting shot. He couldn't prevent the many of questions from forming in his mind. Neither could he prevent the thoughts of rage and violence that soon filled his head. Voorheeze couldn't believe somebody actually shot his mothafucking brother. Somebody really tried to erase his folks, and Voorheeze wasn't about to let that shit ride. He wondered why T'Rida didn't call him, why he went kamikaze without getting at him first.

As he drove, he smoked a blunt and allowed his mind to do whatever it felt. He saw all the police cars and caution tape on the block, as he turned on Pulgas so he slowed down and drove looking just like a concerned citizen. He couldn't see the body, slumped over in the car that the police were surrounding, but he knew the Lexus belonged to the faggot Lynch. From this, and hearing what Jenn told him on the phone, he knew, somehow this scene was connected to what happened to his brother. He continued past the scene and made a right turn at the corner of Camellia Way and headed for Jenn's house.

Cautiously, Voorheeze parked his Suburban two houses down the street from Jenn's house. He checked to make sure his double shoulder rig was firmly secured on him before he opened his door. Only then did he decide to exit the truck and walk to the house. Taking in the scene around him as he did, making sure no one was paying too close attention to him or the house. Jenn and Anne were sitting in the living room looking out the window as Voorheeze approached. Jenn stood up to greet Voorheeze, giving him a hug.

He returned her warm embrace with one of his own, then told her to take him directly to his fallen comrade. The two of them walked into the garage hoping and praying. Doc had been working on T'Rida now for over an hour with his assistant. He removed three of the bullets in T'Rida's body. Doc also had an IV hooked up to him, sending morphine into his veins to dull the pain. He was just finishing up the dressing-on his wounds when they walked in.

The sight of his brother all bandaged up laying like a Desert Storm survivor brought tears to the gangsta's eyes. Never in his life had Voorheeze considered and called someone his brother after the death of Jay, so many years ago. He had a few close patnas or whatever, but he didn't trust anyone enough to consider them a brother like he did T'Rida. He just didn't have that type of bond with anyone else, not even young Gunz. To Voorheeze, niggaz nowadays had their priorities and loyalties all fucked up, but T'Rida was different.

The two of them had shared so many memories and experiences over the years growing up. They had gone through the good and the bad, the thick and the thin and made it through. Of course, over the years they'd had their share of differences, but they always remained true and loyal to each other. Indeed, this was his one and true friend. His one and only brother. Looking down at T'Rida's weak and bandaged body, all shot the fuck up. all Voorheeze could do was stare at his friend with a heavy heart.

As the tears poured out of his eyes and ran down his cheeks like rain, he couldn't look at his brother any longer in this condition. He walked out of the garage and the tears continued to silently fall. "Jenn, I wanna know what the fuck happened. I want to know right now!"

She'd never seen Voorheeze in this condition, she wanted to grab ahold of him and comfort him so bad. But instead, she answered his questions and told him everything she'd heard about the robbery that took place earlier that day. She explained what Anne had shared with her. What Jennifer didn't know, Anne filled in. By the time she and Anne were done telling him everything, all signs of sorrow and hurt vanished from his face, without a trace. What replaced it was a look that portrayed why he was given the name he went by.

DE'KARI

His mouth was as dry as the Mojave Desert sands and he had a taste for nothing but blood. The blood he could now taste in his mouth was the blood that would no doubt be shed by any and everyone related to what transpired with his brother today. Voorheeze walked back into the house with the two women following him, with a look on his face that would scare the Devil himself.

He sat on the couch, Anne handed him an already rolled blunt and Jenn went into her kitchen to make them fresh drinks. Once she was in the kitchen, she thought twice about it, then said fuck it and brought the entire bottle of Patron, along with glasses of ice into the front room. For fifteen minutes or so, Voorheeze just sat on the couch drinking and smoking silently, lost in deep thought. He smoked three blunts by himself, back to back and had three glasses of Patron. He was pouring his fourth drink when he looked up at Jenn with that sad look back on his face, he just shook his head and cried some more.

"I know honey, I know." Was all Jenn could say in response to his pain, as she walked over to him and sat down placing her arms around him.

Voorheeze took another swig from his glass and looked up again. This time the evil glow in his eyes had returned. He couldn't allow himself to be weak at this moment. He was a fucking General in this shit and had to conduct himself as such. He had to think like a General, but most importantly, he had to carry himself like, *Jason mothafucking Voorheeze!*

Snapping back to reality, he stated, "Jenn, check this out. I got some shit I gotta take care of. Is my nigga good here wit' you until I can put something together?"

"Honey, don't worry about him. He's alright, right here where he is. I'll take care of him as long as he needs taking care of." She meant every word.

Looking over at Anne, he said, "Lil momma, a nigga thanks you for what you did for my brother. Forever I am in your debt. If you need anything, just let it be known and it's done. Believe that!"

She just nodded her head, with a look of sincere compassion and empathy on her face. Voorheeze pointed to the two bags on the floor that Jenn had brought from the room earlier, and told Anne they were hers no questions asked. She told him it was at least two hundred thousand dollars in the first bag and five kilos of cocaine in the other. Once again Voorheeze told her it didn't matter, it was hers now. He told her if she knew what to do with it then the coke was her's as well.

Anne thought to herself for a minute as Voorheeze was finishing the clear liquid in his glass. Then she spoke, "Alright then, if you just insist on thanking me, then as my *'thank you'*, I want you to let me fuck with y'all. I wanna be a part of the Neva Die Mob Family."

He wasn't clear on what she meant, so he told her to explain what it was she was actually saying. When she was finished Voorheeze looked at her with a real puzzling look on his face. Voorheeze thought about what she was telling him. He weighed every option and scenario over in his mind. Although, he wasn't too keen on allowing anyone to interject themselves into the family, he had to admit, today's occurrences had already put her in. Not to mention, if it wasn't for her, his brother would no doubt be dead instead of fighting for his life out in the garage.

In reality, she'd proven herself already. So, he told her, "Look the bags are still your's ma, but if you wanna fuck wit' it, then we'll fuck wit' it." Still thinking as he spoke, he continued. "But for now, I need you to stay here wit' Jenn and—" He paused to think, then told her. "As a matter of fact, fuck it! You can roll now. We gon' make it do what it do."

When Doc knocked on the door, Jenn let him in. He explained T'Rida's condition to them. He was now stable. None of the bullets did any critical damage. The shot to his chest was just below his lung and went straight through. Mostly, he had a lot of muscle damage and his body shut down in order to recover the nerve shock it experienced. Doc said he'd still check on T'Rida periodically over the next few days to make sure none of the wounds got infected. T'Rida was not to be moved, but for the most part, he was okay. The amount of Morphine in the IV would keep him under heavy sedation for the next twenty-four hours.

Even still, Doc would stop by in the morning anyway. Voorheeze thanked him for his time and help, then he told him that Jenn would have something for him in the morning as a token of his appreciation. While he was saying this Anne reached into the duffle bag and gave Doc twenty-five thousand. When Voorheeze looked at her she told him they were fucking with it.

Anne knew that giving the money to Doc would impress Voorheeze, but she'd been right there in the thick of the gunfight right along with T'Rida. So, her reasoning for doing what she did went way past impressing Voorheeze. Voorheeze made several phone calls then looked at his watch after the last call. Noticing it was almost time for Gunz's flight to land at the airport, so he made his way back into the house. He told Anne it was time for them to ride out, so they exited the house and made their way to San Jose to meet Gunz. Before leaving, Voorheeze walked back into the garage to check on his brother one last time.

Anne stood outside as he did so, giving him his privacy. She told Jenn to take care of the money for her and to do something with the coke. Jenn wanted to question her little cousin on her choice to get involved with Neva Die, but knowing her cousin, getting in her business would only make things worse. So Jenn kept her thoughts to herself. Besides if she really looked at things, Anne was already in it. After Voorheeze came out, they left.

***

Mucho's had been a little place that all the young D-Boys went and had lunch at in downtown San Jose. Before they went to prison, Voorheeze and T'Rida used to beat the block right out there in San Jose. They chose Mucho's back then as the spot they'd eat at because they loved Mexican food and the food at Mucho's was good. It was a small little hole in the wall joint, that quickly became popular among all of them. Gunz, on the other hand, didn't fuck around with downtown San Jose like they did.

However, on the few occasions he went down there with them and ate, the food was good. So, he knew exactly where to go without directions. Gunz put the blunt he was working on out in the ashtray and checked his double shoulder rig. Relaxing as his hands touched the two revolvers he was legendary for carrying. He made his way to the food joint around the corner from

where he parked. He wasn't expecting Voorheeze to have anyone with him as he walked into the restaurant. He trusted his
folks, so as he sat down at the table, he never questioned his folks
about who she was or why she was there. Voorheeze kept his
voice low so no one else inside the establishment would hear
their conversation, and he filled Gunz in on everything.

Gunz soaked up all the information he was hearing while
battling to keep his composure and anger in check. After Voorheeze finished telling him everything, Gunz's only response
was, "When we moving?"

Voorheeze knew Gunz wanted the same revenge he wanted,
Dollar and his brother were dead already. But, an example
would be made out of their stupidity. Anyone and everyone that
fucked with them would fall. Period point blank, no questions
asked. No answers would be given, just *Neva Die* justice! They
would be dealing with Wendell and everyone associated with
him.

***

Jason 'Double Dragon' Voorheeze was actually born Lamont Simpson. He was born and raised in Menlo Park California, until the age of seventeen. Lamont was known to everyone
as Lamont or 'L'. Since the age of eleven, he was mentored by
a cat named Fast Eddie who was originally from Chicago Illi-
nois. Eddie taught the young, neglected, Lamont everything he
knew about the game and dealing with individuals in the
game. Eddie had five young wolves under his wing at the
time. Five wolf cubs he turned into one of the most known and
feared crews in the Bay Area.

Eddie looked at the young wolves like they were his own
cubs. It was Eddie who gave the children their street
names. Naming them names that fit their characteristics and personalities. Each one of them taking on the names of fictional
characters they were most like. Lamont's alias went so well with
his personality, that his alias soon became the only name he was
known as. T'Rida who wasn't part of Eddie's wolf pack, but still
a friend to Voorheeze was the first person to notice the small
changes in Lamont. All his life Lamont was a bright child but

was commonly known as the class clown and center of attention.

Young Tommy noticed that his friend was becoming quiet and withdrawn. He had become very serious. The biggest change Tommy noticed came after Eddie gave his wolves their guns. Lamont fell in love with and would only use the two .45 Dragon Colts, which Lamont cleaned and played with daily. At first, T'Rida thought that was Lamont's new way of seeking attention. Tommy thought his young friend was playing the role of a real psycho just to gain attention. So, Tommy ignored his friend's actions.

That was until the first time one of their robberies had gone bad. They were boxed in and the situation looked as if they were going to get caught. They were in a jewelry store off Thornton Avenue in Fremont. The jewelry store was supposed to be a simple in and out job. However, two off-duty Fremont Police officers would spoil that. Lamont had left the jewelry store to get the getaway car, leaving one of the other wolves and Tommy to tie up the loose ends and come out with the bags of jewelry.

Three employees were tied up in the back of the store when Officer Prescott walked in with his partner looking for an engagement ring for his woman. By the time Lamont pulled up to the front of the jeweler store, he could see T'Rida laying on the ground facing him, with his hands cuffed behind his back, while the two police officers stood over him with their guns drawn. As Rida looked at the car pulling up to the curb, he knew it was a wrap for him. He could hear one of the officers calling the robbery in on his radio, while his partner was bent over searching him.

The next thing he knew, he was watching Lamont stroll into the jewelry store pistol in each hand like it was nothing. He had the look of a demon from hell on his face, as he slipped in the door like liquid. Making no noise whatsoever, he walked straight up to the officer that was on the radio, standing with his back toward Lamont. The officer who was searching Tommy saw Lamont's shoes as he approached. The officer started to stand up, but before he could Lamont raised both pistols simultaneously and blew the officers heads off.

GORILLAZ IN THE BAY

As the dead bodies crumbled to the floor, Lamont stood over the bodies and shot them two more times. Never saying a word to Tommy, the entire time as he searched the officers for the handcuff key. He freed Tommy and walked right out of the jewelry shop getting back into the getaway car. Right then and there, Tommy realized Lamont Simpson was no longer the person he'd grown up with. For whatever reason he'd changed, he had indeed become Jason Voorheeze.

Over time, T'Rida would add the words Double Dragon to the handle due to the twin .45's that Voorheeze carried. Lamont talked different, walked different, moved different. Hell, even his thought patterns were different. Over the years Lamont would continue to grow more and more vicious, more and more sinister. He stalked the streets of the Bay Area like a lion patrolling the boundaries of his territory.

DE'KARI

Chapter XII

The wolf pack disassembled after the death of Fast Eddie. Ironic as it might be, his death was brought on by one of his own cubs. Fast Eddie had grown untouchable on the streets due to the viciousness of his wolves. No one could get to him and this gave him the feeling of immortality. Unfortunately, this was the same feeling of immortality that made him betray one of his own wolves and sleep with the young wolf's wife.

That act of betrayal was answered by Fast Eddie's untimely demise. However, it was the death of Fast Eddie and the separation of the wolf pack that seemed to bring some of Voorheeze back to his old self. T'Rida overtime was able to get Voorheeze to close the book on that chapter of his life. Years later, T'Rida would often joke to his lifelong friend, that he'd brought him back from the dead.

"Arise Lazarus Arise!" T'Rida would say to him before busting out in a gut-wrenching laugh.

This was just one of the many obstacles they'd overcome together. It had been years since that old Jason Voorheeze had showed its side. Even though, being in the game itself called for its own level of gangstaness. It didn't call for the sinisterness of the old Jason Voorheeze. He learned to differentiate between the two personalities. Once he was able to recognize and admit that he did indeed have two different personalities, and one was more ferocious than the other!

This was the Jason Voorheeze that now stood sentry-like over the old woman sitting in the rocking chair frightened and crying to her eldest son on the phone, while blood ran down the side of her face. Voorheeze slapped the little old lady across the face so many times with his pistol she could barely speak. Growing impatient with the old cow who just kept mumbling and sniffling on the fucking phone, he snatched the phone from her.

"Look, nigga, ain't shit to talk 'bout. If you want this old ass broad to live, I suggest you get here and get here now!" Was all he spewed into the phone.

"Look, son, whatever your ills are God can help you," She began to speak to him earnestly. "Whatever it is you think my son did to you, or even if he did do it. Son, I am sure he is sorry. Son, listen to me, don't blame Wendell for whatever misfortune. It was the Devil that caused it, not Wendell," She pleaded with Voorheeze.

What she didn't realize was that you couldn't rationalize or reason with pure evil. Just as there is no way to make sense out of the senseless. Voorheeze ignored the little old lady and gagged her with an old dirty sock and some tape he'd found in the hallway. After making sure she was gagged and tied securely, he poured two cans of gasoline over the top of her head and laughed as she wiggled and squealed beneath the bondages trying unsuccessfully to free herself. Panting like a wild animal, Voorheeze pulled out a pack of Newport 100s and a lighter from his pants and lit a cigarette.

He stared at Wendell's mother with the soulless stare of the dead as he smoked the cigarette. He took one last drag on the cigarette, then spoke. "Naw ain't da Devil's fault. It's yo' fault, you gave birth to that coward ass mothafucka."

After he spoke the words, he tossed the burning cigarette onto her gasoline-soaked body, and she immediately burst into a big fireball. Voorheeze walked calmly from the house in Union City, laughing while the old woman's body burned. He never intended for Wendell to save his mother. He only had the old goat call him and beg him to come over to ensure he'd be the one to find the old hag burnt to a crisp. The pleasure he received from hearing her cry and plead to her son was indescribable.

Gunz watched as Voorheeze came walking out of the house laughing and thought. *'This is one cold mothafucka!'* He had no idea what Voorheeze had just done, but seeing him laughing so sinisterly, told him he didn't want to know.

"Shit nigga, for a minute I thought you'd gotten lost up in there," Gunz said to him as he started the ignition. "Do I even want to know what you were in there doing?"

Voorheeze thought of the terror and fear he heard in the old woman's voice, as she begged her son to help her. He relished the look in her eyes as he tossed the lit cigarette at her. "Naw, brah, trust me you don't want to know."

GORILLAZ IN THE BAY

***

As Pink walked out of the Albertson's, she bumped into a young street thug almost knocking him down with her shopping cart. Her focus was on her mother, wondering why she wasn't answering her phone. She was so lost in thought, as she pressed redial on her phone that she didn't notice the thug she'd bumped into had turned around and began walking in the same direction she was going. As she marched to her car she kept listening to the ringing phone in her hand.

"Come on Momma, pick up the phone," she mumbled.

Her mother always picked up the phone. Just then her call waiting signaled someone was attempting to call her. She moved the phone from her ear and checked the Caller I.D. and decided to ignore her oldest brother's phone call. Now was not the time to be dealing with him or his drama.

"Not now, Wendell. I don't have time to deal with any of your bullshit," She mumbled as she ignored the call.

After receiving the voicemail for the eleventh time, she put her phone in her purse and made up her mind that she was driving straight over the bridge to check on her mother. It wasn't like her mother not to answer her phone. Pink was praying over and over that her mother hadn't fallen down again or anything like that. Her mother was truly getting old, a fact Pink couldn't ignore considering her mother had fallen down twice this past year. Both times she remained stuck on the floor where she fell until Pink grew tired of not hearing from her and drove over to her house out of concern.

These were her thoughts as she bent over to lower the last grocery bag into the trunk of her Jaguar. Her thoughts were interrupted by something or someone brushing up against her ass.

"What a waste," She heard someone whisper into her ear.

***

Gunz was going to initially plot on Pink for a couple of days just to make sure everything went off as planned. A couple of hours ago, he dropped Voorheeze off and came back over the

Dumbarton Bridge to East Palo Alto to buy some food to take over to Jenn's place. He figured she probably didn't have time to go out and buy groceries and shit with her watching T'Rida. So, he drove over the ramp to Albertson's. As he was activating his car alarm, he couldn't help but realize the parking lot was virtually empty. Besides his car, there were only two other vehicles in the darkened parking lot. A Jaguar and a Buick LeSabre. No cars meant no customers which also meant no long lines, which was cool with him.

He was thinking about the cute mulatto he'd run into at the airport the other day. He was so lost in his lustful thoughts he didn't see the shopping cart nor the woman who was pushing it until the cart knocked into him.

"Excuse me," The woman mumbled briskly as she hurried past him, not even stopping to check and see if he was okay. She held a cell phone to her ear mumbling. *"Come on, come on."* As if she were willing the person on the other end of the line to pick up the phone.

It wasn't the inability to watch where she was going, nor the rude way in which she'd mumbled, *'Excuse me.'* Like it was his fault and he should've watched where he was going and kept going like he was a piece of shit that surprised Gunz. What surprised him was who the hell the woman was that bumped into him. After she bumped into him he kept walking toward the store as if nothing happened. After about ten steps he abruptly touched his pants pocket like he'd forgotten his wallet and turned to go back to his car.

The driver of the scraper was nowhere in sight and no one else had pulled into the parking lot, he noticed. Gunz saw this as an Omen. He didn't believe in coincidences. Him running into her in this parking lot meant it was time for her to die *now*. Which was sad, because she had a beautiful body. She had thighs like Tina Turner and an ass like Serena Williams. On any other day and any other situation Gunz would've loved to stick first his tongue, then his dick into her sweet little pussy. Tonight, he pulled out his .44-colt python and began screwing the silencer on it as he trailed behind her.

As he watched her ass jump from the frantic marching she was doing toward her car, his dick grew in his pants. She never once turned back or looked over her shoulder. Instead, she just kept walking to her car. Gunz scanned the parking lot one last time as he approached her from behind. She was placing the last of her bags into the trunk of her car as he reached her.

"God damn," He said to himself looking at that bubble of an ass she had.

As she was bent over the trunk, he couldn't help but think that her ass looked like a Buffalo's ass. Regretfully, he pushed his lustful thoughts out of his mind. He walked up to her pressing his hard dick up against her ass and bent over her like he was her boyfriend whispering into her ear.

"Such a waste," He whispered into her ear.

He continued whispering this to himself, as he pulled the trigger of the Python blowing her brains out, spraying the inside of the trunk with her blood and brain matter. Pink's body jerked violently from the impact, then slumped over into the trunk. Using his free hand Gunz tossed the rest of her body up-into the trunk and closed it. Leaving the Jaguar where it was in the parking lot, Gunz walked back to his triple black on black Escalade and pulled off forgetting the groceries he was going to buy. It would be a week later before Pink's body would be found in the parking lot.

T'Rida's throat felt like he'd been eating hot dry coals for a week straight. The burning and dryness were almost too much to bear. He tried licking his lips, but they too were dry and cracked. It felt like someone had scratched his lips with sandpaper. His eyes were still closed as he lay wondering where he was and what the fuck happened to him. As he attempted to open his eyes a soft voice spoke to him. At first, he thought he was tripping. Maybe the voice he was hearing was all in his mind. It continued, and it was too clear to be in his mind.

Someone was close by talking to him. The voice was feminine and soft. T'Rida realized the voice sounded familiar, but he couldn't place it. After a few seconds he finally did, it was Jenn's voice. Then it all came back to him. Focusing now he could hear Jenn apologizing to him. She was saying that if she would've never called him none of this would've happened. T'Rida couldn't agree with her, in fact, he was still grateful to her for calling him. Shit as it was, he was going to find out who'd robbed him no matter what and his actions would've been the same regardless.

As Jenn continued to talk to him, T'Rida's dick jumped under the sheets. He couldn't believe it, even after all his body had been through, he still woke up with morning wood. When Jenn saw his dick stretching the sheet covering him, her pussy instantly became wet. She told herself, she was wrong for thinking how good that pole would feel inside of her. After all, he was laying here still fighting for his life. He had been laid up in her garage for over a week unconscious and medicated. T'Rida's eyes had opened by now, but Jenn didn't notice because she was staring down at his dick licking her lips.

Still staring down at his rod, she talked to him unaware that he was listening. "See, look at you. You got a bitch's mouth all watering and shit. I wish I could just take you in my mouth, right now, and suck the shit out of that mothafucka."

"All that talking you over there doing ain't even good for a nigga, ma," T'Rida said startling her. "Now stop all dat woofing and handle yo' business," he told her.

"How long have you been listening to me?" She asked him, now embarrassed.

"Ain't none of that important, right now. The only thing you need to worry about is fulfilling all those empty ass promises you over there making. But before you start, ma, can a nigga get something to drink? My mouth feels like a fucking desert," he said thinking how good her hot pussy would feel, surrounding his dick.

Shit just because he was laid up in bed with a couple of bullet wounds, didn't mean he was out of commission. Jenn went to get him a glass of water. When she returned, she handed him the glass of water and kept her promise. She lifted the covers and took his rock hard shaft into her hands. She stroked his massive shaft a few times savoring the feeling of sliding her hands up and down it. Then after licking her lips, she opened her mouth and swallowed the entire shaft.

Damn her mouth felt wonderful as she swallowed his dick. As good as the head he was receiving was, T'Rida couldn't stop his mind from drifting back to that unfortunate night. He remembered kicking in Melvin's door, remembered vividly as he smoked that faggot at the store. Then his mind floated to the shootout between them and the other queer on Pulgas. As he replayed the events of that night in his mind, he felt a burning in his chest. Then the pain shot down his arm before registering in his mind. His body involuntarily jerked from the pain.

Jenn, however, thought he jerked as a reaction to the blow job she was giving him. This only motivated her to be even more enthusiastic. T'Rida couldn't enjoy the pleasure, though. He was lost in thought. His mind continued to replay the events of that night and he was seeing himself being knocked backward from the force of the 223 hitting his chest. He watched helplessly as Anne ran out from behind the Navigator with the shotgun in her hand and blew Dollar's head off saving his life.

It was only now that T'Rida even realized it was Anne who'd saved his life that night. He was remembering her struggle to get him into the truck. She was the one that got him into safety. The tightening of his stomach and pulling in his groins brought T'Rida back to the present. Before he had a minute to enjoy the talented mouth of Jenn, a jet stream of cum erupted into her mouth and down her throat. She gagged a little from the force of which the cum shot into her mouth, but nevertheless, she swallowed every last drop of his load, gently stroking him while she sucked out the smallest drop of his semen.

"Now that's how you supposed to wake a nigga up in the morning," T'Rida joked.

"Yeah, yeah nigga, whatever," She responded, removing her hands from her hot soaking pussy.

She had grown so horny from all the groaning he was making while she was sucking his dick, that she had slipped one hand into her panties and played with her clit as she sucked him off. Shit, she'd cum twice herself. She covered T'Rida's body back up with the sheet and gently sat on the bed next to him.

"How long have I been out?" He asked her once he caught his breath.

"'Rida baby you've been here for over a week."

When she told him this, T'Rida couldn't believe his ears. *Over a week?* He couldn't believe that was possible. Although he'd never been shot before, he knew his body. He was a savage and he went to the gym regularly. A few gunshots wouldn't have kept him out of commission for that long. She had to have been mistaking.

"Jenn are you telling me honestly, I've been here for over a week?" He asked hoping her answer would somehow change.

"Yeah. Doc worked on you nine days ago. He told us you were out for so long because of the amount of blood you lost. He said it caused your body to go into shock and shut down." She saw that this was upsetting him, but she had to let him know just how close he came to dying. So, she continued, "Every morning he's been coming by to check on you and to change the dressings on your wounds. And I've been here nursing over you the rest of the time." After telling him all the medical stuff Doc had told her, she filled him in on the news reports that followed since the incident.

On the news, it was said that everything that had transpired over the last week and a half had all been drug-related. She didn't know if he knew it or not but felt she had to let him know, so she told him that Marlon hadn't survived the shootout. She finished up her report with the news of how badly Voorheeze had taken what happened to him.

In the little time, he had regained his conscious, T'Rida hadn't the opportunity to reflect on Marlon's death. Fuck! He and Marlon had gone back nearly as long as he and Voorheeze. Marlon was a true down to earth soldier and his death didn't sit well in T'Rida's heart. T'Rida figured Voorheeze wouldn't have taken the news too well, but never did he imagine that his brother would've taken it nearly as hard as Jenn told him he took it. Voorheeze made it his and Gunz's personal business to erase any and everything that was ever connected to Lynch and Dollar.

Lynch ran two weed spots in E.P.A and both of them were shut down. Dollar's house on Camellia way not too far from Jenn's house was sprayed with over three hundred bullets. Not only did they kill Wendell's mother and sister, but two of his cousins as well. Every male over twelve years old in their families were gunned down as well in the onslaught. The message was out. It was loud and crystal clear.

GORILLAZ IN THE BAY

It was heard by everyone in the streets that: *'It was safer for you to fuck the devil's wife than to fuck wit' The Neva Die Family!'*

The only person to get away so far was the nigga, Wendell. No one had seen or heard from him at all. Voorheeze not only had his wolves, street soldias, runners, rippers, and anyone else out looking for him, but he also put ten racks on the niggaz head as an added incentive.

All of the killings took place in just three days and four nights. Voorheeze made sure the retaliation was swift and brutal. In a response to all the bloodshed and bodies the police cracked down on all the drug dealers and hoodlums in E.P.A. known or unknown. The police chief believed he had a full-fledged drug war going on. The violence reminded him of the 1989 killings in the city that made East Palo Alto the murder capital of the United States back then.

All that Jenn was telling him was too much for his head. His body hurt like fuck from the waist up and the mental stress was giving him a headache out of this fucking world. He couldn't tolerate all of this at once, it was just too much. He tried to sit up, but the physical pain shot through his body like lightning bolts, nearly causing him to blackout.

Jenn was alarmed, she asked him if he needed her to call Doc and have him come over? T'Rida told her not to worry about it. He said he was cool, even though, he didn't seem like it. He instructed her to grab him a phone and to bring back one of the bricks of coke she'd told him that Anne left. T'Rida remembered his patna in West Oakland had gotten shot over thirty-something times a few years back. He'd told T'Rida later when he healed that the Doctor told him the amount of cocaine in his system at the time was the only reason he was alive. When T'Rida saw his nigga moving around as well as he was at the time and commented on it.

His nigga told him he didn't feel any pain because he stayed snorting coke. If the coke could take that niggaz pain away, then it most certainly could take T'Rida's pain away. Although T'Rida had his cell phone right next to the bed, he needed a landline just to be safe. When she brought the phone to him, he punched in the numbers he'd memorize not too long ago.

DE'KARI

Chapter XIII

When the phones first hit the market not too many people knew about them. Go phones was the wave of the future. After this invention was created niggaz didn't have to worry about the police tapping into their phones anymore, because they couldn't trace them. It was a trap stars dream. Everyone in the family had Go phones that they used for one week, then got rid of. The changing of the phones was more reliable than clockwork. Clocks broke down and stopped on you. The changing of the phones was Law.

T'Rida, Gunz, and Voorheeze had always gotten two phones in every rotation that no one knew about, except them. These were their emergency phones and nothing else. The crazy part of it all was even if they didn't use the phones that week, they'd still change them out. Considering that a week had gone by already, T'Rida was hoping Voorheeze hadn't changed last week's phone.

After all the bloodshed and get back Voorheeze and Gunz headed out to the beach house in Aptos to lay low for a while. When they pulled up to the house Gunz couldn't believe what his eyes were seeing. The house he was looking at was like some shit out of the movies. Voorheeze told him that other than him, T'Rida was the only other person that knew about the beach house. As the phone began to ring, Voorheeze knew it could only be one person. As he walked over to the phone to answer it, Voorheeze silently thanked God his brother's life was spared.

Now all he could do was hope there wouldn't be any permanent damage from the bullet wounds. Voorheeze never had too much faith in hospitals and doctors, but he was hopeful that Doc had worked a miracle.

"Hello?" He finally brought himself to pick up the phone.

"V, it's me brah, what's hood wit' it?" T'Rida asked hoarsely.

"Brah, I'm just glad to hear your voice," Voorheeze told him sincerely.

DE'KARI

"Shit, brah, I'm the one that's glad. Jenn put me down on everything, so I know what's up—" T'Rida paused as pain shot through his body again.

Although V never liked mentioning names over the phone, he knew these lines were secure, so he didn't say anything as Rida mentioned Jenn's name.

Voorheeze responded back to T'Rida. "What's the business wit' you, though? Brah, is everything a'ight?'

"Sit tight where you at brah, I'm good. Ain't no need in you moving. I'm making some arrangements as we speak, then I'm on my way to you.

Voorheeze could hear his brother fighting the pain he was feeling. He responded back to T'Rida with concern in his own voice. "You really don't wanna make dat journey in your condition. Brah, I know you Gangsta as fuck and all, but driving in yo' condition ain't cool. Let me send you one of the boys to drive you."

"Naw, it's hood, brah. I'ma have little mama push me down there after I take care of some shit. Did you call wifey for a nigga and put her mind at ease?"

"Yeah, but I didn't go into too much detail. You know how she be wildin' out and shit, nigga I didn't want her getting on everybody's head and shit. So, I just told her you were laying low for a minute and you'd get at her when you could."

"Foe sho, let me get on this shit, I'll see you in like three."

"Alright, big brah, luv you, my nigga."

"Luv you too, cousin. One!"

"One." Voorheeze hung up the phone and walked down to the beach, so he could let Gunz know what was up.

Gunz had never been to a beach in his life. The serenity he felt when they arrived engulfed him. It was a tranquil feeling, he'd never known before. He'd spent all day yesterday and today lounging and just listening to the surf. He would've enjoyed it, even more, had he been alone, but Anne was next to him laying back as well. To Gunz, Anne was a cool bitch, she looked good enough and from what he'd heard and seen, she had potential.

Nevertheless, Gunz wasn't on that page. He was maxing and relaxing. Anne had never been to the beach either and was trying to absorb as much of the beautiful ocean scene as he was.

GORILLAZ IN THE BAY

Jenn sat in silence, while T'Rida spoke on the phone. She was impressed with the little system he and Voorheeze had, but she kept her admiration to herself. She rolled a blunt while she waited for the phone call to end.

Handing the blunt to T'Rida, she asked once he was off the phone. "So where is it that I am supposed to be taking you to?"

He took a drag of the blunt, then told her. "To this lil' spot down the freeway." He didn't ask, he stated matter-of-factly. She didn't mind though, she'd help him with whatever he needed.

T'Rida picked up the brick of coke Jenn had brought him that was lying next to the bed. He cut a small slit in the middle of it and with the credit card scooped out some of the powder. He snorted two huge lines. He expected the powder to burn his nostrils, yet the feeling he received was cool as the dope made its way into his system. Following what he'd seen his father do so many times, he closed his eyes and tilted his head back.

Jenn walked out of the garage, so she wouldn't have to see him do this. She didn't judge him for what he was doing, but at the same time, she didn't agree with it. She kept her opinion to herself as she walked out, trying to understand the physical pain he was in, knowing that it was because of the pain that he was fucking with the coke.

"Where you going?" He asked her when she stood up.

"I gotta check on something in the house," She lied, not able to tell him how she felt at the moment.

"While you're in there, could you fix me a drink?" He asked. "Sure."

By the time she returned with the drink, he had the brick sitting on the nightstand. He snorted about two grams in that time and was experiencing a good drain when she walked in. He took out roughly five ounces of coke from the brick for himself and handed the rest back to her to put up. Dressed in a new beige velour sweat suite that Voorheeze left for him, T'Rida and Jenn walked out of the garage, jumped into the Expedition and headed down the freeway.

He didn't tell her the city they were going to. Instead, he just told her to take 101 South until she hit highway 17 and headed toward Santa Cruz. Two hours later, they exited onto Sea Cliff

Avenue, in Aptos. The neighborhood was real quiet. Aptos was one of them small uppity cities with people who had what they call Old Money. For the most part, the people stayed to themselves, but you could sense the unspoken racism that was in the air all the time.

As they turned onto the street the beach house was on, Jenn was breathless. She'd never seen anything as beautiful as what laid before her eyes now. Every house on Beach Drive was huge and beautiful. They were all two and three-story houses. There was even a couple of four-story houses on the street. When T'Rida pointed out the house they were going to, it was the largest house on the street. It stood four and a half stories tall.

The first floor of the house was made of some type of rock, but the other three and a half stories were made of all glass. She would later find out that the second story was one huge glass sliding door that led to an over-head terrace. The third floor was laid out in a similar fashion as the second. The fourth floor, however, was just one large window. On the first floor of the house was a floor to ceiling painted mural that was eye-catching. The room was complete with its own bathroom.

Directly, to her right side was a walkway leading to a spiral staircase that ran up the center of the entire house. Next to the stairs, by the side wall was an elevator. The second level was the living room, dining room, kitchen, and a den. The carpeting under her feet was the thickest and softest, she'd ever felt or imagined walking on. The third floor held three bedrooms, one of which was a master bedroom with a Jacuzzi.

The fourth floor was the largest of the three master bedrooms. It took up the entire fourth floor, it had a California King, Four Poster bed directly in the middle of the room. On the wall was something she'd never seen before. It was a forty-inch plasma flat screen television. The bathroom had his and her sinks, a shower complete with a bathtub as well as a Jacuzzi. This was the most expensive state of the art shit she'd ever seen.

Gunz and Voorheeze were in the living room watching the 49ers game on one of the plasma screens and Anne was upstairs taking a nap when T'Rida and Jenn walked into the room. The reunion of the young drug lords was brief but heartfelt. Behind the walls of the lavish beach house, no one was worried about upholding any thug personas. They embraced one another with full emotions. The three of them had been through some difficult and trying times together, but throughout all the drama, never had one of them come this close to losing their lives.

More importantly, they knew what they were capable of and stopped caring about other people's opinions a long time ago. So, they didn't give a fuck if anyone saw or heard their display of emotions, after almost losing one of the three. They all stayed at the beach house for two weeks discussing their plans for the future. The only person who didn't participate in the discussions was Jenn because she had no intentions of changing the relationship she had with them. She wasn't Neva Die, and she didn't intend on becoming a part of the family.

The five of them remained at the beach house for four weeks. The guys spent most of the time discussing business. All three of them wanted the family to grow. The plan had always been for Neva Die to become the largest organization the United States had ever housed. Each of them had a different idea of how they would reach that level.

Voorheeze felt they could achieve this goal through financial gain and a little muscle; keeping the family to only those who were a part of it now. To him, there really wasn't a need for expansion. He believed that at the level they were at now, if they just allowed a little expansion and grinded harder, they'd leave a great legacy. If they utilized consistency, everything would work out. Too much expansion he believed would open the doors for all types of problems from snitches and snakes, to cowards and suckas.

Anything that was too big always attracted attention and most of the time it was the wrong kind of attention. Gunz, on the other hand, felt they needed to expand quickly and allow the momentum of the influences they were gaining to open new gates and different avenues. He felt the way to do this was to open new chapters in as many other states as possible.

As for T'Rida, he didn't think shit. He knew very well what needed to be done and what was going to be done. He understood Voorheeze's point of view, as far as not expanding too quickly or too large for that matter. Because the more people they allowed to become a part of the family, the more chances they stood of allowing an informant in or even allowing in a weasel. In prison, he recalled reading a letter written by Jonathan Jackson to his brother George in Soledad Brothers.

In that letter, Jonathan was explaining the need to put potential soldias through extensive training and background checking as a way to sort out all the poisonous weeds and branches. Strength, he realized was in character and not in numbers. On the other hand, Gunz was right to an extent. In order to accomplish what was desired by all, they would indeed need to expand and create not just new chapters, but new avenues in other districts and states.

The key was all in how, when and where, they'd expand and this was what he had already known. No matter where a chapter was started, it would be done so under the supervision of one of them, each chapter would adhere to the same rules, policies, and procedures.

But the most important rule, they'd install and live by, would be the fact that family members would be chosen and couldn't choose! A potential member would be watched and studied closely before being approached and groomed. Essentially, their power would be through financial growth and influence. A believer in Socialism himself, T'Rida knew that in today's society the practice of socialism for the family was one thing, yet they'd need capitalistic ideas in order to achieve enough stability for them to live as Socialist, or even better as a family.

Gunz shared his idea of the Philadelphia venture with his two Patna's and the three of them chewed over the idea for a while weighing the pros and the cons. By the end of their discussion, it was set. The venture would happen, they would just have to wait a while and make sure all their eggs were in line before they made the move.

As he snorted another two lines of powder, T'Rida felt he was indestructible. The effects the drug had on his body was unbelievable. He couldn't remember the last time he felt so wonderfully powerful. It had been nearly three weeks since he'd been shot. Although his body still felt and showed some signs of what happened, T'Rida was oblivious to it because of the powder. All he felt was the surge of power and adrenaline that surged through his veins with each snort that he took.

He liked how his mind seemed to work more precise and more analytically, bringing in each detail more clearly. It seemed as if a part of his mind that normally was closed, had been opened and allowed him to solve problems that he wouldn't have normally been able to solve. As he took another snort of the deliciously white powder he could hear his family downstairs and a sense of warm admiration washed over him. He was proud of how far they'd come in such a short amount of time.

Sure, it seemed like it had been forever since that fateful night they'd jacked the nigga in the apartment in West Oakland. But it had only been about a year and some change. Now he owned three houses. The beach house alone was worth two-point-four million dollars. The cars he drove today were the shit he'd only seen in movies and rap videos.

He could continue thinking about all the luxurious things he had for an hour. As he wiped the sweat from his forehead, he smiled realizing all that mattered, was that they were all eating. Not just him, but the entire family was eating. It felt good since they'd only just begun what they were going to do.

"From that shit-eating grin, you got on your face. A nigga might think you had an imaginary bitch on her knees bossing you up," Voorheeze stated as he walked into the room snapping T'Rida out of his daydream.

T'Rida looked at his second in command, with love and admiration in his eyes. "Naw, my nigga, just thinking 'bout how far we've come."

"Real talk, I feel you on dat shit, brah."

"Man, I told you niggaz we was gon' eat." Voorheeze could hear in T'Rida's voice how proud he was, and he couldn't blame him.

This was T'Rida's dream, sure, they'd all contributed to making shit happen, but T'Rida had the plan for them to put the shit together and they did it. This ran through his mind, as he bent down over the table, to help his nostrils to a hefty snort of the powder lying in the plate on the nightstand. After he took two big snorts, Voorheeze stood up to look at his patna.

"Brah, you, know we can't stay away for too much longer. Our lieutenants are holding it down, but if we stay away too long mothafuckaz will start to get the wrong idea."

"I know, my nigga, I've been running over the plans for our next move in my head," T'Rida commented right before he bent down to take another snort. He lifted his head and continued. "My nigga, Imma need you to rock how we rock, you know what I mean? But now on the same token I'ma need you to step it up a little more and handle my end of shit too for a while." As he wiped the sweat off his head, he continued, "You know I feel cool, but I'm not back cool enough to hit dem blocks like I needs to"

Voorheeze had been snorting powder since he was eleven, so he knew first-hand, how powerful and alluring the drug was. He'd seen too many good niggaz get caught up not being strong enough to tame the beast. So, he knew the signs and as he looked at T'Rida he saw some of the signs of a nigga wide open. He had real concern and love in his voice, as he told him. "My nigga don't trip off dat shit, Rogue. I got you on this mob shit, my nigga."

Wondering if he should just leave well enough alone and see if T'Rida would chain the beast himself or not. He figured if the shoe was on the other foot, he hoped his brother would do the same, so he said fuck it. "Rida on some real shit, though, brah check dis out. You know I've been rocking wit' my cock out and snorting dis bitch since I was yay high to a camel. So, my nigga, I ain't neva gon' judge you." Shaking his head Voorheeze continued. "But blood, you hitting dat bitch a little too hard yada mean? Fall back some, my nigga, you slipping."

"Slipping?" Rida asked with a puzzled look on his face.

"My nigga, you been up like four-five days Rogue," Voorheeze pointed out.

"Brah, I've just been organizing shit mentally. I luv you for the concern, brah, but I'm good."

"A'ight, Rogue only you know, my nigga."

"V, it's good, brah," T'Rida reassured him. "I'ma shoot down the way, spend some time wit' Moe, and finish healing."

"Do you, my nigga. I'ma hold the streets down and make sure we keep dem bitches on lock. Get yo' shit back on point, by the time you ready to bounce back in, shit gon' be where you want it to be." Voorheeze started to walk out. As he got to the doorway he turned back for a brief moment. "T, make sure you come back, nigga. This our family, not my family." Then he walked out.

Voorheeze went down to the second level of the beach house looking for Gunz. The two of them talked for hours. Although, he hoped T'Rida wouldn't fall victim to dat white bitch, somehow, he just knew he would. It wasn't like T'Rida had been down with her for long or anything like that. It was in the way he took to the bitch that spoke to Voorheeze.

He couldn't neglect their business. The plans Gunz had for Philadelphia seemed like a good look to Voorheeze. Gunz had family out there who were doing thangs. Now they were in dire need for a real connect. From what Gunz put out there, his relatives were talking 'bout moving a thousand bricks a month. Gunz's older cousin had a pilot who owned his own private airstrip in Bryn Mawr, Pennsylvania.

The pilot also had a cousin out in Gilroy who was a pilot with his own flight school. They would alternate flying back and forth dropping off the packages and money. They'd pay each pilot fifteen thousand a trip. Voorheeze and Gunz decided, they'd send five hundred bricks on the first run as a test. Gunz would remain in Cali long enough to help Voorheeze reorganize some shit and make sure Cali was running like a well-oiled machine.

Voorheeze knew he'd have to make a few promotions throughout the ranks. His first order of business would be to make both C-Murda and Styles Capo's. They'd both put in enough work as Lieutenants and were as loyal as they came.

Initially, T'Rida didn't like the idea of Voorheeze bringing Anne so close to the family. True, T'Rida was the one to give her the green light, but he was going to start her off small and see what she could do. He really didn't want her knowing about the beach house. Hell, even their lieutenants and capos didn't know about the beach house. But he figured what was done was done. Shit, no matter how much power a nigga had, he didn't have enough power to go back in time and change shit.

Not to mention, he felt he was indebted to her for saving his life. On top of that, he guessed she'd already proven she would hold her own and bust that thang when needed. Nevertheless, he decided she would be Voorheeze's responsibility. He would have to break her in and find a suitable position for her to play, that would be beneficial to the family. However, as the days passed and the five-spent time together at the beach house. He noticed little things about the dark chocolate cutie that he couldn't help but find intriguing. On more than one occasion, he had told her how indebted he was to her for shit she'd done for him. Each time she would humbly downplay her role or brush off the gratitude, like it was all in a day's work, only impressing him more. In the end, he changed his mind and decided she'd stay close to him.

Shit, as gangsta as he was, he could always use a hitta close to him. Convincing himself that his reasons were strictly from a strategic standpoint. After all, he was still pretty weak and fucked up from the shooting and she could handle a pistol.

As he watched her walk out of the shower, T'Rida knew he was full of shit and had been lying to himself. As the water ran down her body onto the floor towel she was standing on, so did his eyes. He was drinking in the dark chocolate tones in her curvaceous body. Anne stood six-feet-one and weighed one-hundred and ninety-pounds of firm thick beauty.

Her deep dark chocolate skin glistened with a natural glossy radiance, that came from the numerous amounts of water she drank daily. Unlike most women, she didn't clog her pores with a lot of different beauty products that were loaded with different chemicals. Her 42C breasts sat nice and high on her chest, so perky you'd think the natural mounds were fake. She had the prettiest set of nipples he'd ever seen. Not to mention, her smooth tight and firm apple bottom booty. As she bent over to rub coconut baby oil on her legs, T'Rida's dick instantly began pulsating and growing hard. Full of cocaine and mesmerized by her beauty, he stood up from the bed, walked over and stood behind her. Feeling his dick pressing up against her, Anne's pussy immediately became soaking wet from the knowledge of how good it felt deep inside her last night.

Thoughts of how it stretched her walls and touched every hidden corner of her pussy like she'd never before experienced. She pressed her ass firmly against his dick and rocked back and forth. She attempted to stand up, but T'Rida placed his hand on the center of her back bending her over even further, with his other hand he rammed his dick deep into her pulsating and waiting pussy.

Thrusting deep and hard inside of her with a carnal hunger too strong to deny. Anne's cries of pleasure and ecstasy excited him more and more, feeding his hunger.

"Yes—yes! Fuck that pussy, daddy! Fuck it," She cried just as an earth-shattering orgasm ripped thru her body.

They went from the center of the room to the bathroom sink, on the floor up against the wall and finally finished in the shower. After they were finished, the two of them took a shower and went out on the third story patio to stare out at the ocean and relax. While outside T'Rida rolled a sweet one, the two of them smoked and laid back. T'Rida had lost count of how many days they remained at the beach house getting high and fucking. What he did know was that Monique was furious with him.

He hadn't been home in over a month. Although he told her, he had to stay out of the area 'cause shit was too hot on the streets, she wasn't listening to any of that. If he didn't want her going off the deep end, T'Rida knew, he would have to go home soon. Not to mention, the powder he'd brought from Jenn's house was gone and he didn't feel like taking another trip to get more.

When it was time to leave the beach house. He dropped Anne off with a list of instructions for her to carry out. Once she was done carrying out those instructions she was to hook up with Voorheeze. After he dropped Anne off, T'Rida picked up a few ounces of coke from one of the stash houses and jumped on the freeway, headed home to Monique and the kids.

DE'KARI

Chapter XIV

Monique was in the backyard swimming laps in the Olympic size, heated pool, when T'Rida walked in the house. She didn't hear him walk in until she'd finished her laps and was standing by the pool toweling off. She heard noise coming from inside the house, knowing she was the only person home, she reached under the copy of *'Brittney's Secret'*, a book she'd been reading and grabbed the 9mm Glock from under it.

She jacked a round into the chamber and headed toward her house to investigate. She knew damn well no one had the audacity to be breaking into her Goddamned house. As stressed out and as pissed off she was at her husband, didn't nobody want to fuck with her. The noise was coming from upstairs. She wasn't too sure, but she swore the sound was coming from her bedroom. The first thing that came to mind was the master safe. Throughout the house was a total of three safes hidden, but the master safe was hidden in the Master bedroom.

She took a deep breath, held it in and proceeded to climb the stairs as silently as she could. Every step she took caused her heart to pound violently in her chest. Just outside the double doors of the Master suite, Monique could hear the dresser drawers open and close. She could tell from the sounds that someone was searching the drawers looking for something. At that exact moment, she silently wished her man was there to protect her.

Just the thought of her having to be there by herself turned her fears into anger. Anger for a nigga that would leave her and their kids alone in an eight-bedroom mansion. A mansion that some mothafucka just broke into and was at this very moment robbing. That same anger now channeled in the right direction, she kicked the double doors open, with her bare feet and stood with the pistol pointed directly at the chest of T'Rida, who was standing butt naked in the middle of the room putting on a pair of boxer briefs. The sound of the doors crashing open made him jump at attention.

"What you gon' shoot a mothafucka for washing his ass?" He smirked as he looked at her.

DE'KARI

Monique was ready to give this mothafucka a piece of her mind. She opened her mouth to speak and just then she saw the new bandages he had on his body. She lowered the pistol and closed her mouth. Immediately, her heart broke into a million pieces at the sight of her man all bandaged up and wounded.

She rushed over to him, "Oh, Daddy, I'm sorry baby. I didn't know it was you." She hugged him long and strong, giving him the hug you give someone you hadn't seen in a long time. "I thought someone was coming in here trying to rob us."

The mere sight of him brought tears to her eyes. As Monique hugged her man, she could tell he'd lost ten to fifteen pounds. She also noticed that his embrace wasn't the same. He felt weak, her heart sank at the thought of her man being shot.

"It looks a lot worse than it actually is, Babe," T'Rida told his woman trying his best to sound pain-free.

Just the way she melted into his arms, instead of cursing him out after being gone so long, showed him just how scared she'd been. It killed him to know, he'd caused his woman that much pain. Monique couldn't even speak her emotions were so strong tears choked her voice in her throat. The tightness in her heart felt like it was going to blow her chest up. So, all she could do was hold the man she loved as tight as she could.

She knew he could feel her pain. He held her in his arms and continued to soothe her. After what seemed like a lifetime, T'Rida guided Monique toward the bed where they climbed in and fell asleep with Monique's head resting snuggly on his chest, and her body wrapped in his big arms.

Although he laid perfectly still, while Monique slept in his arms, T'Rida was wide awake. He laid there with a million thoughts roaming through his mind, going over one-thousand and one different plans. Finally, after accepting that sleep would inevitably escape him, T'Rida climbed out of bed silently, so he wouldn't wake Monique. Out on the back porch, he sat under the awning smoking a sweet one, continuing to allow his mind to drift.

Not even realizing he was smoking on his third one, T'Rida heard a noise inside the house. Monique was sleeping and the kids were at her mother's house. Veronica was keeping the kids until Monday, so there shouldn't have been any sounds coming from the house. He slipped through the sliding glass door with his Cannon in hand and sweat pouring down his face, holding his breath. First, the dining room and kitchen, then the living room, T'Rida walked without caution.

One by one he checked all the rooms and bathrooms. Where was the mothafucka? T'Rida knew someone was in the house. His senses were screaming at him! His skin was crawling all over his body! Finally, he opened the door to the bedroom. The room was pitch black though the cocaine heightened his night vision. His eyeballs were the size of a dinner saucer. His heart was racing a thousand miles an hour as he scanned the room. He was shocked no one was in there, except Monique laying sound asleep in the exact position he'd left her.

T'Rida doubled back checking all the bathrooms and rooms again, gripping the gun tight in his hand, as he walked. He just knew somebody was in the house. He didn't know that the cocaine had him tweaking.

***

As the Camaro turned the corner Anne's eyes were already sizing up the Block. For a month now, Cantalope had been schooling her on the art of pickups and drops. Anne prided herself for being street-smart and sharp all the way around. But, Cantalope was by far the sharpest bitch she'd ever met. From day one, Anne was beyond impressed with the abundance of game she'd been receiving. Although Cantalope was a beautiful, high-yellow, red-bone, with so much elegance and class; at the drop of a hat, she could turn on the switch and become the most ruthless bitch to ever hold a pistol!

Her intellect and strategic mind were so far advanced, Anne couldn't help but wonder why she wasn't running someone's security unit at a Fortune 500 Club. Or maybe even a private event security. None of the cars that were parked along the street looked out of place, Cantalope had told her that was the first and most obvious way to know if something was up. A car that didn't belong usually meant a person or people who didn't belong. She didn't see any shadows, in any of the windows of the parked cars nor did she notice anyone out of place.

She caught movement out of the corner of her right eye. Looking in that direction Anne saw a little girl running out of her front door to play in the front yard. Anne pulled the car over three houses down from where the girl was. She made sure not to pull into the driveway of the house. She remembered Cantalope's explanation, *'when you pull into the driveway, you not only box yourself in, but you also cut your visibility in half. When you're parked on the street, you can see all the way down the street in both directions!'*

After checking and double checking the rearview and her pistol at the same time, she climbed out of the car. She popped the trunk remotely, as she approached the back of the car. Still, her eyes scanned everything while reaching in the trunk and retrieving a shopping bags. She looked like a woman who'd just came from the mall. Once she was in the house, she locked the door and stood completely still listening to all sound. She looked out a hidden peephole as she listened, making sure no cars suddenly pulled up at the house.

Once she was satisfied that no one was in the house and she wasn't followed, she climbed the stairs to the second story. There a safe was in the wall of the closet, in the master bedroom. She emptied two of the bags she carried into the safe that was already three-quarters of the way full. The twenty-five stacks of ten-thousand she placed into the safe filled it completely. When she first started dropping the money at the stash houses, the sight of so much money made her freeze, but now she was used to it.

Hell, there were safes in the closet of all five bedrooms and under the sinks of all four bathrooms. She made her way downstairs, then headed to the basement. No matter how many times she looked at it, she could not get used to what stood in front of her. She took a deep breath to brace herself. She struggled to open the six by four floor safe and couldn't believe her eyes.

The safe was a good two-feet deep and had stack on stacks of one-hundred-dollar bills in it. One by one, she placed the twenty-five stacks that were in the last eight bags in the safe. This shit was ridiculous! She stood there admiring the mountains of money, as she shook her head in disbelief. Anne snapped herself out of her trance. After struggling to close the heavy iron safe , she walked out of the basement.

Voorheeze watched Anne on the screen of the monitors as she climbed the stairs. He knew how she was feeling. He felt the same euphoric feeling himself when looking into the giant free-standing safes. There were over thirty cameras positioned throughout the house so that every inch of the house you could see from three sets of monitors. Monitors owned by Voorheeze, T'Rida, and Gunz. There were also sensors and detectors throughout the house.

Anne chirped once on her Nextel signaling that everything was cool, and she was ready to exit the house. The double-chirp from Cantalope let her know the outside was secure. Anne locked the house up and walked back to the door. The same thought crossed her mind every time she left the stash house. Considering all the money inside, why didn't they have an alarm on the house? What she didn't know was there was an alarm on the house and the only one with the code was Jason Voorheeze. The moment he watched her lock the door on the hidden camera's outside porch, he activated the alarm.

Anne pulled off from the house. Two minutes later, an all-black Mustang GT that was parked halfway down the street on the opposite side, pulled off heading in the opposite direction. Its tinted windows concealed Cantalope as she drove off. Cantalope loved her sistas above anyone else. They grew up to-gether, fought together, laughed together and even cried to-gether! From day one she was all about her and her sisters.

She and her cousin French Tip had always been close. Growing up, they were like sisters. French Tip was Voorheeze's baby sister and Cantalope's right hand and best friend. If you saw one, you saw the other and if you had a problem with one, no questions asked, you had a problem with the other. In middle and junior high school the duo would beat girls down. By the end of high school, the two became four. These were four of the baddest and deadliest bitches to ever come out of the Bay Area.

Rumor had it that Cantalope's freshman year biology teacher had the hots for her. When his continual advances went unanswered she received a 'D' that everyone knew should have been an 'A'. Two weeks after school let out for the summer, he was found locked inside of his classroom with his throat cut from ear-to-ear. His dick had been hacked off and shoved into his mouth. Someone had written the words, *'Reap What You Sow!'* in bold and black letters on the blackboard behind his body.

Even though she'd never been arrested or questioned about it, the entire City knew who was responsible for the murder. The next year both her and French Tip received straight A's and had an all-female teaching staff. That began what would become the *'She-Wolves'*. It began as a legend of Urban chicks that killed in a way, all their killings were done without a trace. Hood legends quickly became reality at the formation of Neva Die.

It was well known that Neva Die had its very own Hit Squad known as the *'Wolf Pack'*! They were vicious, they were bloody, and they were elite. Anytime there was a point to be made or a message sent. Marlon and his hungry Wolves did so with efficiency. But, whenever the family needed killing done quickly and efficiently T'Rida would let his *'She-Wolves'* loose. It never set well with Voorheeze that his baby sister was a stone-cold assassin. But, considering his way of living, he knew he couldn't judge her.

In the hood, you were either predator or prey. Voorheeze was just glad his little sister didn't turn out to be prey. In fact, French Tip was the most vicious and feared out of the entire pack! Her jet-black flawless skin and beautiful features made many niggaz think God had shown a display of perfection when he created the Chocolate China Doll. She had eyes that were passed captivating, they were hypnotic! However, if you really stared into them, you saw the death and destruction, along with the pain and suffering.

Even her own sistas who were all stone cold killas felt nervous around her. Often wondering if she truly was biologically connected to Hades and the Devil himself! Although Cantalope ran the She-Wolves, French Tip controlled them hands down! Anne drove the Camaro to the meet spot, to go over some shit with French Tip and Cantalope. It didn't bother her that the two She-Devils were critiquing every move she made and how she made them. She knew she was in training.

GORILLAZ IN THE BAY

The shit they were schooling her with was priceless! Not to mention, in the few months she'd been fucking with the family, her money game was already ridiculous. Back on that day when T'Rida and them came through her front door, she never would've imagined they'd turn out the way they did. All her life she'd been either abused or fucked over by no good, nothing-ass niggaz. The abuse had grown so common in her life, she figured it was normal.

She didn't have friends or family, so she didn't have other females, she could compare her struggles with. So, she became expectant of the abuse and bullshit. The day she saved T'Rida's life was the first time she'd ever killed someone. But, fuck remorse, it never came! From the moment she pulled the trigger, all she felt was exhilaration! It had felt so good to finally be the one inflicting the pain. The gun gave her power!

She didn't have to feel helpless any longer. Using the slightest pressure of her finger just an inch or so, in a fraction of a second, she could alter or end somebody's life. No smelly dick, trifling-ass niggaz would ever lay his fucking hands on her again! She slid her hand over the cold steel laying in her lap, her pussy twitched at the feel of it. As she pulled to a stop light, her Nextel chirped drawing her attention. Only her new family used the chirps, so she chirped back without hesitation.

"Wassup, sis?"

"Change of plans, T'Rida needs you. Drive over to the white house. He's on his way. I'll hit you up later," Cantalope relayed the new instructions to her.

"Aight bet," Anne responded.

"You did good." Cantalope wasn't good at complimenting people, but from the very first hand to hand combat, she saw something special in Anne.

The way she picked up on strategical formations, Cantalope knew Anne was a bad bitch in the making. The type of bitch that only came around once in a generation. She knew because her mom had been that bitch.

Chirp! Chirp!

Feeling uncomfortable herself from receiving the compliment Anne chirped back her acknowledgment.

He picked up the dry washcloth and wiped the sweat off his forehead for the umpteenth time. Thousands of thoughts raced through his mind at once. He, Murda and Styles was due back in a little while with the new shipment. Monique was on his ass all the time, he had missed a meeting with Johnny and two with Voorheeze. He knew that Voorheeeze was hot, but the mothafuckaz didn't know the strain of all the shit he had on his shoulders. Shaking his head after he marveled over the situation, T'Rida picked up the glass tube sitting on the table.

After packing it, he placed the glass pipe to his lips and took another hit. The feeling was exhilarating. T'Rida knew now why mothafuckaz were spending so much money on this shit. Although his thoughts were still rapid, they came clear and orderly. Just that fast he knew exactly how he was going to handle everything.

The motion detector attached to the camera at the front gate got his attention. He tucked the crack pipe in his pocket, grabbed his thumper off the table and tucked it into his waist. The camera at the gate was equipped with a new 3-D imaging that allows the dark tint of the windows to be seen. So, he knew it was Anne inside of the Camaro. Even still, he walked out and waited for her to drive into the yard.

As she exited the car T'Rida couldn't help but admire her body, especially that phat print peaking at him through the tights she was wearing. T'Rida may have been a married man, but that didn't change the fact that Anne was one sexy bitch. As his eyes took in her beauty his G took in the new aura about her. He could feel a new confidence in her, that wasn't there the last time he'd seen her.

As they greeted each other, embraced and caught up, T'Rida took it all in. While he was sizing her up and reading the changes, Anne noticed the changes in his weight, His wet clammy skin and the way his eyes kept darting all over the place. But, she held her tongue and played her position. Hell, this was the nigga that put her on and gave her a shot. T'Rida in truth was her meal ticket and now that she was just starting to see some dough, she wasn't going to fuck that up!

GORILLAZ IN THE BAY

Not long after Anne pulled up C-Murda and J Styles pulled up. C-Murda was in a U-Haul truck and Styles was following behind him in a Lincoln Navigator. When they got out of the vehicles there was no small talk. They all walked to the back of the U-Haul. C-Murda looked back at the gate double-checking that it was closed before he turned to unlock the back of the truck. Considering that T'Rida had told her Styles and Murda were dropping off a shipment. She already knew what was on the truck. So, while everyone else's eyes were on the truck and its cargo, Anne's back was to the truck. She stood with her thumpa in her hand, while her eyes continuously scanned the yard and the gate.

She was ready to act a fool at the first sign of a problem! After moving a few items out of the way that were merely props, Murda and Styles reached the two barrels of cocaine. This was the first of what would become the regular shipment from now on. Once both barrels were off the truck, T'Rida stepped up and took a look at one-hundred kilos of raw cocaine. All types of shit went through his mind at that moment, but you couldn't tell.

Quickly he gave his Capo C-Murda instructions on the distribution. Next, he had a word with Anne and walked back inside the warehouse. Although the White House was the main holding for the supply, these first one-hundred kilos would hit the streets immediately. C-Murda basically oversaw the distribution of all the product. He would disburse the work evenly between three teams. J Styles and T'Rida's first Lieutenant and third in command under C-Murda, would take twenty-five keys and get them to their trap houses. C-Murda would get the rest to its destination. Twenty-five keys were to go to Clarkola and Twenty-five keys to DeeDee to let them do what they do, and the other twenty-five got stashed.

T'Rida neva wanted to get caught without work, so they would tuck a third away in case there was ever a drought. After today's run the She-Wolves would resume the shipments and once the drop was secure at the White-House, C-Murda would take over and do his thang. This is why French-Tip sat low in the seat of her Camaro overseeing the whole play. Not only was she extra protection in case Murda and Styles ran into a problem, she was also ironing out the details her and her sistas would implement. T'Rida and Cantalope were the only ones aware of her presence.

Chapter XV

The way the growing empire was set up was unbelievable. Its intricate structure was organized from the blueprint of T'Rida's very own organization. *The Black Guerilla Family!* In the design of things, there were Cadres within Cadres. A Cadre for a better understanding was a self-sustaining, independent, full-functioning Unit. A governing body so to say or a chain of command. Each chain had its five links: The overseer or the C, this is who oversaw the entire chain. Next, you had your line Lieutenant or your M.O.J. Your line Lieutenant ran the day to day activities thus most would see him as the shot caller.

Only the Line Lieutenant himself knew who the C was. Depending on your links sometimes the line lieutenant would also wear the hat of the Minister of Justice who passed down discipline. After the M.O.J you had the M.O.S. and M.O.E. Your M.O.S. or Minster of Security was just that, head of security. Your next minister often wore two hats as well. Minister of Economics as well as Minister of Education. Both of which was self-explanatory.

The C and his Ministers made up the five links in the Chain of Command. This was your 'Round Table,' each had just as much say as the next and each was the head of his own Cadre. Orders were passed down the chain of command and grievances were passed up the chain. By this design, each member of the organization only knew the man directly above and below him in the chain of command. If shit ever went sour, one man could bring down the entire organization. Shit was tight!

T'Rida checked the monitors, then grabbed a change of outfit and headed to the bathroom. Inside he took a couple more hits off his pipe, then hopped in the shower to freshen up. He walked out of the bathroom dressed in his new Armani suit looking like new money. His cannon was in a shoulder holster concealed under the suit. Although his eyes bulged out of his head they were on point.

"Did Cantalope fill you in on what's needed of you?" T'Rida asked Anne as he approached the desk.

Anne was seated with her back toward him watching the monitors with her thumper in her hand resting on the top of the desk.

"Naw we mobile, you know sis ain't gonna do no talking over the phone. So, she just told me to meet you over here."

"Well for the next few weeks you wit' me. A lot of moves about to be made, so I need you glued to my hip as my extra eyes."

"Just tell me a position and bet I play it," Anne responded full of conviction neva taking her eyes off the monitors.

As T'Rida rounded the corner of the desk and came into view, Anne let her mouth speak her thoughts, "Goddamn, G.Q. in dis mothafucka!"

"We about to be making some power moves. So, for now on a nigga gotta dress like power. You gotta look the part to play the part," Rida explained as he beamed from Anne's reaction to his looks.

The way this nigga was looking Anne's pussy wanted him to play the part on her!

"You can leave yo' whip. We'll double-back and pick it up later."

"A'ight." Anne stood up, taking his comment as the cue to leave.

She was thrown off as he made his way toward the back of the warehouse instead of the front. But, she didn't break not one stride as she followed. They approached a door in the back corner of the warehouse. Anne didn't hesitate, she stepped quickly in front of T'Rida, so she would be the one to open the door. A panel on the right of the door had an emerald green light showing on it.

She took it as a sign to go so she opened the door. It opened to a long-carpeted corridor. Once the heavy door closed, Anne watched as T'Rida pushed one button and green lasers scanned his face. After the recognition, he pushed one other button and what seemed like thirty different bolts were being locked.

What she didn't know was the exact same thing was being done to the opposite warehouse. The heavy doors and the door panel itself was made of light titanium alloy that coated steel reinforcements. A Tank couldn't get through the doors. And the concrete walls themselves were two-feet with crisscross rebar built into the concrete. Unless your face was logged into the memory of digital pad you were not getting into the White House period! At the end of the core door, was the door with an identical security pad, leading to a business office.

Securing the door T'Rida then crossed the office and opened the other door. To Anne's amazement, French-Tip was at the desk in an office directly across from the one they were exiting. A quick head nod was all the acknowledgment between her and T'Rida, as he and Anne kept moving. Anne couldn't believe they had walked out of the White House, right into *'Satin Doll Fashionista'* that's what you call Gangsta Shit!

While there weren't any murders needed, the She-Wolves handled all the supply pick-ups and money drops to the stash houses. Naturally, the elite killing force would stand as watchful guardians over the warehouse that was built to house most of their product. This shit was ingenious! Exiting the front office, they made their way to a cranberry colored, big body, Benz. The interior was butterscotch and mahogany wood grain with butterscotch leather seats. The rims were custom made twenty-two-inch Mercedes rims.

The fragrance of the car was identical to the Issey Miyake Cologne T'Rida was wearing. Anne couldn't help but think, *'God, damn, this nigga is clean!'*

They drove around the bay area for a few hours, while T'Rida busted some moves and handled some business. Anne had zero clue how big Neva Die was or how much responsibility T'Rida had. He handled all his business with precision and efficiency from what she could tell. But, he wasn't so tight on his security she noticed. Twice he'd started to climb out of the Benz without grabbing his Banger from the stash spot until she reminded him. She also noticed that he snorted cocaine continuously and even smoked on a couple of sweet ones. All which she noted and stored away.

Exiting off highway 880 on the Dixon Landing exit, T'Rida made his way to Vienna Drive. He had bought a house over in Milpitas that would be known as the War Room. The place where the hierarchy of Neva Die would come to meet. Tonight would be the first of many of the organization's meetings. The

War Room had to be a place located away from any hood. Being a place for all the heads to meet, it couldn't be risked meeting up where nosey eyes could report what needed to remain anonymous.

The nice Victorian house had a wrap-around driveway connected to the back of the house. Parking wouldn't be a problem either with the minicars visible from the street as to not draw unwanted attention. The meeting consisted of each General along with the top two members of each team, plus the top two of the Wolf-Pack and the She-Wolves.

C-Murda and Styles were the first to show up. After that, everyone else began pulling in until all thirteen bosses and under-bosses were in the house. They all sat around the family room smoking on that good, sipping drinks and enjoying small talk. It had been one helluva year for the Family. Building and rebuilding, shipping and shaping.

A few problems arose here and there, but between the Wolf-Pack and the She-Wolves, no situation was ever allowed to grow and fester. The entire Family was eating and happy. But, the thirteen in the house, shit, they were doing the fool financially. Everything was so good Voorheeze had begun a saying that they all began using, *'Life is Good Like the LG phone!'* For them it really was.

"Alright, check me out. Let me get everyone's attention right quick, so we can get this crackin'," T'Rida announced as he entered the room.

All conversations in the room ceased and everyone's eyes and attention were on T'Rida as he continued. "It's been one crazy azz year, but nigga we made it and we here!"

Applause and cheers went up all around the room. None of the cheers were forced. For most of them, this was the best they had ever experienced life. T'Rida allowed the celebrations to go on for a brief moment.

"I'm 'bout to sit my ass down and let V do him, but before I do, I have to say something to my two brothas."

Both Gunz and Voorheeze glanced at each other briefly before turning back to T'Rida and listening a little more intently on what it was that was going to be said next.

GORILLAZ IN THE BAY

"Nigga, it seems like just yesterday when niggaz was Section eight'n it and curb serving. I had a vision and you two niggaz believed in it. Y'all believed in me."

This was a rare moment of emotional display for T'Rida and the room was quiet as he professed his love for his brothas.

"We busted our asses and put it all on the line, but it was well worth it, Look at us! And although you niggaz give me plenty of room to do what I do. I'll neva forget that this is *our shit!* This ain't no one man show! When a nigga got hit up a while back, I ain't even gon' lie, I thought it was ova. You, niggaz, rode foe me like the Hounds of Hell! And Blood I Love You niggaz!"

Voorheeze had neva seen his brother get this emotional, and it really touched his heart. As his and T'Rida's eyes teared up, he rose and embraced his brother. Although his eyes were as dry as the Mohave Desert, Gunz rose from where he was seated, walked over and embraced his brothas as well. After the three finished their brief embrace, Voorheeze took over and was straight business.

"Peep game and check play, because I ain't into repeating myself! Some of you in this room are actual blood relatives but believe me we are *one family* straight the fuck up," he informed. "Now with the exception of Tip, I love each and every one of you equally. I won't hesitate to lay shit down for you! And I won't hesitate to correct you if you make a mistake. All of you know French is my sister and my world. niggaz understand I will kill God behind her! No questions asked! Every nigga and bitch in here need to feel the same way about each other or you on the *wrong fucking team—*" He paused to let the shit sink in. "We have a large family, right now. A family that is both feared and respected, but we tryna build an empire. The way we moving dat ain't gon' be hard at all, but Empires have come and Empires have gone. Look at Felix Mitchell, look at the Firm, The Mo-Mo's, The Dust Man. The hard part is lasting after everything is built. You, mothafuckaz know why none of them lasted?"

D.J. was the first to speak up. "Shit, that's the easiest question in the world, *punk ass snitches.*"

DE'KARI

"Mothafuckaz ain't have no discipline," Cantelope called out.

"Both of y'all wrong," Voorheeze told them.

French Tip knew the answer. She'd heard her brother lacing niggaz on security all her life, so she knew the intimacy of how his mind worked. "Everybody knew too fucking much!"

Voorheeze smiled at his little sister. He knew years of preaching the importance of security to her over and over, again and again, would eventually pay off.

"Speak dat shit, French! Let me break it down for y'all real quick. Every organization is gonna breed snitches. I don't give a fuck what organization it is! And the bigger the organization the more snitches it will have. You can bet your ass we got at least thirty potential snitches on our payroll, right the fuck now—" Voorheeze took an extra-long time pausing this time, as he eyed each Boss in the room.

He could see everybody's wheels turning in their heads. Good at least mothafuckaz were thinking. This was a thinking man's game and if you weren't always thinking, believe shit would start sinking.

"The way we ensure survival and longevity is through the isolation of the ranks. No matter what, we follow the chain of command. If a mothafucka turn Rat, he can only tell on two people. The mothafucka he gives his orders to and who he gets his orders from. He can't tell on nobody else if he don't know nobody else!" Fuck pausing now, Voorheeze was in full Beast Mode. "Safety and Security is what we do! On da real, I'm telling y'all enforce the chain of command! If you don't I will! I don't give a fuck who it is, if the chain is broken, I will break you! I'm not gon' watch what we built fall apart cause a mothafucka street punk comes home and finds his bitch mouth on anotha nigga's dick. He speeds off in a rage and gets pulled over wit' a banger on him and instead of riding his beef he brings us down? Fuck that!"

The next few hours were spent going over the mechanics of how things would be running from henceforth. No one questioned Voorheeze's authority, not to mention the shit he was spitting was some real shit! Niggaz only needed as much info as it took for them to play their position. No more, no less. Knowing who was who and who did what was above their pay grade. All they needed to know was if the nigga above you respected a mothafucka, then you'd better respect him, it was as simple as that!

After the death of Marlon, Johnny Spitz stepped up as the head of the Wolf Pack. Though he had the intellect, charisma and raw brutality it took to lead a squad of enforcers, Johnny took shit to the next level. The handle Spitz was added to his name because he let his bangers spit without question, thought or hesitation. He appointment Stone Cold as his Second in Command and under their leadership the Wolf Pack was not just an average enforcement squad, they were the most feared Murder Team in California next to the She-Wolves. They were getting job offers from as far as Florida for their wet work.

DeeDee and AJ were Gunz' Second and Third in Command and they were the spitting image of Gunz as far as how they rocked. Both young goons were abandoned by dope fiend parents. They were left to either die in the mean streets of East Oakland or learn how to survive. They were both taken under his wings and raised by Gunz. No bond could ever know a loyalty stronger than the one they had for Gunz. He found them, raised them and taught them how to make it. He didn't make them gangsta, he taught and showed them what gangsta was and they followed.

Clark had taken off since that day his little brother had dropped that work on him at Three Brother's Tacos. Officially, he locked East Palo Alto down without having to use any force. The Blue Print Voorheeze had given him was sweeter than honey and ran smoother than butter. The Coke that his little brother was hitting him off with was so raw, niggaz added, *'Ola'* which was short for that *'Yola'* onto his name. Now he was known as Clarkola. Fuck the Mexicans!

'Clarkola got the Yola,' and with Tut being his Right-Hand Man and Enforcer, they didn't have no problems. After all, everybody in the Town knew that Tut from C Street wasn't playing with a full deck. The whole hood knew he knocked a nigga down one day for not putting the King in front of his name when he addressed him.

DE'KARI

The three brothers all had a team of their own, that only *'they'* were responsible for. Each one of their teams had their own council which governed itself. However, the thirteen that were present were the council that held it all together. Neva Die began as a dream that soon became reality. From a small family of friends to a Mob of dope dealers they had grown. But, they were well on their way to becoming an organized crime syndicate. Fuck them old fat Italians! The niggaz were here, and the very first Black Mafia was born that night!

Chapter XVI

A.J.'s phone kept vibrating. He ignored it due to the meeting. He figured after the fourth time it had to be an emergency, so he picked up.

"Yeah?" He whispered into the phone.

He listened quietly and intently. He walked over to Gunz and whispered something into his ear. Gunz looked up at A.J. in amazement and disbelief. Although, the focal point was on Voorheeze, as he spoke curiosity snuck into the room, this was evident by the glances at A.J. and Gunz.

"Aye, V, hold up, big brah," Gunz called out cutting Voorheeze off, getting everybody's attention. "We need to turn the T.V. on, right now, brah!"

T'Rida heard the alarm in Gunz voice and reached for the remote. "What channel?"

"Shit nigga any channel."

The T.V. came on, with all eyes centered on it. On the screen, there were about forty police cars chasing a tricked-out Box Chev. The high-speed chase was taking place on highway 880. The news helicopter was so close that the view camera could see directly inside the car. Voorheeze could tell it was Big Joe driving and Dame in the passenger seat. He couldn't make out the third person sitting behind the driver, but he didn't have to wait long to find out.

First, Lil Twan's head came out of the window, then the top half of his body. He was holding an AR-15 in his hands. On live T.V. Lil' Twan let the AR-15 do its thang. When the bullets hit the windshield of the first police car, its driver yanked the steering wheel hard to the left trying to avoid the hail of bullets. The car slammed into the car directly opposite of it, causing it to crash into the center-divide.

"Goddamn, lil' nigga do yo thang," Tut called out showing his approval of that goon shit.

As if led on by the cheering, Twan let loose another hail of bullets. The footage was so clear you could see the sparks flying off the cars as the bullets ricocheted off them. While the scene was playing out, the announcer was in the background talking.

"Again, we are being told that the occupants in the vehicle being chased by officers are three of the founding members of the violent and notorious gang out of Oakland called The Nutt Case Gang. Earlier today, law enforcement attempted to execute a joint task force raid on the suspected headquarters of the gang." A shot of the house in East Oakland came on to the screen.

"It was during the initial attempted raid, that pandemonium erupted. It was chaos from the start. As officers tried to make entry, gunfire came from everywhere. The gun battle and stand-off lasted nearly four hours. The aftermath, I'm sorry to report left eight officers fatally wounded. While six others were rushed off to the hospital. Under the cover for the gunfire, the suspects that are being pursued made it out of the house along with two others who are still at large. Authorities were led by an anonymous source to a Chevron Gas Station where a possible sighting had occurred. Authorities quickly arrived on the scene where another brief gun battle transpired. Then the suspects sped off and the current pursuit is the result," The announcer finished speaking but the chase was still on.

Dame was now partaking in the shootout as well. It looked like he was waving an Uzi or Tech-9 out the window. The cops had no choice, but to fall back and pursue the shooters from a distance. Twan ducked back into the window leaving only Dame shooting. The bottom of the screen had 93mph on it indicating their speed. Twan was back out of the window. The camera zoomed in on Dame. It looked like he was dialing numbers on his cell phone.

"I cannot believe the audacity of these guys," the announcer's voice came back. *"It would appear, ladies and gentlemen, that one of the suspects is actually making a phone call during this high-speed chase,"* He said as if everyone watching couldn't see that for themselves.

Everyone was wondering who or what was so important, they required a phone call at a time like this. When Voorheeze's cell phone started ringing, the entire room turned from the T.V. screen to him.

GORILLAZ IN THE BAY

"Hello," he answered putting the phone on speaker.

"Habari Gani ndugu! Say, I got some bad news, big brah," Dame shouted into the phone. His voice full of excitement.

"Yeah, Mwezi we can all see dat, right now. Rogue, I'm watching while talking to you."

Dame looked up toward the helicopter and waved. Voorheeze started cracking up. "Nigga, did you see me wave at you?" Dame was laughing too.

"Brah, you fucking stupid."

"So, check it out, cuzzo on dat last little thang you dropped off—" He waited for Voorheeze to speak.

"What about it, lil' brah?" Voorheeze was curious now.

"You gon' have to chalk dat shit up, nigga!" Dame was laughing so hard he started choking. When he finished he kept going. "Brah, I ain't gon' be able to pay you shit!"

"Nigga, I luv you. You know, I ain't trippin' on dat shit, you niggaz just try to make it out." He already knew what Dame was saying. He just didn't wanna hear it.

"You don't get it, big brah! We casing it til' the wheels fall off!" He was serious as a heart attack too.

The moment he spoke the Box Chev hit a spike strip. Joe tried to correct the spin but at the speed, they were traveling that was impossible. Twan's body went flying out of the car. A squad car barely missed him. His body tumbled for a good fifty yards before finally sliding into the median. The chance of someone surviving that was highly unlikely. Big Joe and Dame weren't so lucky. The Chev fish-tailed four times before it finally came to a stop on its roof. Everyone watching the footage, just knew Joe and Dame were dead.

Squad cars came to a screeching halt all around the vehicle. Every cop that jumped out had their weapons drawn. They could see the two bodies in the mangled car, motionless. Gas was leaking from the car, and something caused a spark. While everyone watched the car ignited. The cops just stood there.

"I know they ain't about to just let them boys burn up on national television," French Tip said shocked.

No one answered her. They couldn't. They were all thinking the same thing. "What if they were alive?"

161

DE'KARI

Just then a Captain was seen on T.V. barking out orders. Next, some officers jumped like a fire was lit under their ass. They scrambled to pull the two bodies out of the car. Moments later the entire car erupted into flames. An ambulance arrived on the scene and started working on Big Joe. Miraculously Twan was in handcuffs walking as he was being placed in a squad car. Another ambulance pulled up. Dame was placed into that one. Then the screen went to a visual of the announcer who began recapping the story.

"T'Rida looked over at Voorheeze, "Is this gon' be a problem?" It was an honest question. A question that Voorheeze didn't like, but still an honest question.

"Naw, we ain't gotta worry 'bout nothing! Them niggaz brick solid!" Voorheeze vouched for them. There was neva any doubt!

6 months later

T'Rida looked at himself in the floor length mirror, as he dried himself off. He couldn't believe how small he was. But, he wasn't gon' let small shit worry him. He was a busy mothafucking man. He was always doing this or taking care of that. So, if a nigga missed a meal or two fuck it! He noticed that his six-pack was back.

"Bitch, Mr. Strippa Man, Strippa Man," he sang out and started laughing as he did a little shimmy in front of the mirror.

T'Rida was a mothafucking Boss. Like most niggaz when he was in prison, he dreamed of coming home and becoming somebody. Niggaz in the pen was always lying about the shit they had or did. Or they were fantasizing about the shit they wanted or wanted to do. No exceptions! Everybody either fed a pipe-dream or was feeding somebody a pipe-dream. Not T'Rida, he came home and did the shit niggaz made pipe dreams about!

He had the money, the cars, and the women. Okay, he smoked a little Coke, but he didn't let the shit change who he was. He still handled his business. So, fucking what he'd lost some weight! He would just go buy some new shit! He walked over to the nightstand, grabbed his stem and took a hit. When he exhaled, he felt the Coke running thru his body. The all familiar sensations he experienced when he took a hit erupted through every cell in his body.

"Anne wake up, we got shit to do," he called out a little too loud, but he was unaware of that fact.

"I've been awake, Strippa Man," she told him.

"Then why you laying there like you dead and shit."

"First of all, Bitch can't get no sleep with all that noise you be making in the shower thinking you're Gerald Levert or somebody. And second, it ain't no reason for me to get out of this warm bed with you hogging the shower!"

"Yeah, yeah, if a nigga doesn't jump in there yo' ass know you gon' lock the bathroom down with that death you be doing every morning," he teased as he playfully snatched the comforter off her.

"Fuck you, T! You act like you full of roses!" She shot back as she threw her pillow at him, before jumping up.

The sight of her flawless body immediately caused his dick to rock up. Anne was ready to playfully tussle as they had a few times. But, as he closed in on her T'Rida had another thing in mind. Anne saw the lustful look in his eyes and allowed her eyes to drop to his fully engorged dick that was giving her a full salute. Just the sight of it caused her mouth to water at the anticipation of what he would do to her. She dropped to her knees and hungrily took him into her mouth.

After they finished their morning fuck session, they hopped in the shower, got dressed and headed to the mall. Along the way, Anne was having mixed emotions. Her time with T'Rida was cool and his dick game was off the Richter scale, but he was walking a very tight rope. When she had first found a crack pipe that fell onto the car seat from his pocket, she put that shit on the table fast! Even though he played it off and told her it was only an every now and then extracurricular thang, she knew inevitably what the end result would be.

She'd seen it way too many times. Being from Oakland, Anne had seen some of the biggest playas in the game succumb to the shit. Niggaz like Bone Crusher, the Original Ball Playa Rickie Lovett, the list just ran on and on and it broke her heart. Especially when she thought of her own mother. Anne had wondered if she should mention something to Voorheeze, but she quickly checked herself.

T'Rida was the one that had given her an opportunity. It was because of him that her life had changed. How in the fuck could she betray that by putting his business out in the streets? Besides, for all she knew Voorheeze already knew about the shit. For all, she knew T'Rida could've been a functioning addict for years. Naw Anne wasn't about to fuck hers up!

T'Rida had bought so much shit that he paid one of the workers at the last store to help them carry their shit to his truck. As they were exiting the mall, they walked past a set of bathrooms. T'Rida gave Anne the keys to the truck and told her he'd catch up to her. He had to take a piss almost every fifteen minutes or so. T'Rida walked into one of the stalls and locked the latch. He pulled out a plastic bag, his pipe stem and a lighter. His hands were shaking in anticipation of taking a hit. He placed a nice size rock on the tip of his pipe and licked his dry lips.

Just knowing that he was about to tighten himself up, he farted loud and long. It was an involuntary muscle spasm that crackheads did when they knew, they were about to get high. He took a full pull leaned back against the stall and closed his eyes. Just before he passed out he exhaled. His body screamed, *'Fuck yeah'* in extreme pleasure. Wasting no time, he took another hit. This time he exited the stall and began washing his hands before he let the smoke out. After wiping the sweat off his forehead he left the bathroom and headed outside to his truck. His heart was racing a thousand miles an hour as he neared his truck.

"Look, mothafucka now I done tried to be polite with yo' stupid ass and tell you I'm not interested! Don't make me have to act a fool, because you don't know how to accept no!" He heard Anne's voice before he got to the truck.

A Yukon Denali was parked next to his H2, so he couldn't see who she was talking to. Still, he pulled his thumpa off his hip.

"Bitch, what the fuck you mean act a fool! Bitch, I'll knock yo' fucking head off!"

GORILLAZ IN THE BAY

T'Rida instantly started laughing louder than a mothafucka! The baldheaded buff nigga spun around hella fast.

"Nigga, you find something funny wit' yo' bitch ass?"

"Actually, my nigga, I really do. It's too bad your ass will neva know what it was, though." T'Rida let the nigga know as he raised his hand and sent two slugs into the niggaz head.

At such a close-range blood and brain matter sprayed both the H2 and Anne's face. It was actually a miracle that one of the bullets stayed lodged in his dome and the other ricocheted off his front skull and curved as it exited the back-right side of his head. If it were not for that mere chance of luck, it would've no doubt exited the buff niggaz head and entered Anne's. Instead, it knocked out the driver's side window of the Yuko.

T'Rida walked casually over to the driver's side of the H2 and hopped in just like nothing happened. As he was backing out of his parking spot, he put the big truck in park and hopped out. Just as casual as before, he walked in front of the H2 and crossed over to a car parked a space down and calmly raised his hand.

Boca! Boca! Boca! Boca!

He sent four back to back shots into the head of a white woman who was kneeled down trying to hide between two parked cars.

"No witnesses, no evidence," He spoke to no one in particular then walked back to his truck and drove off.

He drove to a gas station and drove through the car wash. Anne grabbed one of his spare face towels off the back seat and went into the bathroom to wash the blood off her face. When she came out of the bathroom he was parked and waiting for her. When she climbed into the truck the smell let her know that he'd been smoking. Even though he tried to cover the smell with air freshener, she could still make out the sweet, acrid smell of melted crack rock. Instead of saying anything, she simply pulled her blood ruined shirt over her head, put one of the new shirts he bought her on and sat back.

"No Nigga that disrespects anybody in this family will ever get a chance to think about his actions. Dead that shit right then and there!" His tone let her know that it wasn't a topic for discussion.

It was a directive to which she simply replied, "No problem."

It had been a couple of days since he made it home, so he dropped Anne off at her place in Oakland and told her he'd pick her up in the morning on his way back down the freeway. Then he made his way home to Monique and the kids. When he walked into the house Na'Shay rushed into his arms, causing him to drop some of the things he was carrying.

"Daddy! Daddy! Mommy, Daddy's home," She screamed as her tiny arms tried to wrap around both of his legs.

"Hey Princess, gimme some sugar," he told her forgetting the bags and dropping them onto the floor as he bent down to pick up his baby girl! Na'Shay squealed with excitement as he tossed her into the air. "Who's daddy's favorite lil' Princess?" He called out as he tossed her high above his head.

"Meeee!" She screamed, between laughing.

After a few more times tossing her in the air, he placed Shay Shay down. "Come on baby and see what Daddy got for you." T'Rida turned and set the code for the alarm system before picking up the money bags and making his way into the living room with Shay right by his side matching him stride for stride.

"Moe, babe, why wasn't the alarm set when I walked into the house?" T'Rida questioned as he sat on the long butter-soft leather couch.

Nashay immediately jumped up into his lap.

"I missed you too, damn! I saw you pull into the driveway from the camera monitor and I disabled the alarm for you, Tommy."

"Baby, you know I've missed you. I just gotta make sure you ain't slipping on your security," he told her.

"Now Princess look, you know, you're my favorite lady, but you have to share half of these bags with your momma so she doesn't be jealous."

"Daddy, mommy not gonna get jealous," Shay Shay told him giggling.

"Just share with her anyway, Baby. Do it for, Daddy, okay?"

"Okay, Daddy."

T'Rida stood up from the sofa and walked over to Monique with six of the bags in one of his hands. He bent over and gave her and his son who was laying in her lap a kiss. Then he went and jumped in the shower to wash the streets off him. The water not only cleaned him off, but the steamy hot water also sobered him the rest of the way. When he walked back into the living room, Moe was watching the news. Breaking news was across the bottom of the screen, a report of a double homicide at the Great Mall in Milpitas just hours ago.

"Baby, don't that look like your truck?" Moe asked him as an image of him driving out of the parking lot was being played.

"You ain't neva lied, baby. That looks just like my shit. Good thing I've been out in the Valley with you and the kids all day," He told her making sure his alibi was intact.

T'Rida sat next to the love of his life and scooped up his son from her lap, paying close attention to the news. The angle of the video neva showed his license plate and there were no eyewitnesses. So, as the screen flashed to the police, they were asking anyone who may have witnessed the murders or had any information on the truck in the video to call a one-eight-hundred number.

T'Rida asked, "How's Momma doing?"

"Oh, momma's good, she asked about you today when I talked to her on the phone."

"We gonna have to go see my momma. What about taking the kids down to see her and your sister one of these weekends?"

"Daddy, you know I'd love that! And momma would love it, too."

"You know your momma don't like me. She blames me for all yo' negativity. Not knowing you the one that turned me out." He chuckled knowing he was lying his ass off.

Monique got up and walked into the kitchen. She grabbed him a beer and handed it to him before she headed back to the kitchen to make him something to eat. Titas lay sleeping soundly on his lap while Shay Shay was in her own little world playing with the new computer toy he brought her. T'Rida loved both of his children. Even though, Shay Shay wasn't his biological daughter he'd been there from day one and couldn't nobody tell him that she wasn't his.

He sat and reminisced on all the shit he and Moe had gone through and dealt with over the years. Hell, he remembered having her in the kitchen when they were younger, and he taught her how to cook. They met when they were eleven, growing up and learning together. Both had hurt the other over the years, but the love only grew as they got older. He thought about that night so many years ago when he moved to Fremont from East Palo Alto. He had a newspaper job and as he was walking down the street, he saw the most beautiful girl he'd ever seen walking toward him with a little girl holding her hand.

Lil Tommy couldn't believe something so beautiful could walk the earth. Even at age eleven he had seen and done a lot of shit being from E.P.A., so macking a cutie was nothing to him. But, as she was just a couple feet away from him he froze up. He couldn't believe he froze like a little lame boy, but her beauty had him stunned.

He thought, *'How in the hell did she have curves like that? She couldn't have been much older than him.'* Before he realized it, she had passed him by and was down the street. Tommy was kicking himself in the ass for blowing his chance when suddenly—

"Hey, Boy! Hey, Boy!" It was the little girl that was just walking by with the cutie.

"What's up, Shorty, you alright?" Tommy asked her alarmed that she'd be running back to him.

He looked up wondering what happened to ole girl. Maybe she needed his help. At age eleven Tommy was already a little protector and was more than with the shit!

"My Tee-Tee—my Tee-Tee wanna talk to you," She said while trying to catch her breath.

Thanks to little Ashley from that night on everything else was on wrap.

"What's her name?" Monique brought him back from memory lane as she stood in front of him, with a plate of fried chicken, macaroni & cheese and broccoli in her hand. "The only time you get that silly look on your face is when you thinking about some chick. So, what's her name?"

"Lil' Ashley," He responded as he told her about his little trip down memory lane.

It brought a smile to her face as well. They'd had some good times. It would have been more times like that if it wasn't for all the time T'Rida had served. Monique put his plate down on the coffee table along with another beer and grabbed Titas off his lap and carried him off to bed.

"Come on, Shay Shay."

"Okay, Mommy!" Nashay quickly put things away and gave her daddy a kiss. "Good night, daddy, I love you," She told him, then ran down the hall behind her mother.

T'Rida loved his family. He couldn't see living life no other way than with them. Monique and the kids was why he hit them streets. Although she neva brought it up, Monique knew he fucked other women. But, she long knew that T'Rida loved her. She rationed a man was gonna be a man. As long as she alone had his heart, she could put up with him sharing his phys-ical. As long as no bitch ever disrespect her or her family! Lonely and no problem playing trophy wife, but she would for-ever be Deep East Oakland. T'Rida knew that better than any-body.

Before T'Rida took one bite of his food, he picked up his cell phone and punched in some numbers.

"Yeah, what's up, Blood?" The voice on the other line an-swered.

"What's up, Brah? Check me out, I'ma need to stop by the coffee shop in the morning. This cup of coffee that's too hot. It's liable to burn a niggaz taste buds and shit," T'Rida explained to Gunz he was going to need a new ride because the H2 was on fire.

"Say no more. I saw steam rising from the cup myself. You know we go when the rooster crow," Gunz responded letting his little brother know he'd caught the news already.

"A'ight then I'ma make sure I beat traffic."

"Bet that then."

"Bet." T'Rida hung up just as Monique was walking in the room.

"Damn. You know I loved that truck," She told him as she sat down next to him on the sofa.

"You want me to get another one?" He asked as he chewed on a humongous mouth full of chicken.

"Nah, Daddy, you know the rules, don't change coats change the entire outfit," She told him as she stole a fork full of macaroni.

It was cooked just the way he'd taught her, with extra cream and cheese. After adding the macaroni, it went into a Pyrex dish with a layer of shredded cheese and crumbled Ritz Crackers. Then into the oven for a couple of minutes.

After she fed him a mouthful of the creamy macaroni, she told him, "Anyways that new Cadillac EXT is out of this world."

T'Rida told her, "You'll have one tomorrow then." Then he asked her, "What color you want?"

To which she replied, "You already know."

When it came to vehicles, Monique only loved two things; Old Schools, which was her first love and Big Trucks, her second love.

They both sang in unison, "Black and Yellow! Black and Yellow!"

They sat and talked while he ate his meal. Later, they made love and laid in the bed talking until they fell asleep. He may have fucked other bitches when the need to nut got the best of him, but hands down, nobody came close to Moe in the bedroom! They talked about their future and how she wanted to open a small investment company when the kids got a little older.

T'Rida's birthday was coming up so they discussed that. It was marked to be one of the biggest events in the Bay Area. At first, T'Rida didn't want to come because most times people's behavior was unpredictable and that's what caused shit to pop off. But, Moe wasn't tryna hear none of that dumb shit. There was no way she would not be at her Baby's birthday bash! She made sure that shit was clear before she dozed off.

T'Rida was glad he was getting rid of the big truck. On mornings like today, driving from the Valley into the Bay was a real bitch! The traffic was like none other on Interstate 580 and you couldn't maneuver the truck in traffic like you could everything else. At one point, T'Rida was so pissed off at cars cutting in front of him, that when an Uncle Tom looking nigga tried to cut him off, T'Rida held his hand down on the truck's horn to get the driver's attention.

When the bootlicking mothafucka looked over, he instantly hit the brakes and forgot all about trying to cut the big truck off. Staring down the barrel of a Big Ass Gun tended to have that effect on people. As the truck made it up the block, the whistles sounded. The *'Koffee Shop'* was Gunz main headquarters for his operation. It was an auto body, custom shop and a used car lot all in one. It was the closest thing to a legal chop shop you could find.

No matter what your flavor, you neva drove off with what you drove up in. As T'Rida was pulling up to the massive iron gates, they opened without hesitation. He pulled into the massive parking lot that set to the side of the building. Driving all the way to the back of the parking lot that wrapped around the building, T'Rida saw Gunz standing with eight guys all wearing mechanic suits and various mechanic gear.

Gunz started giving his orders before T'Rida climbed out of the truck. "Y'all already know the business. I want it cleaned, stripped, broke-down, re-rocked and rebuilt before lunch! This mothafucka gotta take the truck to Texas today. No exceptions!"

Gunz stopped talking, then turned to embrace T'Rida. "What's up, Blood?" After the brotherly embrace, Gunz asked T'Rida. "Damn nigga, why you sweating early in the morning and shit? Don't tell me yo' ass got it poppin' dis early in da morning?"

"Naw, brah, that traffic gotta nigga on fire, though."

"I don't know why you moved all the fuck da way down to the Valley. Ain't no way in hell I could sit through all that traffic. Nigga you hit traffic coming and going! Fuck that!" He shook his head in astonishment and said, "Come on let's get da Boss in something right."

The Koffee Shop was once an actual car lot with its main building and offices sitting directly in the middle. There was a parking lot full of cars in front of the main building that stretched all the way around the right side of the building. Three other buildings sat to the back of the complex. One building was an auto mechanic shop. The other building was used to do all custom body repairs and alterations. The last and final building was all custom sounds. When it came to your vehicle, the Koffee Shop was indeed a one stop shop!

"I just got two trailers in last night with some nice shit on it, big brah," Gunz was telling him as they made their way from the back of the main building, across the showroom floor. "I ain't gon' even lie to you, big brah, I'll neva deny you shit and you know dat. But, it's one thing on one of the trailers I was planning on showcasing at yo' party—"

T'Rida cut him off right there. "Then showcase that shit. Hell, it ain't even no need for us to go see them trailers. This him right there, brah-brah." T'Rida had stopped walking and was staring at a beauty right in the middle of the showroom floor. "I need dis lil' bitch, right here, brah."

He was looking at the new Infiniti M-45 big body sedan. It was forest green sitting on 22-inch custom forest green Forgiato Estremos. It also had a custom chrome kit with window tints. As it sat there on the floor with its doors open, the inside was killing the game with Olive green interior mixed with Mahogany wood grain. The Butter-Soft leather seats were glistening. The moonroof even had an olive green tractable mesh sun shade. Knowing Gunz, T'Rida knew it was already equipped with custom sounds.

"She all you, big brah. Let me get the windows open and have it pulled out for you." Gunz was just happy T'Rida hadn't seen what he had sitting in the trailer.

While the Infiniti was pulled out they walked to Gunz' office and had a drink. Gunz wasn't tryna accept no money for the whip, but T'Rida wasn't hearing that shit. Especially, when he placed his next order. Now it was a few things Gunz knew well, one was the streets. He was well trained and seasoned. He knew guns, from the smallest Dillinger up to your full assault rifles. You could say he also had a degree in cars. So, after hearing exactly what T'Rida wanted him to track down, Gunz for the first time in a long time was impressed.

"Oh, okay, okay. I see we 'bout to bring Rida-Da-Kid out, huh?" He excitedly asked his big brah.

"It's time to let mothafuckaz know we here," T'Rida said in a voice full of sincerity. "In fact, check this out. This what the fuck, I want you to do." By the time he finished breaking down

GORILLAZ IN THE BAY

everything, he wanted done, Leonard 'Two Gunz' Johnson was beyond impressed and speechless. T'Rida laughed so loud at the look on Gunz' face that he startled a receptionist as she walked by the door. "I'll make sure Cantalope sees to it, that the bread for everything is taken care of and in your office by lunch," T'Rida told Gunz just before downing his shot of Don Julio and heading out the door. As he drove off, he thought to himself, that his birthday would indeed be a day that would go down in history!

It wasn't even eight-o'clock in the morning by the time Rida pulled in front of Anne's house, but the yard was filled with about eight or nine hard-looking little mothafuckaz. Not only was the Infiniti a car they didn't know, but the money they could get for it was something cool. The tinted windows on the car made one of the youngstas uneasy. As he watched the car it was clear that the driver wasn't going to get out. The youngsta rose off the porch and as he began to approach the car his hand was going to his waistline.

"Don't even think about it. Sutton, boy, you better sit yo' young ass right back down on that porch," Anne told her little brother as she came walking out of the house.

"Got you a new boyfriend, huh?" Sutton questioned without taking his hungry eyes off the car.

"Not that I need to start reporting or checking in with you, but that's my Boss, now boy move," She told him, already getting irritated by his antics so early in the morning. "And I don't want you lil' hoodlums tearing up the house while I'm gone."

After learning that the great T'Rida was actually the person driving the car. He didn't hear anything else his sister said. All Sutton could think about was money and the nigga behind the wheel represented just that. The rest of his young team all had similar thoughts. They all needed to achieve that same goal, everybody else in the hood wanted!

"See that right there? That's the type of hype I'm talking 'bout taking us to. We gon' be on some next level-shit!" Young Sutton yelled out to his team as his sister and the head of the most powerful organization in the Bay Area drove off.

As a reply, they all yelled in unison, "Young Nigga Mafia!"

She wasn't questioning his directive, Anne just wanted to make sure she heard him correctly. "You want me to tell her that?"

"Yeah! And tell her I said to have it there before twelve-o'clock," T'Rida instructed Anne as he merged on to 880 South, loving the way the luxury car handled.

"A'ight, Boss, I'm on it," she replied.

Next Anne scrolled through her contacts, found the right one and sent the chirp. Thirty seconds later, her phone rang, Anne was nervous about the directive that T'Rida had given her, but she kept herself calm so the nervousness didn't portray her fears as she repeated her orders. She could tell the person on the other end of the phone felt just as uncomfortable as she did. However, both women conducted themselves professionally.

After the call ended, Anne sat in the passenger seat playing out scenarios in her mind. Could that have been a test to see if she could give orders without wavering, regardless of what the orders were or who they were given to? Was some type of play going down? All types of questions were going on in her mind. The ringing of T'Rida's phone took her attention away from the analysis she was weighing out.

"Where dey do that at?" Cantalope didn't even wait for T'Rida to greet her when he picked up the phone.

"What's good, lil' sis?" T'Rida spoke casually not picking up on her mood.

"What's good is you running that play down to me."

"Whatcha mean? Since when we start questioning shit?" He was beginning to get upset.

Cantalope had neva questioned anything he told her to do. He knew the amount was a lot, but that didn't give her the excuse to question his call.

"Questioning shit?" Cantalope was furious. "My nigga, I just got off da phone from receiving an order from one of my soldias! One of mine!" She yelled into the phone! "Fuck a chain of command. Nigga to me it's like you questioning my authority or my loyalty! So, once again I'ma ask you, brah. Where dey do that at?" Cantalope didn't care that she was yelling at the head of the Family.

GORILLAZ IN THE BAY

She was loyal, but she was neva gonna be nobody's sucka ass bitch! She'd been there from the jump playing her position with no larceny or disloyalty! If T'Rida was playing her pussy ova some side pussy nigga, then she was really gonna show her Gangsta!

Realizing his error, T'Rida softened his tone. "Sis, my bad, blood! It ain't nuttin' like that! That's on the Family lil' sis! A nigga just in a good as mood about what I got in mind and a nigga allowed excitement to override and cloud his judgment."

She heard the sincerity in his voice and the genuineness of his words. Cantalope calmed down and instantly pulled off the gas pedal.

"Brah, you had a girl ova here seeing red and shit. I don't know what got you all excited, that you of all people would break protocol. But, brah, you gotta be easy. That shit wasn't cool, brah, for real." Even though she was calm, she still had to let him know, that shit was real straight up! She wouldn't be herself if she didn't. "Real women did real shit and real niggaz respected it."

"My bad lil' sis. Speak no more, I got you."

"A'ight bet. And about that, consider it done Family." She hung up before even hearing a response.

He didn't take offense because he knew that's how Cantalope was. Give her an order and she was on it right then and there.

After hanging up with Cantalope he told Anne, "My bad, about that lil' momma. A nigga didn't think 'bout the situation I was putting you in when I told you to make that call. But, you handled that shit right by not questioning a command, not to mention, you showed no sign of fear or hesitation giving an order to someone of more power. That's that Gangsta shit a nigga talking 'bout!"

Anne couldn't pat herself on the back. Shit, she only did what she was supposed to do, follow orders. What she was wondering, though, was what T'Rida was about to do or have done with three-point-five million dollars.

DE'KARI

Chapter XVII
NIGGA WE NEVA DIE

Stone Cold sat in the chair with a bottle of Remy Martin in one hand and his Desert Eagle in the other hand, gently resting on his lap. As he took a swig from the bottle, he wished it was still chilled. The cool liquid would've done wonders to his sweat-drenched, overheated body. Looking at the bitch nigga a few feet in front of him sniveling and whimpering, Stones anger was quickly aroused again. It was this pussy ass niggaz fault, his drink had grown hot. It had sat on the cheap coffee table for the last hour in the hot and humid house, while Stone was beating the shit out of him.

As his anger peaked, Stone jumped up and broke the bottle across the niggaz head, causing him to cry out behind the duct tape covering his mouth. Realizing he'd wasted the alcohol on this pussy, Stone then slapped him hard across his face, before plopping down hard in the chair. Stone hated a bitch nigga down to the core of him. The nigga in the chair was entrusted with a position of love and trust. In the ultimate sign of disrespect, he'd bit the hand that fed him when he stole from the Family. He was an ungrateful ass nigga.

Stone hawked up a lugi and spit a fat, slimy slug into his face. He wished he could kill the pussy ass nigga, but he was ordered to keep him alive. Which meant under no circumstance could death befall him. Being first lieutenant of the Wolf Pack, Stone was used to giving orders. But, he was a loyal and dedicated soldier first and foremost, so he knew how to follow an order.

"They just pulled up," One of his young Wolves came into the house and told him before resuming his post on the front porch.

Anne made sure she was cocked and locked before she opened the car door to get out. The four niggaz that were standing guard outside the house didn't even draw her attention. Even if they weren't on her team, it would not have mattered. She sized their viciousness up in five seconds as they were pulling up. None of them were a threat! She followed behind T'Rida as he made his way to the front door and inside. Before she crossed the threshold of the house, she paused and looked at the young Wolf.

"If it moves wrong, lay it down!"

He gave her a head nod of understanding and she kept it moving. In the house, T'Rida wiped sweat off his face and got straight to the point.

"Ain't nothing you can do to save yo' life, so we ain't gonna pretend like shit is good. How you die and how much pain you feel is completely up to you." He peeled the duct tape off Twin's mouth and continued.

"Tell me where your brother is and your death will be quick and painless. Fuck with me and for the remainder of your pathetic, short life, you will wish you were dead already!"

In response, Twin hawked up a nice, fat bloody slimy lugi. Before he could spit in T'Rida's face a lightning, hot pain shot through his head, as he was violently knocked to the side. She moved with such speed no one saw Anne as she pivoted around T'Rida and did a spinning back kick that resounded loudly when her heel made contact with his jaw. Shattering the bone in three places.

"Make it painful," was all T'Rida told Anne.

She placed the small black case she was carrying on the coffee table, unzipped it and spread it open. Stone Cold stared along with the rest of the killas in the room in anticipation. This would be the first time anyone other than the She-Wolves themselves would see one of them in action. Even though she was the newest among the assassins, word was already spreading throughout the family that she was rumored to be the worst of them all.

Anne leaned forward and placed two fresh strips of duct tape over Twin's mouth. The added layer would be needed to mask the sounds that were about to emit from his mouth. Next, she pulled on a pair of black latex gloves and smiled seductively at her victim. The poor fool. In her hand magically appeared a small straight razor, and no one knew where it came from. Using speed and precision, she began smacking the razor in such a way that just the short tip sank into his skin. Each cut was barely a centimeter in length, but its depth was enough to cause droplets of blood to appear. After five minutes of this, there were thousands of droplets all over his body.

Anne pulled a small hairspray bottle full of the solution of water, vinegar, and bleach out of the case. She began spraying the cuts. The sound that erupted from Twin's body was so deafening it came through the duct tape. His body rocked so violently he resembled an old convict in the electric chair. When the violent shakes subsided, Anne sprayed a fresh coat over the wounds. This time the pain was so intense Twin passed out.

An hour later, Anne and T'Rida were exiting the house. To his credit Twin had held out longer than the men watching him thought he could ever have. Once he gave them his brothers hideaway address Anne figured she would make him feel one last pain for making her waste her time. They laid Twin's body on the floor with his hands bound behind him and his legs spread wide open. Anne asked Stone to retrieve the canvas sack out of the trunk.

While he did that she slathered a healthy layer of peanut butter all over his dick and balls. Stone came in with the canvas sack just as she finished. She laid the canvas sack so that the top of it laid only inches from his testicles. When she untied the sack three malnourished looking rats raced out of it. The rats hadn't eaten in weeks and the smell of peanut butter sent them in a frenzy. They attacked the peanut butter with determination and once they were getting accustomed to eating they continued with his balls, then his dick.

The pain was so fierce it gave twenty-six-year Twin a heart attack. The scene was so gruesome the other killers turned their heads not wanting to give up their lunches. Before leaving T'Rida gave Stone his orders. He wanted the other Judas found and an example made before the sun rose. The next day began with the gruesome story on every news channel statewide. The body of a twenty-six-year-old African American was discovered in the early morning work hours mutilated and hanging from a traffic light. No witnesses were found, and everybody wanted to know how you hang a body with no arms or legs from a traffic light in the middle of the busy four-way intersection.

To make matters even worse the arms and legs were laid, each limb at the beginning of each street in all four directions. Once the body was later identified as the body of La'Shawn Williams whose twin brother Marshawn was found mutilated and murdered in the living room of his house in Redwood City. It was clear to the Underworld that Johnny Spitz and Stone Cold were signifying the New Leadership of the Wolf Pack, as well as setting the tone to a *Zero Tolerance* for any Bullshit!

***

The only exceptions to the chain of command Voorheeze implemented that night in Milpitas was regarding the Wolf Pack and the She-Wolves. Since they were both security and enforcement, the entire organization from block lieutenants and up, needed to know who they were. That way, if they were called to aide one of the teams in trouble, there would be no friendly fire killings. Since war and destruction was their specialty if it was a matter of safety and security, their command superseded any rank or position among the organization. It was with this authority that Anne picked up her cell phone.

"We need to talk," She spoke with conviction into the phone.

"I'm in my area," was the response.

"I'll be there in an hour," She informed her caller, disconnecting the line.

Next, she called Chocolate and gave her the address where she was. She instructed her to get to her now! For weeks she struggled with the heavy burden on her shoulders. Loyalty fought a battle in her mind with duty. She lost countless nights of sleep trying to figure out what was the best decision for her. To say, she was torn would be an understatement! Finally, duty won the fight. She realized in fulfilling her duties she was still being loyal. In fact, it was the greatest act of loyalty she could give under the circumstances. That was being loyal to the dream. Chocolate arrived in fifteen minutes and Anne jumped on highway 237 headed toward 101 north and on to E.P.A.

Clarkola had a spot at the back of Cypress Street in the Gardens. Whenever Voorheeze was '*in his area*' he was at his brothas spot. When Anne pulled up to the house, Clarkola and a few of his team was in front of the house discussing some things. When Anne climbed out of the car, he told her that Voorheeze was in the house waiting on her, then he turned back to his conversation. Anne walked into the house and immediately saw Voorheeze sitting at a dining room table with his cell phone to his ear. He gestured for her to have a seat. She sat down on the leather sofa in the front room, giving him his privacy and patiently waited for him to end his phone call.

When his call ended, Voorheeze stated, "From the conviction in your voice and the fact, that you've neva used this number before, I already know we got a problem. Just tell me how severe it is."

Anne stood up from the sofa, walked over to the table, sat down and began. "Brah, I can't sugar coat it, even though, I want to. I gotta give it to you raw so it's like this—" For the next thirty minutes Anne filled Voorheeze in on everything that had been going on, while she was running security on T'Rida.

The news she was feeding him nearly brought Voorheeze to tears. He hadn't even known! He couldn't even begin to imagine his homeboy smoking Coke. From what Anne was telling him, T'Rida was not only smoking Coke, but he was actually a full-blown crack head. She told him initially, she didn't want to betray her loyalty to T'Rida by putting his business out there. Plus, Cantelope had issued her new orders two months ago.

It seemed a small situation was potentially becoming a huge problem. So, Anne's orders were to become T'Rida's full-time eyes and ears. Since she had him, she silently prayed he was just in a phase and would bring himself out of it. But that didn't happen. He lost weight rapidly, became paranoid and was constantly slipping.

Last week Anne heard T'Rida and Voorheeze discussing a new connect that T'Rida was scheduled to meet in a few hours. Their original connect J. Blaze had been struggling to keep up with their weekly order of product. They were vastly gaining new territory and were looking to double their product not to mention begin expanding into new areas.

Anne knew the importance of the meeting and what it meant to the organization. More importantly, she knew that T'Rida was in no way capable of meeting anyone on a major business level in the condition he was in. Voorheeze chocked back the tears. Although the information she'd just dropped on him was a major blow, he had to analyze the body of facts and boss up. Taking a few deep breaths, he cut her off as Clarkola entered the house with a couple of goons.

It was one thing having to hear the news himself, but Voorheeze wasn't going to allow his brothas business to spill out into the streets. The Family would lose respect for their General in a heartbeat. He gave Clark a few orders and let him know he would meet up with him in a day or so. Then, he and Anne walked out of the house and jumped into their cars headed to T'Rida's fuck spot. Chocolate was still sitting in her truck when she saw Anne's Camaro turn the corner and come up the block.

When she saw Voorheeze's Denali bend the block after Chocolate's phone chirped twice. It was Anne letting her know that she was approaching. She chirped back once letting her know she'd seen her. When her response was not followed by another chirp, Chocolate rested her thumpa on her lap, but stayed on point. Had Anne needed her, she would've followed Chocolate's chirp with one more of her own.

The smell that assaulted Voorheeze's nostrils was unbelievable. Not wanting to further embarrass T'Rida, Anne chose to post up outside on the porch. Voorheeze couldn't comprehend what the fuck he was seeing. The inside of the house was a fucking mess. It looked like it hadn't been clean for days. Spoiled food, half-eaten boxes of old pizza lay everywhere. But the sight of his big brotha left him speechless.

T'Rida looked like he hadn't slept in days. His signature, oily, razor-sharp waves were unmaintained and in dire need of a haircut. A once well-trimmed beard was now wild and out of control. Gone was the once manicured, precision cut, G.Q. looking T'Rida. What stood before him was some shit he couldn't quite understand. His heart swelled with emotions. Staring at T'Rida, Voorheeze let his eyes drop and instantly all sadness evaporated.

In T'Ridas right hand was a burnt glass rose stem that crackheads used for a pipe the sight enraged. Voorheeze! "Nigga, what the fuck is yo problem? What the fuck is going on in this bitch?" Voorheeze spewed forth the question still hoping his eyes were fooling him. Praying there was some type of explanation for the bullshit that he saw.

"V, it ain't even all like you thinking, brah."

"Fuck you mean, it ain't like I'm thinking, nigga! You, up in dis bitch all smoked out!"

"Naw, naw, brah. I'm just relieving a little stress that's all." T'Rida stumbled to get the words out of his mouth. "I'm just doing me, blood! That's all, brah, ain't nobody smoked out."

"Doing you?" Voorheeze couldn't believe his fucking ears. "Nigga you in here living like a fucking Vagabond! Talking to me wit' a fuckin' crack-pipe in yo' hand." As the words left Voorheeze mouth T'Rida looked down at the pipe in his hands like it was a snake. Quickly he shoved his hands into his dingy pockets.

Voorheeze just shook his head. He was beyond a loss for words. "Rogue, look, you ain't in any condition to meet this new connect.".

T'Rida had forgotten all about his meeting with Samori. "Was today really the day of the meeting already? V, I'm on it, brah. I just gotta—"

Voorheeze cut him off, not even tryna hear whatever the fuck he was about to say. "Naw, brah, you ain't on shit!"

"Nigga, this is exactly what we've been waiting on. This is the majors, big brah. Now I know you ain't intentionally tryna fuck up what we built. But rather it's intentional or inadvertently, my job is to make sure it doesn't happen."

Voorheeze took a deep breath, so he could get the rest of his emotions in check. "I'ma go meet this cat, get everything right and secure our future. This is still your shit, I ain't neva gonna try to play you to the left. But, Rogue, get yo' shit together. Cause this ain't you."

T'Rida tried, but he couldn't get through the cloud of confusion and drugs that involved his mind. Voorheeze's words were landing on deaf ears. Not because T'Rida didn't care about what his brotha was sharing with him, but because he was way too high to understand. He couldn't remember how many days he'd been up. The only thing he could think about was taking another hit.

DE'KARI

He silently wished Voorheeze would just shut the fuck up and leave! Even though he smelled like shit, Voorheeze embraced his brotha then left the house to prepare to meet the connect. As he left, he told himself, *'he would have to keep an eye on his brotha*. He couldn't afford to let T'Rida succumb to the Demon that claimed so many in the streets.

Chapter XVIII

As they entered the dimly lit restaurant, the exotic smells that engulfed his nose was both exciting and alluring to Voorheeze. The smells were Foreign, yet, pleasant to his nose. As his eyes adjusted to the darkness, he was surprised that the only security he noticed was the one man who now escorted him and Anne to the table where a lone man awaited them.

Voorheeze wondered how someone so important could be so derelict about his security. Even more surprising was the youthfulness of the man who sat patiently awaiting them to make it to the table with a gentle smile on his face. His dark skin and strong features betrayed his African descent. Yet, it was his strong accent that conveyed his Mandingo heritage.

"Brother Jason Voorheeze," Samori Toure spoke as he stood and extended his hand in greeting.

"Mr. Toure—" Voorheeze began, but Samori cut him off.

"I insist, call me Samori! For we two are brothers, are we not?" His English was surprisingly clear with such a strong accent.

Voorheeze gestured toward Anne and was once again taken back when Samori spoke.

"Aaah the beautiful, Annabelle La'Trisha Combs!" When Anne smiled with a puzzling look on her face, he spoke again. "My sister both beauty and your fast-growing reputation proceed you. Please have a seat."

As they took their seats a sense of uneasiness came over Voorheeze. He naturally expected the new connect to be enraged at his presence at the meeting instead of T'Rida. In fact, he half didn't expect the meeting to take place. Just when he was getting ready to address the issue, Samori spoke up as if he was reading his mind.

"I see our friend, Mr. Smith decided it would be best if you took this meet instead."

"My brotha's uh—he ain't quite physically able to attend such an important affair.

DE'KARI

"Interesting choice of words, not physically in a position to attend such an important meeting."

Voorheeze could sense there was more to the words the man sitting across from him spoke. Instead of jumping he sat and listened intently!

"The fact that you were not searched or that you see no bodyguards or security, may give the illusion that I am very relaxed or perhaps I have no sense of security." As tempting as it was to respond, Voorheeze held his tongue and his patience. He knew whatever the catch was, sooner or later the African would get to it.

"However, I assure you, the truth is much more to the contrary. You see Mr. Simpson, or should I say, Mr. LaMont Simpson. I take my security as serious as humanly possible, without losing my mind. I do my—how do you say, homework, on any and everyone. I do business with or may potentially begin doing business with. Had Mr. Smith showed to this meeting himself, I would've taken it as a sign of utmost disrespect and he would not have walked back out these doors."

Voorheeze leaned forward placing his forearms on the wooden table and looked Samori Toure directly in his eyes before asking him. "You wanna run that by me again, brah?"

"My brotha, I assure you, I mean you no disrespect. I am however not a man to dance around things. I've been aware of Mr. Smith's drug problem since our mutual acquaintance first spoke of your family. Normally, I would have left the request drifting in the breeze, once I learned of the problem. But, I must say two things gave me a reason to look further. The first was the level of sophistication your family achieved and operates on and considering the speed in which you've put everything together. Which speaks of a unique and advanced analytical mind. Your mind!"

There it was, Samori wasn't in the dark after all. In fact, it would seem, he was more informed than Voorheeze was. Voorheeze stole a quick glance with his eyes at Anne. He wondered just how long had she fought with the idea of coming to him.

"As me and some of my closest associates watched and studied your Neva Die Family. Not only were we intrigued by you, but it became obviously clear from the beginning that it was you and your security around your family that is responsible for such discipline organizational skills."

Voorheeze glanced around the restaurant mapping out exit routes hoping Anne who sat quietly listening, was doing the same thing.

"As for security or the lack thereof, it became clear not too long ago that indeed, it would be you to take this meeting." Samori smiled at the confirmation of his little prediction. "It was also clear to me, that you would in no way disrespect me or your family's future by bringing a weapon into my establishment! I'm sure Miss Combs has her weapons on her, though. She will find no need for them here. And even if I misjudged my assessment, believe me when I tell you more than one pair of eyes are trained on this table as we speak. One could never be too careful in this world we live in."

"You said a lot, brah. Now, I mean this with all due respect, when I ask you this. Yet, I gotta ask all the same! What you saying, though? I mean clearly, the ball is in your court, so what's your move?" Voorheeze clearly hadn't thought when he walked through the doors of the restaurant that he was walking into his death. But if that's what it was, he was ready to embrace it. What he wasn't gonna do was run like no little bitch or beg and plead.

Anne adjusted her weight in the chair. Although, this fine ass African nigga impressed her with all that he revealed, showing her he was game tight. He had the game seriously fucked up if he thought he'd walk away from this table if shit jumped off. Apparently, he ain't did all his research on her!

Samori let out a small chuckle, "If business was not on my mind, surely you would have never been seated! My friend, let us eat so that pleasantness may replace the tension in the room. Afterward, we can discuss our business arrangements and the future of our dealings. I will however, impose on you if we decide to go further, the responsibility rests on your shoulders."

Samori picked up a fork and gently struck the crystal wine glass in front of him. Immediately, people surfaced out of thin air and rushed about placing a meal in front of them that was fit for a King! They dined on some of the best food, Anne and Voorheeze had ever tasted. The conversation was casually pleasant and all through the meal, Samori looked at Anne in a way that made her pussy moist. After a dessert made of Nokia Chocolate, Samori and Voorheeze retired to another section of the restaurant that held a smoke lounge.

There they discussed the terms of their relationship and ironed-out any loose kinks. After the agreement-was made, Neva Die was about to take things to a level that had neva been seen before. Not only could Samori supply them with whatever amount of Coke they needed. But he was also able to hit them with some of the purists China White the Bay Area had seen since the days of the Dust Man.

If shit couldn't get more perfect than that, Samori believed in protecting his investments to the utmost, so he told Voorheeze he'd supply him and the family with all the weapons they'd need free of charge. The first shipment of product would be on consignment. Upon the second delivery, the product would double but the prices would stay the same. So essentially for everything they bought he would front them the exact amount they purchased.

When he and Anne left the restaurant, Voorheeze had a level for his new connect that he'd neva previously had for any connect. Little did he know he'd left one hell of an impression on the twenty-five-year-old drug Lord himself.

***

The biggest trial of the decade was getting ready to commence at the Oakland Superior Court. The front of the courthouse was jam-packed with spectators, police, news crews and even undercover federal agents. Most just wanted to get a glimpse of the notorious Nutt Case Gang. The young brazen guys who'd killed so many police, then took them on that widely watched and talked about high-speed car chase. The feds were hoping to identify more members by watching the people who would attend the trial. There were more photos being taken of today's event than at any award show.

Gunz sat in the last row in the back of the courtroom. Beside him was DeeDee, A.J. and D.J. A courtroom surrounded by police was the last place any of them wanted to be, but if they were nervous you couldn't tell. Gunz scanned the courtroom. He knew the feds were there. He could smell them. The room was full of excited chatter and nervous energy.

"All rise," the Bailiff called out as the judge entered. "The Honorable Judge Brooks presiding."

Everyone stood until the Bailiff gave the okay to sit. Moments later, the side door was opened. The room was completely silent and still waiting for the first glimpse of the youngsters. Dame entered the room first smiling. Big Joe walked in looking like a grizzly bear. Boome followed him and Lil' Twan strolled in after him looking like he wanted to knock down everybody in the room.

The Bailiff made the mistake of putting his hand on the back of Twan's shoulder to help usher him along. Twan instantly stopped. The look he gave the Bailiff would kill death. "If you eva do that again, you'll retire early."

The room erupted! Reporters were shocked, people were whispering and pointing.

Twan wasn't the only one to stop, all three had stopped. Now they continued to their seats.

Gunz was tryna catch one of their attention, but couldn't succeed. He leaned over and whispered something into A.J.'s ear. A.J. smiled, looked around the courtroom and nodded. A.J., in turn, whispered into D.J.'s ear. D.J. just looked at A.J. The judge was saying something about the magnitude of the case and some other shit, D.J. wasn't giving a fuck about.

He reached into his pocket to retrieve his phone. He put it to his ear, then yelled at the top of his voice. "Trick Bitch! What the fuck you mean you gave me Chlamydia? Do I look like I give a fuck 'bout you crying now, hoe?" D.J. was standing up faking like he was on the phone.

"Order! Order! Order in the court, young man?" The judge was banging the shit out of that gavel.

"What the fuck you want?" D.J. was glaring at the judge like a wild animal.

"Young man there are no phones allowed in this courtroom." While the judge was talking the Bailiff started making his way toward D.J.

"And watch your tone when you address this court."

DE'KARI

Since the Bailiff was making his way over there, the judge was feeling a little bit courageous. DeeDee and A.J. quickly bounced up. Gunz slowly came to his feet as well.

"You really don't wanna do that, homeboy," Gunz said calm and collective, but even a dead or deaf mothafucka could've heard that threat.

The entire room was looking at the four black men who clearly didn't give a fuck about respecting the courtroom or its judge. Big Joe and Gunz locked eyes. They stared at each other for a long time.

Then Gunz nodded his head ever so slightly and said, "What's up?" He broke eye contact finally with Big Joe and locked eyes with Dame.

Fear seeped out of everyone's pores as they wondered what it was they were witnessing.

"Blood, whateva y'all need. Get at yo' brotha, it's good," Gunz called out. Dame smiled in recognition.

The four turned and walked out of the courtroom. Mission accomplished!

***

Today was the day everybody who was anybody in Northern California had been waiting on. The long anticipated and much talked about night everybody was eager for. Not only was it T'Rida's birthday bash, but it was also the record release party for Dem Hoodstarz. Their new album, 'Hood Reality' was expected to be a banger! The jump-off spot was the hottest new club in Northern California, Club Carsjanae (pronounced Cars-ja-nay) was the shit, hands down! One of Voorheeze's homeboys had opened the club just a month ago, and the club had everybody talking.

It was the only two-story full functioning club in California with five dance floors, threefold bars, three DeeJays, and six VIP rooms. Club Carsjanae's had it all! It's owner Linell had a zero tolerance, no-nonsense security team that was ready to pop off. Linell himself stood six feet five and weigh three-hundred and fifty pounds but standing next to his security he looked small.

His security team were all handpicked homeboys of his, mostly ex-convicts, and they often joked calling him Lil' Man

Voorheeze had just got off the phone with Linell, making sure everything was in order for the night. Linell assured him that shit was perfect. Tonight, wasn't just about T'Rida's birthday for the family. Tonight, California would officially be introduced to Neva Die! It was the night that would seal their hold on the Under World! Each of the four Cadres would be represented by their five top links in their Cadre. Also added to that would be their top five soldias. Except the Wolf Pack and the She-Wolves. They were each bringing their top ten.

Neva Die was fa'sho finna show up! If anybody wanted a problem, they no doubt was gon' show out! Fifty killas all under the same Banner was about to be in the building, only a fool would test their hand against that!

T'Rida had told Voorheeze he wanted everybody to meet up at the Koffee Shop two hours before it was time to hit the club. As they all sat inside the main showroom, Voorheeze wondered what was up. Though, he didn't let it show, he was hella nervous. He hadn't seen T'Rida in the last few days since his meeting with Samori and his brotha was in bad shape. He'd intended to drop back in on him, but when that first mega shipment was dropped off, shit had gotten crazy as hell and Voorheeze had been too fucking busy to even think straight.

Even with his brotha going through whatever it was he was going thru. Shit had to keep flowing and somebody had to step up to the plate and navigate the ship.

Voorheeze looked at his watch, T'Rida was twenty minutes late. *'Come on, brah, don't fuck up tonight. Not tonight, while you got us all assembled.'* Voorheeze silently thought just as the tinted glass doors opened.

When Monique stepped through the door, she got everyone's attention with her fire engine red sheer, sequin, Vera Wang dress and matching red six-inch Louis Vuitton red-bottom heels against her deep chocolate skin. Monique was killing shit! She had matching diamond and ruby earrings, necklace, and a ring trio set off her red Mac lipstick. *Beyoncé, Rihanna, Alicia Keys, Gabrielle Union*, shit it don't matter who you thought of,

Monique was fucking them all up! *Kerry Washington* sit down! *Stacey Dash* fall back!

But, it wasn't Monique that silenced the room, when T'Rida crossed the threshold in a blood red silk Armani suit that made his dark chocolate skin a shade darker. His burnt black ostrich skin, red bottom shoes matched the black ostrich belt wrapped around his waist. The black handkerchief with red swirls was the opposite of the red Fedora with black swirls that was on his head. You could tell T'Rida had lost a considerable amount of weight, but Boss is all you saw as you looked at him.

The twin bulges under his suit jacket told you that shit wasn't a game? In case somebody looking at his ten-carat diamond pinky ring or his iced-out Dragon chain that hung twenty-five inches down his chest made a mothafucka have foolish thoughts.

"One Aim! One Struggle! One Goal!" He yelled as he stepped into the middle of the showroom.

In unison, everyone responded, "Neva Die!"

The room erupted in cheers and loud shouts! T'Rida told Voorheeze to make sure everybody dressed like they were going to the Playas Ball. Everyone except the soldias, they were all in hood apparel so mothafuckaz' would know not to get it fucked up! Everyone was fitted in their finest, wearing different forms of G.Q. and Vogue apparel.

"Alright, look, we ain't 'bout to be up in this piece for hella long. I apologize for being late, but my shit wasn't ready." On cue, Monique pulled two small boxes out of her Vera Wang purse and handed it to him. "I got some shit for everybody, then we gon' dip. But right now, I need my two little brothas."

Voorheeze and Gunz walked up to him. He handed both of them a box with the biggest fucking smile either of them had ever seen on his face.

"Rogue, why you giving *us* presents and it's your birthday?" Voorheeze asked.

"It might be my birthday, but it's *our* night! Now nigga, hurry up and open that shit." T'Rida was enjoying himself.

Gunz had his box open first, but Voorheeze wasn't far behind him. Each box revealed matching necklaces. Now all three had matching chains that were invisible set, clear, flawless Diamonds. The Dragon piece was a mixture of whole set, crushed and bezel set. The only difference between the pieces were the eyes. T'Rida's dragon held blood red Ruby eyes, Voorheeze's Dragon had green Emeralds and Gunz Dragon had ocean blue Sapphires.

"The pieces will speak our new and final awakening and that tonight the Mobb Family will no longer be a part of our name. From now on this is *'Neva Die Dragon Gang'*. Let everyone fear the Dragon!"

The room erupted again, it was a wonderful mood. Everyone was feeling good vibes. The soldias were tryna keep looking as hard as possible, but each one was excited as hell on the Low Key. Shit, they were the ones selected to roll with the Bosses. Tonight would elevate their street cred, that much more. T'Rida motioned to Gunz and Gunz walked to his back office. Voorheeze grabbed T'Rida in a tight brotherly hug.

"It's good to see my brotha back," he whispered.

"I ain't neva left, brah, only paused."

Gunz walked in holding a tote bag in his hands. "Check me out, everybody listen up. Everybody in this room has an envelope with their name on it in this bag. When I call you, come grab yo' envelopes. But, I'm only gon' say this shit one time, play with me if you want to. Don't open or fuck wit' yo' envelope. Just grab it and wait." Even though he was smiling like a Cheshire Cat, everyone heard the seriousness in his voice and saw it in his eyes.

Nobody was going to be hardheaded and not listen. One by one, Gunz called names out until everyone was holding an envelope.

Laughing like a little kid Gunz looked to T'Rida and said, "Brah, you hella fucking stupid! Nigga, let's do it!" No one in the room had ever seen Gunz act so excited. The stone cold killa was as giddy as a little kid. His excitement made everyone else excited!

"Let's go!" Was all T'Rida said and everyone walked out of the building, headed toward the steel gate that secured the side parking lot. Everyone was on edge. T'Rida spoke for the last time. "Let's introduce these niggaz to Neva Die!"

DE'KARI

***

The night was perfect and the music was off the Richter! To say Dem Hoodstarz new album was slap was an understatement. That mothafucka was the truth. Band-Aid and Scoot had the mothafucking place near riot-ready. The center floor housed a stage and each dance floor had screens with the live performance playing. There were multiple flat screens in all the VIP lounges that were playing the performance as well. Bottles were flying out of the triple wide storage freezers and security was on point.

This was the shit Linell had been planning all his life. Tonight, was the culmination of all the nights he'd spent working his ass off, legitimately! He did it, he'd really did it. As he was making his way to the next VIP lounge to greet his top customers and big spenders, his cell phone rang.

"Yeah, what's up, Rogue! Where you niggaz at?" He yelled in the phone over the music.

"Brah, we about to bend in a couple of minutes," Voorheeze's voice was barely audible due to the loud music in Linell's ear.

"A'ight it's showtime, nigga. Let 'em know! Let 'em know!" Linell couldn't wait for the crazy-ass shit.

He hit the button on his hip signaling Band-Aid that it was time. In the middle of his performance, he stopped and signaled for the music to stop. Immediately, every eye in the building was on him either live or on the screen.

"Check it out! Check it out! Check it," He called into the mic making sure he had their undivided attention. "I thank all you mothafuckaz for coming out tonight to show us some luv for our record release! Y'all the ones that make this shit live for us, for real! But, now as everybody know tonight ain't all about Hoodstarz. Off top I don't want nobody to get shit confused, it's all lawless over here!" All throughout the Club the P.A. niggaz were barking and going crazy. The Little City by the water always represented. "But now, I want everybody in dis bitch to help me welcome the new King of Northern Cali as him and his team get ready to join us and celebrate his birthday! If any of you mothafuckaz don't know who I'm talking 'bout, Nigga my Nigga, T-Mothafuckin' Rida!"

All the screens turned to a live feed outside the club. The lines were still packed with mothafuckaz eager to step in the club and join the festivities. The sound of loud engines and music caught everyone's attention. What they saw would forever be remembered in the Bay Area.   Headlights lit up the street as everyone in the club watched the screens with anticipation! Car after car after car of brand-new high-performance vehicles filled the screens.

The first eight cars to fill the screen were all brand-new Chevy Camaro SS's. All eight were in the same color yet each cars representation of the black and pink were uniquely different. Every single car was high-performance with racing kits on them and were super hot. That was merely the beginning, behind the Camaro two Dodge Challengers roared down the street. The ground vibrated from the two muscle cars' racing package. Everyone was dying to see who would step out of the vehicles.

The first Challenger was all black with pink highlights and trim package. Its twenty-two-inch custom Forgiatos were black, with pink trim and the windows on the beast of a car were pink mirror tints. Everybody was impressed. The second challenger was identical in design and color scheme. Yet, all the colors were reversed. The car itself was hot pink with a black trim package and matching deep dark tints. However, it road on twenty-two-inch pink and black deep dish Asantis. The eight Camaros parked in a reversed V angle sealing off the end of the street. The two Challengers pulled in behind each other. The total formation making an arrowhead.

Outside everyone went crazy as the cars stopped and blocked the four-lane one-way street. The streets went from raucous and chaotic to complete silence as all ten cars opened their doors in unison. Even though, all ten had never before been seen together, there was no mistaking the She-Wolves; especially since it was Cantalope who stepped out of the Black Challenger and French Tip who stepped out of the pink. When the cars pulled up they were all playing, 'That's What's Up' off Dem Hoodstarz album.

DE'KARI

All the women were dressed in everything from Vera Wang, Donna Karan, Dolce & Gabanna, and Chanel. Directly behind the She-Wolves pulled in fifteen black and red Dodge Avengers. Wasn't no mistaking the soldias as they stepped out in all-black wit' bangas in their hands. The crowd outside the club were trembling at the display of power and muscle. The only people still going crazy was the crowd of E.P.A. niggaz! They loved and lived for that Gangsta shit, so what they were seeing on the screen had them niggaz super animated.

This time the sound of power and muscle was different. The sounds of the V-8 engines of the muscle cars were nothing in comparison to the sound of the four V12, high powered racing vehicles pulling up in unison. mothafuckaz went Ape-Shit when they saw fifteen black and red custom Dodge Daytona Chargers follow them and seal off the other end of the street. As the Cap's and Lieutenants exited their muscle cars, forty-five members of Neva Die made their way to the front of the club without anything being said. Another thirty-five niggaz with guns drawn took up stances in front of the entrance.

The She-Wolves didn't need to display their Gangst! 'That wasn't lady-like'. But, the poisonous aura seeping off of them, installed more than enough fear. The first of the four exotic cars caught everyone's attention. An all red Porsche 911 twin turbo. The driver's door opened and one of the sexiest sistas to ever walk the streets of the Bay Area stepped out in six-inch red-bottom stilettos. The catcalls instantly erupted but were silenced just as quick when the soldias cocked their hammers.

"Show some fuckin' respect!" one of them yelled.

Just then, the modified Lamborghini doors on the all-black Aston Martin One-77 opened, revealing all red interior, with blood-red butter-soft leather seats. What drew everyone's attention was the red halogen lights that displayed a red Dragon on the ground under the drivers and passenger side door. Gunz stepped out of the Aston Martin looking clean like Max Julien from the Mack.

The third exotic car a Lamborghini, a cherry-red Ferrari La-Ferrari, it was a site to see with its custom black and diamond encrusted Asantis. Voorheeze stood and smiled as he admired the dragon emblem on the ground as all the ladies admired him in his cream-colored, silk, Armani suit and albino snakeskin Louboutin shoes.

Inside and out the club the loud-speakers came to life when the song, 'Let's Go' blasted at full volume. Just then the custom Falcon doors on the triple-black and red Bugatti Veyron opened. Red and black from head to toe the new King of Northern California climbed out of the three-point million-dollar vehicle. In total, almost nine-million-dollars worth of vehicles sat in the middle of the street. All paid for and bought along with the dragon pieces hanging from everyone's neck by T'Rida as a thank you and token of luv for his family!

Loyalty and hard work had built this organization and he felt every chosen person should enjoy the benefits of their labor.

(song playing) "Chea! And everybody knows me. I'm Neva Die Dragon Gangs own Lil Dee. I'm not Moses can't split the Red Sea. But, I can split yo' head and leave red on yo' white T."

Band-Aid began his verse to the song altering it to fit T'Rida's entrance. The crowd went ranky! After a momentary pause, T'Rida headed toward the doors. He stopped when he got to Monique and if the his or hers Maximillion red and black mink coats didn't tell you that Monique was the First Lady of Neva Die, the kiss T'Rida gave her sure did. After the long juicy kiss, T'Rida made his way inside the club with Monique at his side and an army of proven killas behind him.

By the time Neal, the head of security had them walking up the stairs to the main VIP lounge, Linell was already at the lounge. "Welcome to Carsjanae's," he spoke greeting T'Rida.

"I love this place, family! This a real elegant spot you got here, I'm impressed," T'Rida truthfully spoke.

"Trust me fam this is only the beginning."

"Is this the lovely, Monique I've heard so much about?" Linell turned his attention toward the First Lady, displaying charm and respect, but the warm charm showed his hosting talents.

"Nice to meet you," was all a blushing Monique could get out.

"L, you did it. Rogue this mothafucka's phat!" Voorheeze greeted his homeboy as he entered the lounge.

"We did it, Rogue. We did it," Linell told his patna.

DE'KARI

The VIP lounge overlooked two of the three dance floors on the first floor. It catered to their needs. It was comfortable with ten sofas, five couches, lounge chairs and tables throughout the lounge. The thick plush carpet felt like pillows under their feet. All around the lounge were flat screen televisions and buckets with bottles of liquor and ice sat on each table. There were over two-hundred different bottles throughout the lounge. The shit was plush! Just as the family was getting settled, three beautiful and thick sistas walked into the lounge each carrying a punch bowl full of Cush.

They said the three bowels on the main table was nine-feet long and already housed one-hundred bottles of alcohol. Then they each reached into an apron tied around their waste and placed twenty packs of Swishers on the table next to the bowls. As they were turning to leave, Clarkola grabbed the hand of one.

"Hold on, beautiful, spend some time with me. You're way too mothafucking fine to be working."

On the stage, the Hoodstarz begin the East Palo Alto's anthem. "P.A., E.P.A., Rogue that's where I'm from nigga!"

The night was promising to be special. Everyone had their different glasses or bottles. T'Rida had smoked a few rocks on the drive over so he was already feeling himself.

When Linell walked out of the VIP lounge, he met up with Neal. "Rogue, I want you to have security round up seventy-five of the baddest bitches in the building and outside in line waiting to get in. Round them hoes up and meet me at the bottom of the main stairs. I want dis shit done in under ten minutes.

"A'ight little nigga, I told you 'bout barking orders at me," Neal told him playfully. The inside joke with them was always good. Neal was only five-three, but a little nigga he was far from, and everybody in P.A. knew that. Linell and Neal had been friends for years.

"Nigga, you better get me dem bitches!" Linell barked out.

"Everybody listen up!" This was the fourth time T'Rida had called it out. It was so live in the club his niggaz couldn't hear him. After a moment, the lounge was calm and quiet. "Check me out! We've busted our asses and nuts building what we got! Trust and believe when I tell you that shit was part-time compared to what's coming. Ain't no telling when we gon' have another time to celebrate. Shit ain't no telling how long we gon' keep the peace before a mothafucka try us. After all, just as we was hungry and came demanding shit! Another crew more hungry than us gon' try us!"

"Boo! Boo! They all yelled.

"Fuck Dat! niggaz gon' die 'bout dis." The Family didn't like that shit.

"Dat's right, we foe damn sho betta be ready to die 'bout dis shit. Cause if a mothafucka want what we got, they gon' have to get it how we got it! Mothafucka's gon' have to get it like Dracula!" Again, shouts were made and heads nodded as niggaz mumbled their agreements.

T'Rida continued, "But tonight, I want everybody in dis bitch to turn the fuck up! It ain't my party it's *our party*. Tonight, they saw us enter this bitch like the world is ours and it is! Dis neva die and we dem Dragons! Now, it's a lot of mothafuckaz in dis building tonight. Voorheeze peopled showed us tremendous love and respect. And y'all betta make sure to return the gesture. It's a lot of Taliban niggaz in here and although, we're honored guest, we in dey house! So, respect a man in his house! But, I wanna see y'all turn da fuck up!"

Right on cue, Linell stepped into the lounge that was capable of holding two-hundred and fifty people with a train of bitches. It was on and popping for the rest of the night. It felt like each and every member of Neva Die was at the top of the world, cause they were.

T'Rida spent the majority of the night making his woman feel like a Queen. People came up to him to pay their respects and he would always be cordial. But, he would use this time not only to flaunt Monique around, letting everyone know without question who the First Lady was, but he was also using tonight to make up a little for the many nights he was in the streets and didn't make it home.

When Band-Aide and Scoot came through to wish him a happy birthday and best wishes for the future, the two Bosses sat for a while. T'Rida showing his respect and congratulating the older Boss on his much-earned success. They discussed a little business and vowed to get at each other later and chew on some ideas. Ultimately, T'Rida got back to Monique. She was enjoying the respect and attention her man was giving her.

When Voorheeze came and asked her if he could steal her man away from her for a brief moment, naturally she didn't intrude. She knew how close the two were. She could remember when they were so broke, they only had two Cup of Noodles to eat. Voorheeze being a gentleman, he didn't hesitate to share one of the Cup of Noodles with T'Rida and give Monique a cup for herself. Voorheeze grew on her and she loved him like a brother.

Just as she was beginning to wonder what was keeping the two of them so long, Monique saw Voorheeze walking back to the lounge without her man.

"Sis, I need you to come with me." She didn't hesitate nor question him.

Monique just simply got up and followed. Her mind was wondering where T'Rida went, but she kept quiet. As they made their way down the stairs, Method Man and Mary J. Blige's duet came over the speakers.

"You're all I need to get byyyy!" That was her and T'Rida's song and she silently wished he was with her, so he could rap the lyrics when Method Man's verse came on like he always did. She was so lost in her thoughts she didn't realize Voorheeze had led her to the stage until he directed her to sit down in the chair and handed her the microphone she neva saw in his hand. She tried to ask him what was going on, he just smiled down at her, turned and left the stage.

"Monique, I'm, I'm here for you anytime you need me. For real Moe, it's me and yo' world believe me. Nuttin' make dis man feel better than a woman, Queen to wear da crown and be down for whatever—"

Monique couldn't believe it. The lights dimmed and a spotlight shined on her man as he made his way from the bar rapping the lyrics to her as he walked over to the stage. Monique couldn't hold in her excitement. She was both turned on and embarrassed by all the attention as she noticed that was displayed on every screen in the building.

"Word life, you don't need a ring to be my wife. Just be there for me and I'ma make sure we be swimming in

mothafucking luxury. I'm realizing that you neva had to fuck with me"

Monique loved the shit out of this man. He always went out of his way to make her feel like she was the only person in the world that mattered.

"But you did, now I'm going all out kid, cause I got mad love to give. You, my wife!"

He handed her the last Don Perignon that he carried from the bar. "Moe, it's been a lifetime and you done held a nigga down even when a nigga didn't deserve it. You always believed in me, even when I didn't believe in myself. You motivated a nigga and stayed loyal even back when I was only a peanut butter and jelly, Top Ramen and tuna fish nigga. Neva once did you nag me or complain. Niggaz think Nelson Mandela had a winner, but Winne ain't got shit on you ma!

Her heart was fluttering and her eyes moistened as T'Rida poured his heart out and professed his love for all to see. Her pussy was soaking wet, she was loving this man so much. But her lungs stopped working as her breath got stuck in her throat, when T'Rida got down on one knee.

"Moe, I made a lot of promises to you when we were kids. It took a while, but one by one I kept every last one." She nodded her head excitedly in agreement. "Baby, it's time I fulfill the last and most important of all—making you, my Queen. Kipaka, will you marry me?"

She couldn't believe it! She'd been dreaming of this moment for over ten years and it finally was here. The tears flooded down her eyes effortlessly. Monique didn't realize she was still holding her breath until the burning in her chest reminded her. She took a huge gulp of air and downed the champagne.

"Oh, baby, you know I will!" She screamed so loud she didn't need the microphone!

Everyone applauded and cheered. On the low-key, a few gangstas had to turn away from the screen. The moment moved them and they couldn't let niggaz see their momentary vulnerability.

For T'Rida it was the perfect conclusion to the perfect day! When he had the idea back at the Koffee Shop to buy the entire top echelon of the organization brand new vehicles, he knew that he was on some stuntin' shit. He had told Cantalope to go to one of the cash houses there and take Gunz ten million. Sure, it was a lot to fuck off on vehicles, but nearly seven and a half was on Voorheeze, his and Monique's. Gunz' Aston was what was on the back of the trailer. It truly was well worth it! Besides, the level they were about to be on, they would make that bread back in no time!

Chapter XIX

The tires of the Lambo screeched loudly and hugged the side-walk as the vehicle raced around the corner. Voorheeze was pushing that mothafucka as fast as he could through the city, intent on getting to his destination as quickly as possible. He didn't know the bitch that called his phone two minutes ago personally nor did he know how she'd gotten his number. But, he knew who she was. What she told him a minute ago had him seriously fucked up! He couldn't comprehend it! What the fuck did she mean? Is it possible she was confused? Was this a prank? If it was he'd kill her!

So much shit was racing through his mind. He almost didn't see the police car parked in the back of the parking lot of Washington Park. As he was approaching the corner. At the last possible moment, he made out the shadow of the car and downshifted the clutch, slowing down. So consumed by his thoughts regarding what he'd just been told, he almost fucked his shit up. If he would've been pulled over right then, he without a doubt would have been heading back to prison. When ole girl called him, he was on his way to meet Clarkola and Tut. Some shit had popped off and Styles was out of town taking care of business. So, Voorheeze had two crates of AR-15 that he was-taking to his brother.

Everything else was secondary to checking on T'Rida! This bitch had to be out of her mind, surely, she didn't know what she was talking about. *Rida had locked himself in her bathroom and wouldn't come out.* What the fuck? She said he had been up for four days straight smoking crack and tripping! What the fuck was this bitch talking about? He rounded the corner on Pennsylvania Avenue doing sixty miles per hour. Desperately trying to clear his mind at the same time. When he turned into the parking lot of the apartment, he saw a slim, chocolate sista, standing at the far end of the park and wondered if she was Tonya.

He brought the Lambo to a screeching halt and jumped out of the car neva taking his eyes off the woman standing on the sidewalk.

'Goddamn,' he thought.

If this was Tonya, he tilted his hat to T'Rida. Having something so bad and sophisticated fucked off. But, he didn't have time to be lusting after some bitch regardless of how bad she was, he had to keep his mind focused. T'Rida had told him about Tonya a while back, so when she called him, Voorheeze knew of her. He just didn't know her personally.

"Are you Voorheeze?" She asked once he was approaching the sidewalk, her voice was angelic.

"Where my brotha at?" Was his only reply.

She pointed to her apartment, then walked off in the same direction without saying another word. She confessed that she'd known about his problem for some time. However, she didn't feel it was her place to put his business all out there, but now she was scared for him. Her concern for him certainly outweighed any need for privacy!

Voorheeze followed her into the apartment and the stairs leading to the bedrooms. As he made his way up the staircase a familiar aroma assaulted his nose, it was the sweet stench of burning crack. Before they reached the level that they arose to in the game, Voorheeze spent more than his fair share of time in Crack Houses selling dope. So, he knew this smell all too well. Once they reached the top of the landing, there were three doors. She approached the door on the right and got ready to knock on it, but he stopped her.

He motioned for her to go back downstairs. He needed to do this alone. Anger boiled inside of him at the same time as sorrow filled his heart. It was going to be hard enough for him to confront his brother, he didn't want to further embarrass him by having the confrontation in front of his chick.

He opened the door slowly. The stench mutilated his nose like someone blowing a full cloud into his face. It caused him to take a step backward. He looked around the room taking in the sights not seeing T'Rida. Everything was a complete mess, a total contrast to the rest of the apartment. Things were thrown all over the place. Shit was cluttered on the floor, dirty dishes were everywhere, and the bed was a mess. Voorheeze shook his head in disbelief and prepared himself for what was next. He knocked on the bathroom door.

GORILLAZ IN THE BAY

"Babe, please just give me a few more minutes and I'll be out," Rida called out, thinking that it was Tonya knocking at the door.

What he heard next caused him to choke on the smoke he had just inhaled.

"Bruh bruh, you need to open the door and come out and holla at yo' nigga."

T'Rida wondered if he'd been up for too long, or was the dope that good. Either way it went, it didn't matter, he was tripping. That didn't sound like Tonya, it sounded like Voorheeze, but it couldn't be his nigga because Voorheeze didn't know where Tonya lived. He looked at his pipe with a confused look on his face and asked it, "Why are you doing this to me?" He wanted to cry he was so ashamed, but instead, he put more of the sweet evil on his pipe and was getting ready to take another hit when the knock at the door came again.

This time there was no mistaking it, it was Voorheeze who called out to him and asked him to open the door. T'Rida was fucked up, he didn't know how Voorheeze was in his O.G.'s house, but he was. T'Rida took the hit and asked his friend why he was there. Voorheeze didn't answer the question, instead, he told him to open the door. Although T'Rida was ashamed of what he was doing more than ever, he told his friend he was on his way out. He took one last hit and opened the door.

T'Rida opened the door and Voorheeze was shocked. His friend was sweating harder than a track star. His eyes were wide open like he was spooked and looking over his should past him. Voorheeze could see dope all over the bathroom sink, but the worst thing was the foul stench that emitted from T'Rida's body. He smelled as he hadn't bathed in over a month. Voorheeze almost threw up, the smell was so horrible. T'Rida tried to put a smile on his face but the attempt was pathetic.

"Why?" Voorheeze asked himself. "Why his folks, or better yet, how?"

They walked over to the bed, where T'Rida grabbed a dirty glass off the nightstand and poured himself a drink. For the next hour and a half, T'Rida opened up to his friend, hoping what he was saying wouldn't cause Voorheeze to look at him differently.

DE'KARI

It all started that night T'Rida woke up and found himself in Jenn's garage recovering from his gunshot wounds. The pain was so intense he snorted some powder to ease the pain. For a while, the dope eased his pain, but at the same time, it gave him an energy he'd never known, a sense of power never imaginable to him. Not just a power in the sense of the word, but an inner power, a feeling of being indestructible. He loved the way the cocaine made him feel. In fact, he found that his thinking was a lot quicker and clearer when he snorted the coke.

He enjoyed the feeling or the high so much that soon he began snorting the powder even when he didn't feel the physical pain. He found himself snorting more of the dope and doing so more frequently. He was snorting just for the pleasure of the high. He knew something was wrong, but he didn't care. His God-like feeling from the drug was worth an addiction. But soon, it wasn't enough. He snorted so much of the drug, so quickly, while experiencing this new sensation; that no matter how much he snorted or how often he snorted it, he would get high and wouldn't achieve that feeling any longer.

He was depressed for a while from not being able to reach that invisible plain he'd been achieving from using the drug. He wondered what he could do about it but couldn't come up with any solutions until one night he was watching a special about cocaine on 20-20. It had mentioned how many people who started snorting cocaine quickly began smoking it to achieve that familiar sense of getting high.

He couldn't imagine himself smoking coke at all, but according to the news special, that would be the only way he could feel indestructible again. He fought over all of this in his mind for over two weeks, all the while feeling miserable. Finally, he said fuck it, his urge for that feeling of power was greater than his judgment on people who smoked crack. Besides, maybe they all knew something that he and the rest of the world didn't. Maybe they were the ones missing something, not the crack heads. He didn't realize, he was already addicted to the cocaine and this was his drug-polluted mind talking to him and not his reasonable mind.

Later that night, when Monique and the kids were asleep, he walked out into the garage and made him a pipe out of

GORILLAZ IN THE BAY

aluminum foil. He grabbed a quarter ounce of crack and locked the garage door. When he put the rock on the pipe and took his first hit, nothing would be the same. He pulled on the pipe slow and steady while smelling the pleasant aroma. He pulled consistently until he could no longer take anything in and then he inhaled. He didn't know how long he was supposed to hold the smoke in, so he held it in until he could no longer hold his breath. While doing so, he didn't experience anything except tasting the sweet smoke as it rolled over his tongue and down his throat, but when he exhaled the smoke, his perception of everything magically changed.

His ear popped like cork-screws, he could hear a cricket fart through the door and across the yard, and his heart began pumping faster as his adrenal glands flooded his body with adrenaline, his mind became clearer, no problem was unsolvable to him at that moment, and his entire body became electrified as if he was full of energy. Shit, he felt like God. This was the best feeling he had ever known in his life. Nothing was greater, not sex, no sport he'd ever played, fighting, nothing! He chipped off another rock from the quarter and took another hit. For a brief moment, the feeling was magnified and T'Rida was good. That night he ended up smoking that whole quarter-ounce and pondering.

But, just like snorting powder, smoking crack had its downfall of not achieving that same feeling again. Every time he got high, he looked for that same familiar high, but he never experienced it. True, he did get high each time that he used, but never as high as he had gotten on that first night. In the beginning, he thought maybe something was different with the dope that second time, then he thought maybe his tolerance was stronger, so he needed more. He didn't realize, he'd never reach that level again in his life, no matter how much he got high. He was 'Chasing the Dragon' as addicts called it, but he had no way of knowing this.

Voorheeze couldn't believe what he was hearing. He couldn't comprehend what his brother was telling him. But he could see the sincerity of the pain in his face, thus, he knew his folks weren't lying. He wasn't sure if Monique knew, but he felt that he had to ask if she knew. At the mention of her name,

Voorheeze heard a muffled noise outside the door and knew that Tonya was listening to them, and in fact, she had just heard the same confession he did. T'Rida got up and went into the bathroom, Voorheeze knew he was going in there to smoke some more of the dope, but he was so stunned by the story, that he couldn't bring himself to say anything to him.

Instead he opened the room door, and as he expected, she was right there. He asked Tonya if she minded if he smoked a cigarette, she didn't, so he lit a smoke while thinking about what he'd just heard, and wondering what he was going to do next.

His mind was racing a hundred miles an hour. His heart desperately trying to keep up with his mind, raced along at its own alarming speed. The embarrassment he felt was ego-shattering, yet, it didn't matter. No one knew what it was like, no one understood what T'Rida was going through. If he could just experience that feeling one more time, just once more, then he would be cool. But no matter how hard he tried, no matter how much he smoked or how he smoked it, he couldn't reach that level of ecstasy he once felt back when he took his first hit of the alluring drug.

He told himself, he just wanted to feel it again, just once more. Yet, somewhere inside of him was a reality that he chose to ignore. That reality was that he would never again achieve the feeling that he was so desperately searching for. Yet and still, he placed another rock on the pipe, his hands were trembling all while.

'Why?' he was wondering, *'Why him?'* He couldn't grasp the concept of how he became a 'Crack-Head', but that is what he was. T'Rida 'The Goon' had become T'Rida 'The Dope-Fiend.'

He pulled hard and slow on the pipe, as the flame melted the rock it became a sandy-brown oil. He closed his eyes for a moment, but his body screamed for him to open them. His mind needed to watch the smoke fill inside of the crack-pipe. If T'Rida had looked into the mirror at that exact moment and saw the image he portrayed, he would have no doubt, killed himself right then and there. But he wasn't looking at his reflection in the mirror while he was smoking, in fact, in his mind he wasn't in Tonya's bathroom.

GORILLAZ IN THE BAY

He was back in the garage at his home in Tracy. Monique and the children were in the house sleeping. He himself was beginning a journey, he would never return from. As he held his breath in, his eyes became wide with the anticipation of the coke rush that was about to surge through his body. At that moment, a tear formed in the corner of his eye and slowly began rolling down his face. When he finally exhaled the smoke out from his lungs, the taste wasn't sweet like he was used to. Instead, his mouth was filled with a bitter, tangy, tart feeling. And it was because he knew then, that he couldn't allow himself to continue this path of self-loathing and destruction.

T'Rida decided then, he would have to end this battle soon. And the only way he would be able to do so, would be to end his life. Smoking crack was a form of suicide, only it was a slow death, a death he wouldn't endure through. He needed to end his life as quickly as possible.

***

It had been over a year since Voorheeze raced across the Dumbarton Bridge to Tonya's house and witnessed T'Rida smocking crack. A year of headaches and one problem after another, all evolving around T'Rida and his drug addiction. Now, he inhaled the weed smoke and leaned back against the couch. It seemed everything they'd worked so hard to build was all quickly being eradicated like a fuzzy dream easily lost in the night. Although he felt he should've told Gunz about what was going on sometime this past year, he couldn't bring himself to betray Rida's privacy in that fashion.

True, it was wrong for Voorheeze not to tell Gunz, but he thought when push came to shove, his and Rida's friendship and bond was far stronger, than his and Gunz's. But, he felt he had to say something to somebody. Shyt, Rida was really fucking up. He was making piss poor decisions, neglecting important meetings and shit, constantly. T'Rida was throwing coke parties at his house in Milpitas, and although, he didn't want to admit it, Voorheeze knew 'Rida was quickly submerging to the dope. Voorheeze decided he'd go against his better judgment and stick to his loyalties by keeping it to himself.

DE'KARI

To begin with, he wasn't the type of nigga to gossip, and couldn't see himself speaking badly on his patna. They had gotten into a few shootouts and other uncalled for situations, yet, whether it was right, wrong or indifferent, he was riding for his niggaz no matter what. Over the years, he and T'Rida had spent more time together. He was being loyal to his comrade and being there for him for whatever moral support he could give him.

T'Rida, on the other hand, was preparing Voorheeze for the day he would have to take over as Commander and Chief of the organization that they'd built. They had gotten away from just selling drugs and street life over the years. They had actually developed a format and a foundation that would make anyone proud. They contributed to the community and different charities, helping children and other things. This was one of the many reasons T'Rida decided he could no longer be a part of the family and their dealings. Although the dope was affecting T'Rida in certain ways, it wasn't taking away all of his realism.

Monique came in the den to see if Voorheeze needed anything else before she gave Titas a bath. In truth, the things she held inside were killing her, yet, she refused to show weakness. She refused to allow anyone to see her suffer. Being from East Oakland, she'd been through it all, seen it all and done it all. All her life she'd experience the short end of the stick and the poor end of the fucked-up situations.

For the past few years she had been given a taste of the good life. The days of Food Stamps and AFDC were long behind her, and no matter what, she refused to ever imagine going back to that bullshit. Voorheeze didn't need anything, so she left him downstairs in the den and headed upstairs to her son, still thinking about the things going on.

At first, T'Rida's behavior was throwing her off. She had no idea what was wrong with her husband, but she knew something was. Staying out a few nights of the week to take care of business wasn't out of the ordinary for him, but he had begun staying away longer than necessary and coming up with off the wall excuses. She didn't know if it was her female intuition or just her heart that was crying out to her, but something told her things weren't right. So, she bought a little used white Toyota Camry and began following him.

GORILLAZ IN THE BAY

She didn't know if he was living a separate life or what, but something was wrong. Hell, if he wasn't cheating on her, she would've been surprised, but what she found out, she wasn't ready for. A woman could never be ready to learn that her man was using dope, and yet, that is what she learned one night while she was following him. All types of thoughts ran through her mind that night, from questioning why he'd do so, to questioning herself, figuring that perhaps she was to blame somehow, till finally, she began questioning his manhood.

What type of mothafucka would start smoking crack after all the shit they'd been through, she had to ask herself. A pussy nigga, that's who! There was no other explanation she could come up with, other than her man had become a pussy. She followed T'Rida for nearly a month and some of the things she saw him do really sickened her. Some of the places she observed him go into just to get high caused her skin to crawl.

He was a Boss nigga. How could he allow himself to move around with the peasants? No, not the peasants, move around with the vermin! Yet, she never changed her attitude toward him. She never let on to him that she knew what he was doing, or what she herself was up to. Not even last week, when, while following him she noticed someone else following T'Rida. At first, she thought it was some undercover cops or something, but it wasn't. They were just some niggaz who were about to jack him.

She followed them and when T'Rida went inside of a crack house on Weeks Street in East Palo Alto. She saw them getting ready and figured they were going to rob him when he came out. Ever since she started following him, she carried the little mini .380 he'd given her as a gift. After T'Rida went inside the house, one of the guys got out of the car and hid in some bushes while the other guy drove a little down the street and hid the car .

She herself drove further down the street and parked her Camry. She looked around the car and found a screwdriver under one of the seats. Grabbing the screwdriver, she walked back down the street in the direction of the crack house. As she was passing the car that the nigga was sitting in, she heard him open the door and get out. Like most dumb niggaz he tried to holla at her, instead of focusing on what he and his patna was trying to do.

DE'KARI

She played along really well, allowing the nigga to get all close up on her. He was so busy feeling on her and thinking with his dick, that he never questioned why a woman would be out at that time of the night walking the streets, until she was removing the screwdriver from his neck for the third time. After she stabbed that nigga she proceeded down the street to the other.

He was nothing like his patna, he didn't try to get at her or anything. Hell, he didn't even budge inside of the bushes. If she hadn't seen him going into the bush, she would have never known he was there. As she walked by, she could see the pistol he was holding. Faking like she'd forgotten her purse, she mumbled out loud, stumbled and headed back toward her car. All the while, she scanned the streets making sure no one else was out, then she said fuck it and aimed the little gun at the nigga in the bushes.

Hearing her when she said fuck it, the nigga took his eyes off her ass and looked up at her face, but he too had been distracted and didn't see the gun she was holding, until the flash of the muzzle lit up the night.

Pop! Pop! Pop! Pop! Pop! Pop!

Firing all six bullets inside of the gun in rapid shots, Monique spun around on her heels and walked briskly, yet casually, to her car and drove off.

She thought of all of this while she was bathing her son. No one could tell her that she didn't love T'Rida. He was the love her life, yet, all the respect she had for him was gone. But, it was her love for him that kept her by his side. She told herself she took a vow for better or for worse, good or bad, in sickness and in health, right or wrong, or indifferent; and she would uphold that vow. As she reflected on all the thoughts plaguing her mind since she found out about T'Rida using crack, an image flashed before her eyes. It was an image of a dream she had so many nights ago.

Remembering that dream, she realized she had pre-dreamed killing the two niggaz that she killed that night. She dreamed about T'Rida and his drug usage, and in fact, she dreamed about giving Titas the bath she was giving him right at that moment. When all of this came into her mind, her heart sank in her chest as she told her son to get out of the bathtub. She half dried him off as quickly as possible, calling out for Voorheeze as she was doing so. When he didn't respond, she told Titas to follow her and she ran down the stairs heading for the den.

Once she got to the den, she realized the house was empty. That's when she listened to the silence, which was eerie and nerve shattering. She walked out of the den to turn the television off in the next room, but stopped in her tracks as she saw the breaking news report. The house that was on the news, was the Milpitas house T'Rida had bought. The news person was saying a shootout had just taken place at that house and all its occupants were killed.

The scream that escaped her lips was a glass-shattering shriek as she fell to her knees in tears.

***

Downstairs, similar thoughts of loyalty were running through Voorheeze's mind as he played Madden. In the next room another T.V. was playing. He didn't pay attention to it, but it was playing so loud he couldn't ignore it. Subconsciously he was hearing everything that was being said. Sure, T'Rida was fucking up, but T'Rida was his brotha, and regardless of what, a real nigga rode for his brotha without asking any questions.

These weren't just thoughts going through his mind, this was reality! It was his reality! All of this, he attempted to get out of his mind, while he played the game. Gunz should've been arriving at the house at any minute. They were supposed to meet T'Rida there and discuss the future of the family. Voorheeze was debating on confronting T'Rida and letting Gunz know the business. He was turning on T'Rida. Shit, Gunz was their brotha too. Voorheeze knew Gunz would put the shit on the table. So, fuck it, he was gonna put the shit on the table, too.

Voorheeze heard knocking at the front door. Pausing his game, Voorheeze got up to answer the door, knowing Monique was upstairs and he was the only man in the house. As he was walking by, his attention was drawn to what was on the television in the next to the den.

There was a breaking news segment about a shootout that was taking place in Milpitas. He didn't stop to see what was going on, although his attention was caught, he continued toward the front room to answer the door. After Voorheeze let Gunz in, they walked back to the spare room. He wanted to catch the rest of the news coverage that was going on. It turned out to be the Channel 12 news station. Dennis Richmond was saying that a reporter was live on the scene of the shootout taking place and they were transferring to the live scene.

Gunz and Voorheeze looked at one another at the same time, when the house the police had the shootout at came on the screen. Voorheeze couldn't believe what the fuck he was seeing. The War Room was on the television. Immediately, they went into action purely on instinct. Both of them bolted out the front door and headed for their vehicles. Voorheeze was on the phone with his man Spitz giving orders to assemble the Wolf Pack and the She-Wolves cause it was time to get the kids ready for Church and meet him on highway 680 by the Calaveras Blvd exit.

He told his goon that he and Gunz would come speeding by in less than twenty-five minutes and they were to be waiting there for them. Gunz himself was on his cell phone doing the same thing. Not one word was muttered between the two. There wasn't a need for talk, everything was obvious. Their boss and friend was in trouble and needed them and they were going. *The Mobb was on the way!*

Voorheeze couldn't believe what the fuck was going on. After finally building an empire that could possibly control the entire West Coast, it was all on the verge of being erased. He was speeding so fast in his Lambo, his mind wasn't concerned with anything else. He picked up his cell phone and called T'Rida.

When he heard the phone pick up, he immediately started talking. "T'Rida, we on the way, my nigga! Just hold them mothafuckaz off for a few more minutes. Nigga Da Squad is on the way! We gon' turn dat bitch into the O.K. Corral."

Voorheeze was filled with emotion as he vowed to be there for his Boss and Brotha. In his heart, it was over, and if it was going to end, they would end it all with a bang. In his speakers,

GORILLAZ IN THE BAY

Magic's 'Ride Foe My niggaz Foe Eva' blasted from his speakers. T'Rida was telling him, he didn't want him to come to his aid, he was talking about how this is the way it all had to end and shit, but Voorheeze wasn't trying to hear none of that bullshit. They'd taken an oath to never break their stride or leave one of their comrades' side and he was intent on keeping his word.

It had started off as some BGF shit, but now this was some Neva Die shit! Some Dragon Gang shit! However, T'Rida was explaining to him why things had to end this way, and why Voorheeze couldn't get involved or get the family involved.

He could hear in T'Rida's voice that he was high, but something was different in his voice than all the other times he'd talked to T'Rida. This time he could hear a genuine sincerity. He could feel through T'Rida's voice all the pain that the young goon was feeling, all the mixed-up emotions.

Just then he was passing the Calaveras exit on the freeway. Parked along the freeway just before the exit was fifteen vehicles, all of which he knew were his people.

"V, by the time you make it to me, dis shit is gonna be over. You know I'm not gonna let these mothafuckaz put me back in some fucking cage!"

As he was speeding down the freeway, listening to T'Rida on the phone tears began filling his eyes and Voorheeze did nothing to try and wipe them away. He couldn't help but think that he wasn't a man who easily shed tears, yet, this was the second time he'd cried for the man yelling at him on the phone. If he couldn't understand anything else T'Rida was saying on the phone, he understood what he meant when he said he wouldn't allow them to put him back in a cage.

Briefly, he remembered when T'Rida saved his life in prison. If it wasn't for T'Rida, Voorheeze would've been dead.

He'd exited onto Milpitas Boulevard. The night sky camouflaged his face and emotions. Against his feelings and judgment, he honored the last request and pulled over. He stepped out of the truck with tears staining his face and a fire in his heart like he'd never felt before. He was blacking in and out as T'Rida continued yelling, the phone now on speaker.

"Tell da Fam, it's *Neva Die* for life! I gotta end dis shit now, so I gotta go. *One Aim, One Struggle, One Goal, Neva Die!*"

DE'KARI

Those were the last words Voorheeze ever heard T'Rida speak. He and the rest of the team with him that day, listened as their leader's life came to an end. A lone, single tear escaped Voorheeze' eye and at that moment, something in him snapped!

The Saga Has Just Begun!

To Be Continued...
Gorillaz in the Bay 2
Coming Soon

Submission Guideline

Submit the first three chapters of your completed manuscript to ldpsubmissions@gmail.com, subject line: Your book's title. The manuscript must be in a .doc file and sent as an attachment. Document should be in Times New Roman, double spaced and in size 12 font. Also, provide your synopsis and full contact information. If sending multiple submissions, they must each be in a separate email.

Have a story but no way to send it electronically? You can still submit to LDP/Ca$h Presents. Send in the first three chapters, written or typed, of your completed manuscript to:

LDP: Submissions Dept
Po Box 870494
Mesquite, Tx 75187

DO NOT send original manuscript. Must be a duplicate.

Provide your synopsis and a cover letter containing your full contact information.

Thanks for considering LDP and Ca$h Presents.

DE'KARI

GORILLAZ IN THE BAY

KILL ZONE **II**

By **Aryanna**

THE COST OF LOYALTY **II**

By **Kweli**

SHE FELL IN LOVE WITH A REAL ONE **II**

By **Tamara Butler**

LOVE SHOULDN'T HURT **III**

RENEGADE BOYS **II**

By **Meesha**

CORRUPTED BY A GANGSTA **III**

By **Destiny Skai**

A GANGSTER'S CODE **III**

By **J-Blunt**

KING OF NEW YORK III

By **T.J. Edwards**

CUM FOR ME **IV**

By **Ca$h & Company**

GORILLAS IN THE BAY

De'Kari

THE STREETS ARE CALLING

Duquie Wilson

KINGPIN KILLAZ II

Hood Rich

STEADY MOBBIN' **III**

Marcellus Allen

SINS OF A HUSTLER

ASAD

HER MAN, MINE'S TOO **II**

Nicole Goosby

GORILLAZ IN THE BAY **II**

DE'KARI

DE'KARI

GORILLAZ IN THE BAY

A GANGSTER'S CODE I & II

By J-Blunt

PUSH IT TO THE LIMIT

By **Bre' Hayes**

BLOOD OF A BOSS **I, II, III & IV**

By **Askari**

THE STREETS BLEED MURDER **I, II & III**

THE HEART OF A GANGSTA I II& III

By **Jerry Jackson**

CUM FOR ME

CUM FOR ME 2

CUM FOR ME 3

An **LDP Erotica Collaboration**

BRIDE OF A HUSTLA **I II & II**

THE FETTI GIRLS **I, II& III**

CORRUPTED BY A GANGSTA I & II

By **Destiny Skai**

WHEN A GOOD GIRL GOES BAD

By **Adrienne**

A GANGSTER'S REVENGE **I II III & IV**

THE BOSS MAN'S DAUGHTERS

THE BOSS MAN'S DAUGHTERS II

THE BOSSMAN'S DAUGHTERS III

THE BOSSMAN'S DAUGHTERS IV

THE BOSS MAN'S DAUGHTERS **V**

A SAVAGE LOVE **I & II**

BAE BELONGS TO ME

A HUSTLER'S DECEIT I, II

WHAT BAD BITCHES DO I, II

By **Aryanna**

A KINGPIN'S AMBITON

A KINGPIN'S AMBITION **II**

221

DE'KARI

GORILLAZ IN THE BAY
By **Sonovia**

GANGSTA CITY

By **Teddy Duke**

A DRUG KING AND HIS DIAMOND I & II III

A DOPEMAN'S RICHES

HER MAN, MINE'S TOO

By Nicole Goosby

TRAPHOUSE KING **I II & III**

KINGPIN KILLAZ

By **Hood Rich**

LIPSTICK KILLAH **I, II**

CRIME OF PASSION

By **Mimi**

STEADY MOBBN' **I, II**

By **Marcellus Allen**

WHO SHOT YA **I, II**

Renta

GORILLAZ IN THE BAY

DE'KARI

DE'KARI

GORILLAZ IN THE BAY